EMILY DEBENHAM

Rogue of Taurus

To Kindal, my dearest treasure.

Tandem amor venit

Contents

Chapter 1

Cornelia Africana college was set out like an old Roman Forum. At the very head stood a temple-like structure that housed the student center. Livia Fabius charged up the steps, wanting to beat the lunchline so she could get to her 1:00 class on time. She lifted her eyes up and froze halfway up the staircase.

Corvin Tullius stood to the right of the entrance, dressed casually, instead of in his Legionnaire uniform. If he wasn't wearing his navy cargo pants and sky-blue TARP shirt then he wasn't on duty or he was undercover. Livia assumed the latter. His long legs were clad in dark-wash jeans that hugged his narrow hips in a way that made Livia's gut lurch. He wore a yellow polo that contrasted against his dark brown hair and made his hazel eyes look greener. She hated seeing him when she wasn't prepared. It made those irrational feelings she had for him flare up again. Livia had told herself over a million times and in a million ways that she needed to be over him. Yesterday.

Livia took a breath, bracing herself for when he'd turn and see her. Why was he here? She hadn't caused any trouble. She'd lived outside Caesarea for ages before she'd discovered her House and their accompanying powers. She didn't need a minder. She was angry at the lack of trust but infuriated by the lack of privacy. She should have at least been informed that a TARP officer needed to check up on her.

Corvin turned. Upon seeing her, his eyebrows rose. His eyes shifted, taking her in head to toe. Then he tilted his head in the way he did, puzzled. "You look upset, Livia."

She rolled her eyes. That would be the first thing out of his mouth. He was so condescending. Did he really expect her to believe the concerned acquaintance facade?

"Look, I can take care of myself!"

His chin drew back. "Did I imply you couldn't somehow?"

Livia glared at him. Now, he was acting all offended. As if she didn't have any right to be upset. She'd been glad to leave the backstabbing, gossiping, judgemental Caesareans behind her. Now, they'd followed her here. Livia stomped the rest of the way up the stairs. She stopped right in front of Corvin, ignoring that he stood much taller than her, and snarled directly into his face. "I don't need you to be here. Tell Justin or whoever sent you to leave me alone!"

Corvin's affront melted into amusement. "Oh, you think I'm here on assignment."

"Why else would you be here?" Livia demanded.

Why couldn't he act even a little bit intimidated by her? She was Taurus after all and stronger than him because of it. She slipped past him, slamming the door open so hard it smashed against the wall. Whoops. Livia grabbed it and pulled it away—now there was a dent. She needed to calm down. She looked back at Corvin.

He was giving her a try-being-more-discrete look.

She clenched her fists and bit out her words between clenched teeth. "Go home. I don't need you to watch me."

"I'm here as a student," Corvin said, putting a hand on his hip.

Livia tried to reign in her emotions. Here she was insisting that she didn't need a minder and within seconds of Corvin showing up she was putting holes in walls. She one-upped Corvin and put both hands on her hips. She inhaled slowly three times. Corvin watched her with that infuriatingly calm look that he always wore. Professional. Robotic. Cold. That was Corvin to the core.

"You expect me to believe that?" Livia asked. "You already have a degree—"

He cut her off, a touch of anger in his voice."I'm getting Masters of Science in Organizational and Leadership development," he said.

Livia's body responded immediately to the hint of anger in his tone. Heat rushed along her arms and her heart raced. Her shoulders pulled up toward her ears. She ignored her anxiety and demanded, "Why?"

"So, I can transfer into training," Corvin explained. His voice had returned to passivity. He shifted his arm to hang straight along his side.

Livia hesitated. She removed her hands from her hips and crossed them over her chest. An emotion had flashed across Corvin's face so briefly she didn't know what to name it. He spoke in an unemotional manner but three months ago, he'd been called to a domestic dispute. His squad hadn't been able to prevent an enraged Aquila man from killing his three-year-old daughter and then killing himself. She heard from Alia, Corvin's little sister, that Corvin blamed himself. It'd been a hard case for the entire community, but the man had been drunk and so it had brought back particularly bad memories for Livia's entire family.

It had triggered weeks of nightmares for Livia that had only just started to go away. She inhaled a deep breath. She really didn't want Corvin here. For some reason, his presence always dredged up some baggage or another.

Livia debated on whether or not she should believe him. He had a legitimate motivation to seek another position in his department. However, he was a Caesarean security patrol agent in a specialized unit. This wouldn't be the first time she'd interacted with him while he was on special assignment. That was how Livia found out she was Taurus house in the first place.

Livia needed details to verify Corvin's story. "So, what classes do you have today?"

"At three, I have an Executing Strategic Change course," he said.

"Where?" Livia demanded.

"In the Scipio building—" he looked amused again.

That checked out. "Room number?"

"Are you really quizzing me?" Corvin asked in disbelief.

"Are you deceiving me?" Livia countered. She knew the building only had three levels. She'd gotten lost there when she'd tried to find her healthcare policy class.

"315," he said. "Professor Hodgson."

Livia huffed, annoyed she couldn't call him out.

Corvin grinned at her. "It ends at five. Want to meet me there? I'll pay for dinner."

"No," Livia turned on her heel and marched toward the cafeteria.

By the end of lunch, Livia learned you had to pay 25 cents extra for ranch sauce—lame—and that a Professor Alan Hodgson was indeed employed at Cornelia Africana College.

Chapter 2

Livia expected to meet her new roommate when she got home, instead, she found a lizard on the kitchen floor. It was a light sandy color with a flat belly that spread on the floor like a disk. It wasn't tiny either, definitely over a foot long. Livia's throat tightened as she tried to determine if it was poisonous. Was it a neighbor's pet or had it wandered in from the wilds somewhere? Maybe it had snuck in when Livia left the door open to move in.

"Ares," a voice called from the next room.

Livia looked up as a girl with sandy hair, flip flops, and shorts walked in.

"There you are," the girl bent over and picked the creature up.

Livia bit back the warning shout she's wanted to let out. "That's your pet?"

Blue eyes shot toward her. She smiled. "Oh hey! Yeah, this is Ares. He's a bearded dragon."

"Is he allowed?" Livia asked.

The girl's smile fell. Livia didn't want to get on the wrong side of her new roommate in less than five minutes.

"Tell you what," Livia put out her hands in a placating gesture. "You keep that thing out of my kitchen and I'll keep my mouth shut."

The girl grinned. "Your kitchen?"

"I like to cook," Livia said. "And no matter how tame that thing is he's covered with germs."

The girl stroked the lizard's head with her fingertip. "I'll keep him out of the kitchen, promise. I'll only let him out in my room. Okay?"

Livia nodded. "Deal."

"He's quite sweet," the girl said, continuing to stroke the creature's head. Livia watched in disbelief as the lizard tilted its head to the side, clearly enjoying the affection. The girl disappeared to put the creature away. When she returned she held out her hand to Livia and said. "I'm Whitney, your roommate."

Livia took a step back. "No offense or anything but...wash your hands."

Whitney laughed and went to the sink and washed and dried her hands. She came back and Livia shook her hand. "Livia."

"Where are you from?" Whitney asked.

"Montana," Livia answered.

"Hey, that's only a few hours from here," Whitney smiled. "I'm a local."

"What are you studying?" Livia asked. "You know yet?"

"Ancient Civilizations—Latin Emphasis," she answered. "You?"

"Diagnostic Sonography," Livia said.

"Ah, that's one of the most popular programs here," Whitney said. "You must have had an impressive application to get in."

Livia didn't think she was all that impressive. She had to work part-time all through high school so she needed to take a gap year to pad her application. She'd completed an internship with TARP and volunteered at the medical clinic on the weekends to gain enough hours of related experience to apply.

"Probably, one of the less impressive ones," Livia said.

Whitney smiled. "Probably, more impressive than you think."

Livia and Whitney swapped tales about their first day of classes. Then Livia retreated to her room and googled bearded dragons and started researching.

Livia woke up the next morning worried. Bearded dragons were high-maintenance creatures. She didn't want to be complicit in animal neglect. If the creature was going to stay here, it needed to have competent care. She waited until nine to knock on Whitney's door. Her roommate opened it moments later still in her pajamas.

"Hey, sorry I woke you up," Livia said.

"It's okay." Whitney yawned. "What do you need?"

"Look," Livia cleared her throat. "I have another stipulation if Ares is going to stay here—"

Whitney's friendly face stiffened and suspicion came into her eyes. Livia's heart lurched as she realized her roommate was expecting blackmail of some sort.

"You have to take care of him—" Livia said quickly. "I'm not going to sit here and let some animal get neglected—"

Whitney's face softened. "I do take care of him—"

"So, he has the right sized tank?" Livia challenged. "And a heat lamp, and access to water—"

Whitney stepped back. "Come see, he's fine."

Livia followed her to the cage. Their rooms weren't big, more like closets than actual bedrooms. Whitney had put her bed up on stilts and placed the cage and supplies in the space under the bed. They knelt in front of the cage and Whitney showed her the heat lamp and a heating pad that kept the cage warm. There was a forked climbing branch that Ares was currently sunning himself on. There was also a shaded area under a hammock with some water and greenery to hide under.

Relief made Livia's muscles relax. She went down the bearded dragon care checklist she'd made in her head. Whitney's pet had exactly what he needed.

"He's okay," Livia observed.

Whitney smiled. "Want to hold him?"

Now that she knew that the lizard wasn't dangerous Livia was curious about him. "Sure. As long as he's not aggressive—"

"Nah, he's got a good temperament." Whitney pulled the lizard out of the cage and placed him carefully on Livia's lap. Livia lifted her finger and stroked him the way Whitney had last night. Ares's head tilted again and Livia laughed.

"He likes that," Whitney said. "So, I'll go home on the weekends sometimes. Would you be willing to watch him?"

Livia nodded. "Yeah."

Whitney sighed with relief. "Thanks! My mom said as soon as I went to college she wouldn't let him in the house anymore. I was worried I'd have to get rid of him and I love him, you know?"

"Yeah," Livia said. "He's pretty amazing."

They put the lizard away, washed their hands, and got ready for classes that day.

After dinner, Livia stared at her roommate Whitney as she gushed about her Roman history class about the founding of Rome. "I wish I could go back and be a real live actual Roman!"

Livia had to school her expression. First, being a woman in ancient Rome would suck. Second, a thousand words buzzed inside her, wanting to come out. Livia couldn't say— the next best thing happened to me! I found out my family came from an ancient Roman House and that's why I have a freakish amount of strength, can ignore the extreme cold and heat. I can even keep going for days with little to no sleep. The sleep thing wasn't pleasant though—possible, but extremely unpleasant.

Livia had even moved to their little city, Caesarea, in an abandoned part of Montana after high school. The forum had been amazing and so had some of the festivals, but Livia hadn't fit in there. She planned to make a new life outside Caesarea. So, as long as she avoided Corvin and the other Caesareans here she'd be fine. Livia figured she might run into them once in a while but as long as they kept a distance from each other things should work out the way she wanted them to.

Whitney continued her enthusiastic recap of her Roman history class, moving on to the Kings of Rome. Her blue eyes shone with an eager light that Livia was sure she'd never manage. Livia was too jaded to show that much excitement. It felt like tempting the universe to strike her down. Better to keep a level head so when things went wrong, as they usually did, you didn't get disappointed. So it was easy to move on and start over again.

Livia repeated the maxim that was a source of comfort since she was a child. "The only guarantee in life is change."

Livia wouldn't miss Caesarea for long. She'd moved to new places, adapted to new circumstances dozens of times. She would be fine.

Chapter 3

Livia inhaled a deep breath and approached Whitney. "So, I need your advice…"

Whitney lit up, pleased to be a confidant. "About what?"

Livia looked at her phone nervously. "This boy—"

"Ooh," Whitney suddenly sat up straight and pulled her knees into her chest, and wrapped her arms around them. "Do tell."

Livia sighed. "He's in my chem class and we've formed this study group. So, we exchanged numbers and he said, 'Call me if you're bored this weekend.'"

Whitney laughed. "I see."

"So, is that a friend type of thing or…" Livia shifted her hands, uncertain. "Or is that like a dating type of thing?"

"Do you want it to be a dating type of thing?" Whitney teased.

Livia shook her head. "I am not looking for a boyfriend."

Whitney shrugged. "Just tell him that. Is he hot?"

"He's cute," Livia said. "But he's just nice…clean-cut, good."

"Boring," Whitney said, making a face.

"I like that," Livia said, firmly.

She lifted an eyebrow. "As in you'd consider dating him?"

Livia sighed. "I don't want a relationship right now but I wouldn't mind hanging out with him."

"Then call him," Whitney said. "No harm in getting to know him some more, right? No pressure."

"I might," Livia said.

"I'll be going home on Saturday and won't get back till late Sunday. Spending time with the fam," she said. "So, go hang out with him."

Livia hesitated. "I'll think about it. But you think I should just tell him I'm not into boyfriends right now?"

"Yep," Whitney said.

"Okay," Livia nodded.

"Can I show you how to take care of Ares before I go?" she asked.

"Yeah," Livia said and they spent the rest of the evening chatting and playing with the bearded dragon.

* * *

"It's just me and you Ares," Livia said, as she placed water in his cage. She put a pile of kale and some mealworms next to it. Livia closed the cage door and watched the lizard amble over and snatch up the mealworms one by one. It wasn't the most pleasant of sights but Livia was satisfied that the creature's needs were met. He'd be fine until Whitney returned.

"What do you think? Should I call this boy, Oliver?" Livia asked the lizard. She'd already cleaned the entire apartment and baked fresh bread and a dozen muffins. She needed to get out of the house. Livia scrolled around on her phone, procrastinating.

She pulled up the social media site closed to everyone that wasn't directly related to one of the four Caesarean houses—Lupus, Taurus, Rattus, or Aquila. Livia didn't visit Tabula often. She always had rude comments or messages. She was surprised to find that she had recent friend requests.

There was a Felicity from Rattus house. Livia studied her photo, frowning. She had no memory of ever interacting with Felicity and she didn't look familiar. Livia deleted the friend request. There was a second request from a Terrance, also from Rattus house. Livia deleted his request immediately. She'd learned not to interact with guys on Tabula. She'd been propositioned via message more times than she could count. After breaking up with her boyfriend the offers for non-platonic comfort had poured in leaving Livia with a vile taste on her tongue.

She hovered over her messages icon. She had 5 new ones. It was possible they were nice notes. In her experience, it was more likely harassment or complaints about how she didn't know how to be a proper Caesarean. She wasn't really in the mood to deal with it. Everyone important to her knew how to get a hold of her off of Tabula. She sent the messages to the trash without reading them.

She checked a couple of her friends' pages and then Corvin's page. He'd posted a stunning photo from a hike he'd gone on earlier in the week. It was captioned—*Nice views out here.*

He predictably got a lot of likes and supportive comments. Corvin was popular and well-respected in Caesarea. It helped that his father was Paterfamilias of Lupus house—a position that Corvin would inherit one day.

Livia observed that many of their mutual TARP acquaintances posted on how much they missed him. She pursed her lips. He probably wasn't undercover then, but it also didn't prove he was in school necessarily.

Corvin was tagged in another photo from Friday night. He was at an ice cream parlor and he was with the two people that had requested to be her friends earlier.

Livia felt her cheeks heat. They were probably going to school here and had wanted to connect. Livia debated sending a request back now that she knew their friend requests were probably genuine. If she did that she'd have to explain she thought they were going to harass her. That would require explaining her troubled history with Tabula. She didn't want to get into it with strangers. She decided to log out instead. It was all too much manufactured drama.

Livia pulled up Oliver's number and pressed send.

He answered, gruffly, "Hey, who's this?"

"Uh, Livia," she answered. "From class. Is this a bad time?"

He laughed. "You called? Have you heard of text?"

"I can hang up if you want," Livia growled.

He laughed again. "No, don't."

"Let's keep this short. Want to hang out tonight?" Livia asked.

"Sure. What's the plan?"

Livia panicked for a moment. "Ice Cream?" popped out.

"I'm game. Do you need a ride?" he asked.

"No."

"I heard there's a place on center street," he said.

"Okay, text me the address and I'll meet you there," Livia said.

"What time?"

"Seven?" Livia offered.

"Excellent. See you, Livia," Oliver said.

* * *

When Livia walked into the ice cream shop she recognized it from the Tabula picture she'd seen. Corvin had been here last night. Inexplicably, she regretted not crossing paths with him. Livia took a deep breath and shook the feeling off. Her first impression of him was difficult to shake off, but Livia was two years older and wiser now. Livia didn't know if it would be possible to forget the connection they'd formed the week he'd intervened in her life, but she'd learned that Corvin was not the same person that had captured her teenage devotion.

Oliver interrupted Livia's musings when he walked in. He grinned and strode over. "Hey!"

Livia smiled back. "How are you?"

"Good, you?"

Livia nodded. "Looking forward to the ice cream."

"Alright," he gestured toward the counter. "Let's get some."

They chatted about classes as they stood in line together. There was an awkward moment at the register when Oliver tried to pay for both of them. Livia insisted on paying for her own way. The cashier looked between them. Livia insisted again she'd be paying for her own. Oliver didn't contradict her.

They sat down at a table together. "I wouldn't mind paying, you know."

"I know but this is hanging out," Livia emphasized. "Not a date."

Hurt flashed across Oliver's face. "Why not?"

Livia decided to be blunt. "My last relationship ended in disaster, okay? Nothing personal."

Understanding flashed in Oliver's eyes. "Ah, so you're still smarting from your ex. How long ago did you break up?"

Livia thought back, surprised to realize how much time had passed. "Almost a year…"

Oliver nodded. "That's a pretty long time. Maybe…if we take things slow? You can warm up to the idea?"

Livia shook her head. "No, I don't want a boyfriend."

Oliver took a few bites of his ice cream in silence. "Friends for now, then?"

"Friends for now," Livia agreed.

"So…" Oliver gestured with his spoon. "Fess up. What happened?"

Livia shook her head and pressed her lips together. It would be difficult to explain how her breakup with Arik had impacted her unless Oliver understood how Caesarea worked. She had to have permission from the Senate to reveal any details about Caesarea to a non-civ. "Not up for discussion."

Oliver's eyebrows rose in surprise. "So, what do you want to talk about then?"

"My roommate has a lizard," Livia said.

Oliver laughed. "A lizard?"

"Yeah, it's huge. Over a foot long." Livia approximated Ares' size with her hands.

He gasped. "Serious?"

"Yes. It's a bearded dragon."

"What's that?"

Livia explained about bearded dragons and the intricate care routine required to keep them healthy.

"So, you're feeding the thing mealworms while she's at home?" Oliver sat back and ran his hands through his hair in disbelief. "That's crazy!"

Livia thought the gesture made him rather handsome. She smiled. "He's not too bad. I kind of like him."

Oliver hooted. "You like him! Not me! No way! Creepy crawlies are not my thing."

"I like animals," Livia said. "They're fascinating."

"Yeah, well a dog is one thing—a lizard? Some creatures aren't meant to be pets."

"Well, I agree with that," Livia said. "I'm not super into keeping animals as pets. I'd rather observe them in nature."

"That's not my thing," Oliver said.

"What's your thing then?" Livia asked.

"I have a twitch channel," he explained.

Livia frowned. "What's that? I've never heard of that."

"It's a live stream for gamers," he said.

Livia didn't have a positive opinion of gamers in general, but Oliver broke all her expectations of someone that gamed frequently. He wasn't socially awkward or overweight. He was smart and confident and had good hygiene.

"So, this is a hobby?" Livia asked.

Oliver's lips twisted to the side. "A part-time job—"

Livia laughed. "That would require making money."

"I do."

"You do? Playing games?" Livia asked in disbelief.

"They actually require a lot of skill."

"Then why do college at all?" Livia asked.

Oliver sighed. "Parents, partly. Also, competition is tough. It's getting harder to monetize my audience and well...it's not fun anymore."

"Well, jobs aren't meant to be fun," Livia said.

"Yeah, but if it's not going to be fun why not get a normal job?"

Livia shrugged. "I'd get a normal job."

Oliver's chin drew back and a sad look entered his eyes. Livia realized she made a mistake.

She cleared her throat and straightened up. "I'm supposed to tell you to fight for your dream."

Oliver rolled his eyes. "Yeah, but you know reality and all—"

"I'm good at being realistic," Livia laughed. "My specialty."

"Yeah, huh?" he asked.

"But I've never played a video game so…" Livia shrugged.

Oliver looked surprised.

"You might figure out a way to make it work," Livia said. "I can't advise you what to do."

He smiled. "Why don't we do something together next weekend?"

"Like what?" Livia asked.

"They're asking for volunteers at the elementary school. They need people to help them move books into their renovated library. Want to go help?"

"Yeah," Livia said. "I'd love that!"

She pulled out her phone and prepared to put it in her calendar. "What time should we be there?"

Chapter 4

Livia decided to walk to the elementary school that was only a few blocks away from her dorm. She met Oliver there, who had also walked from his apartment nearby. He greeted her with a half-hug. Livia hugged him back awkwardly and pulled away. She wasn't good at affection. She always misjudged how long she should hold on to someone. Whenever she tried to give someone a quick hug it was too quick, and whenever she tried to give someone a longer hug it was too long. Her ex, Arik, was pro at physical affection and she'd thought that would be a good thing. It hadn't been. Livia had only frustrated and annoyed him. She swallowed down her regrets over that and focused on the present.

She was actually excited about this activity. This was her thing. Hauling books was her specialty. Being Taurus house made her strong and durable and she was ready to work. That was until Oliver could barely heft a box of books, leaving Livia wondering how to play her cards. Did she pretend she was weaker than him to hide her exceptional strength so he didn't ask questions? Or could she pull off being stronger than him?

Livia didn't look muscular. She was about average height and her arms were lean and slim. She held most of her muscles in her thighs, which seemed to be a Taurus house trait. They were noted for their brawny legs. Something the plebian Taurus house members were allowed to show off, but since Livia was patrician she'd been held to a different standard. At least, that's why she thought people freaked out the first few times she wore a short dress in Caesarea. She didn't know any other reason why she'd attract so many negative comments. It wasn't something that had ever happened to her outside Caesarea. Livia stopped the insane comments by wearing things that people didn't comment on.

Livia realized that she hadn't reverted to her pre-Caesarean way of dressing. Being Taurus house meant she wasn't sensitive to changes in temperature. Wearing long pants and sleeves in hot weather didn't bother her. She watched Oliver struggle with his box with a sinking heart. She'd forgotten about this part of being outside of Caesarea. She was going to have to pretend to be a weak girl, who couldn't haul a box by herself. It stung. It really did.

Livia resigned herself to her fate and pasted on a fake smile. "Oh, let's carry them together! That way I can help."

Oliver looked at her with relief, as Livia lifted the opposite side of the box. The boxes were small so it was awkward to walk and carry at the same time. It made things so slow that Livia's excitement for the project ebbed away.

There was only one thing that made it worse. She looked away after faking another smile for Oliver as they carried their fourth box inside. She caught sight of Corvin, Terrance, and Felicity giving her confused looks. Livia's eyes fell to the pavement as her cheeks flooded with heat. She was caught participating in this embarrassing charade. It was humiliating. She dreaded them posting videos on Tabula and having to endure savage mockery for months.

"You need a break?" Oliver asked, breathless.

He was out of shape. He wasn't asking for Livia's benefit but his own.

"Why don't you find us some water?" Livia asked.

When he disappeared she hauled in a box all on her own. The guy on the truck handing boxes down laughed. "That guy was slowing you down!"

Livia hesitated, not wanting to draw attention to herself but she didn't see a way to back out now. She'd committed. "He must not work out," she said.

Livia felt anxious carrying the box to the school library, which was ridiculous. What if Oliver ran into her and called her out? What if someone noticed she was stronger than she should be?

"Ditched the guy, huh?" Corvin said behind her.

Livia jumped, heart pounding. "He's getting water."

"I'll bet," Corvin said.

Livia noticed he handled carrying a box without strain. His arms weren't extremely muscular but they were well-defined nonetheless. Livia let her eyes linger on his attractive muscles a tad too long. She told herself it was to avoid looking into his eyes.

"How are you, Liv?" Corvin asked.

Her eyes shot up to his. "I'm good."

She walked through the doors of the library and set her box down. Corvin followed and put his box on top of hers.

"Who was the guy?" Corvin lifted one eyebrow, playfully.

Great, he was laughing at her. "A kid from one of my classes."

Livia tried to see if slipping out into the hallway would end the conversation. They followed her, though, and she turned to face them when she came to a clear space.

"Are you dating?" Terrance asked, leaning casually against the wall. His bright purple hair looked awful under the fluorescent light. Livia disapproved. Hair color like that would make it difficult to get a decent job.

Livia glared at him. "No."

"We tried to invite you to ice cream over Tabula," Terrance said. "We all left you messages but you didn't respond."

Livia's cheeks heated again. She cleared her throat. "I-I deleted them on accident without reading them."

Terrance's eyes narrowed. He exchanged a look with Felicity that revealed he didn't believe her. Livia looked at Corvin but instead of looking suspicious, he looked concerned.

"Well, this Friday maybe?" Corvin asked.

Oliver rushed up before she could answer.

"Liv! I got water!"

He handed her a mini water bottle. As soon as he'd handed it off to her, he broke the seal on his and drank the entire thing. Everyone watched him in silence. Oliver gestured after he finished drinking.

"Friends of yours, Liv?" he asked. The trio tensed.

Livia remained relaxed and explained, "They're from back home."

"Oh, how nice!" he held out a hand. "I'm Oliver. Livia and I met in class."

Corvin reached out his hand. "I'm Corvin. Livia and I used to work together."

"Sweet," he grinned. He greeted Felicity and Terrance with equal warmth and friendliness.

"Liv," Oliver bumped her hip with his playfully. "How come you never told me about them?"

Livia realized too late that she was supposed to give way when Oliver bumped her. She tried to imitate being knocked into and looked ridiculous. Terrance's lips pressed together and his eyes danced with a laugh. Felicity didn't hide her chuckle. Oliver shot her a baffled look. There was no way she'd be able to ever try and explain her weird reactions to him. It would mean revealing she was Taurus house.

Livia wanted to disappear. She had reached her embarrassment quota for the entire week in a handful of minutes.

She looked Corvin in the face and she found that he wore no expression. Typical. But at least he wasn't mocking her. That was a relief.

"Unless, one of these guys is the ex you refuse to discuss," Oliver joked.

Right when she thought it couldn't get worse. "No," Livia said, irritated.

Oliver took in her expression. "You don't even like to joke about hating him?"

"Hate is too strong a word," Livia said, glancing in Terrance and Felicity's direction. She didn't particularly want other Rattus house members to know how she felt about Arik. She was pretty sure that word would get back to him and she wanted to remain on good terms with his family. His brothers were good friends.

"So you don't hate your ex but won't talk about him?" Oliver asked.

"You realize that's an extremely personal question?" Livia snapped, beyond annoyed.

Oliver's brow furrowed. "I made you angry. Sorry."

He was still curious. Livia could tell. She opened her water bottle and drank out of it hoping it would make the Caesarean trio get bored and walk away. No dice.

"Oliver has a twitch show." Livia decided she could deal with them as long as they no longer talked about her. So, she threw Oliver to the wolves. Livia wanted to laugh. Corvin was Lupus so the idiom took on an amusing literal meaning. The situation was dire when you were laughing at your own internal monologue to survive an encounter.

"A twitch channel," Oliver corrected her terminology.

"Makes money playing video games," Livia explained.

Livia genuinely had no idea what other Caesareans would think about this. She was curious to see others' reactions. Arik and his family liked to play sports. She'd never seen them play video games.

There was a long silence. Corvin's face showed an expression for the first time. He tilted his head to the side and pierced her with an intent gaze. Did she interpret that as disappointment? He was so difficult to read.

Corvin pulled his phone out of his pocket. "Fascinating," he said, toneless. "We don't have much more time. Let's see what else they need help with."

Terrance gave Oliver a thumbs up and a smile. "Good luck with that channel!"

Felicity gave a wave and they followed Corvin back out to the trucks. Livia wasn't sure how to feel about their reaction. Polite and civil but unwilling to engage. Had she been snubbed? She couldn't tell and that was frustrating.

That was how things always went with Corvin though. He was never overtly rude but he wasn't friendly either. It irritated her more than the people who were outright mean to her. At least she knew she needed to avoid them to protect herself. Corvin's lukewarm interactions made Livia feel uncertain around him.

Livia turned to Oliver. "I'm ready to head home."

Oliver looked disappointed. "They have pizza when they're done."

"You stay. Enjoy. I need to get some studying done."

"You sure?" Oliver asked.

"Yeah, I'm fine. Talk to you in class."

Chapter 5

"**D**id you go to that service project with him?" Whitney asked first thing when she walked into the apartment.

"Yes," Livia said.

She squealed. "Annnd?"

"He's nice," Livia said. "But nosy...."

"Nosy? About what?" Whitney asked.

"My ex-boyfriend came up and now he won't stop talking about him."

"Uh oh," Whitney said. "He must sense a story there."

Livia sighed. "I saw some friends from back home too."

"Oh, that's nice," Whitney said. "How were they?"

Livia shrugged. "Same as always. Nice but kind of fake."

Whitney pulled a face. "I hate people like that."

"Yeah, I don't know what to do. They want to hang out—" Livia sighed.

"Why not try it once? Sometimes when you get people in a different situation they surprise you." Whitney hauled her backpack to her room. "How was Ares?" she asked.

Livia followed her. "No problems. How was home?"

"Good. I missed my mom something crazy. It was nice to be back. My brothers were super excited to see me," she smiled. Then she frowned. "Have...you heard from family yet?"

How did Livia explain? Especially, without revealing anything about

Caesarea?

Honor Pius had come to Caesarea the summer she'd turned eighteen and engaged in a romantic fling with Drusus Fabius—rich, patrician class, influential, talented orator. Then she'd returned home to Italy. She returned a year later with their young son—Livia's brother Hyrum— in tow and demanded he marry her, forcing him to break off an engagement with a woman he loved. Their awful marriage had lasted twelve miserable years. Livia knew she shouldn't blame her mother for the fact that her father was an abusive drunk. That was on him. But she was furious that mom had stayed so long. Maybe that was unfair, but Livia didn't care. She'd had to suffer the consequences of her mother's life choices and that was epically unfair.

Honor had left Caesarea and refused to ever return after her abusive Aquila house husband—Livia's father—had been put in prison for life. After that their family had been so poor, their life had been so hard. Her mother hadn't even told Livia about being Taurus house. She had even forced Hyrum to keep the secret from her and her other brother Lucas, too.

That meant that Livia's family was considered Rogue—a status that had made her life very difficult in the past year. People in Caesarea didn't trust her and so had a very difficult time accepting her. Livia's relationship with her mother was strained before she'd found out she was Taurus house. Afterward, she couldn't call it a relationship at all.

"You know, my mom lives with my stepdad," Livia shrugged. "We don't talk much." She'd let Whitney think her stepdad was the reason why she didn't talk to her mom. Livia felt guilty about it because Tad was actually a decent man. He'd done right by Livia and her brothers and sometimes she missed him. She missed him more than her own mother. Livia felt the pain flash across her features.

Whitney's eyes widened. "Seems like a hard situation."

Livia tried to smile. "I'm close with my brothers Hyrum and Lucas."

"Did you grow up around here?" she asked.

"No, we moved all over," Livia said.

"Oh?" Whitney replied with interest. "Where else have you lived? Where did you live before you came here?"

"I lived with my brother Hyrum and his wife in Montana," Livia answered. "We were all over the place growing up."

"Like where?" she asked.

Livia hesitated. "We lived in several places in California. Lived in Arizona, New Mexico, Nevada, Maryland, Delaware, Pennsylvania."

"Wow, you moved a lot. For your parents' work?" she asked.

Livia didn't actually know. They didn't technically have to move for work. If she asked her mom now, Livia knew she wouldn't answer. Mom didn't like to talk about the past. Livia had been too young to ask why they moved all the time back then. Now, Livia guessed that they moved because Mom hadn't wanted to be found. Not by Taurus house, nor Aquila house—Dad's family. She'd gone Rogue.

Livia shrugged, deliberately not answering. "What about you? Where do you come from?"

"I grew up an hour away from here," she said. "The first time I came to Cornelia I was in middle school. We were doing a language arts competition. I fell in love with it. When I got accepted it was my childhood dream coming true," she said.

Livia smiled. It was nice to be reminded that the universe wasn't always cruel. "Sweet."

"What about you?" she asked. "Why'd you come here?" she asked.

"Friend told me about it," Livia said. This was true. Tavian Hall from Rattus house had mentioned it. Livia had looked it up and decided to apply. Livia made her decision when the school offered a half-tuition scholarship.

"Tell me about this friend," Whitney said.

Livia looked at her, startled. What could she say about Tavian? He was Rattus house, which made him an empath, but she couldn't mention that.

"He has a twin," Livia said.

"A boy?" Whitney wiggled her eyebrow.

"No, not like that—" Livia said. "He's only a friend."

"Ummhmm," she said, teasing. "So this boy has a twin?"

"Yeah, Tavian and Adrian."

"Two boys?"

"Yeah. We met in high school. I actually dated their younger brother, Arik. So, they're good friends. Very close to my other brother, Lucas."

"So, you just have the two brothers?" Whitney asked.

"Actually..." Livia said. "I have a step-sister. She's nine months old."

"Whoa! That's a gap," Whitney said.

"Yeah, uh, my Mom almost died," Livia said.

"Is she okay now?" Whitney gasped.

"Better. Not back to how she used to be, but better," Livia said.

Whitney's face fell. "Oh, no. That must have been so hard for your family." Livia nodded. "Very."

Livia had almost gone home to help but Hyrum wouldn't let her. He'd flown out with his wife Caecilia instead and stayed for eight weeks. That meant Livia had been in Caesarea completely alone. She'd had an internship with TARP—the Trauma and Rescue division of the Caesarean Security Patrol. When the chief director, Justin Aurelius, had become aware of her situation he'd taken her into his home. His wife Flavia was also Taurus house and had treated Livia like family. Livia missed Flavia way more than she thought she would.

Whitney put her arms around Livia and hugged her. Her roommate pulled away before it registered to Livia to hug back. Livia's cheeks pinked but Whitney waved it away like it was no big deal. Livia let her embarrassment over her awkwardness fade away. Whitney wasn't the sort to hold it against her and there was no one she could gossip to about it either.

* * *

As if Livia's melancholy over her family situation had summoned Hyrum to the rescue, he called Livia that evening.

"I haven't heard from you so I'm assuming the car didn't break down on you halfway there?" he joked.

Livia scowled. Hyrum had worked hard to convince her to sell her car before she came out to Cornelia Africana. "Still driving," she said.

"Quin collected cars," Hyrum said. "I inherited four. I use one. Caecilia uses one. The other two sit around in the garage. Take one off my hands, Liv."

Their uncle Quin, the previous paterfamilias of Taurus house, had passed away almost two years ago now. His death had been the impetus behind Livia's discovery of Taurus house.

"I like my car," Livia argued.

"It broke down on you last month," Hyrum said.

"But I fixed it. It's fine," Livia insisted.

Hyrum sighed. "I'm worried it's not reliable anymore. You're too far away for me to help you out there. She's done good by you, Liv. You made a smart choice, but it's time to graduate to a new car."

Livia didn't want to part with her car. She had paid money to fix it last month. It would be fine. She didn't want to change anything else right now. She had wanted one thing in her life to stay the same. That meant keeping her car. "Hyrum, I'm fine," Livia said.

"Stop being stubborn," Hyrum growled. "I'm giving you a new car. Take it."

"No." Livia refused. "I told you my car is fine."

There was a tense silence on the line. Livia closed her eyes and waited for Hyrum to erupt into a tirade about how she was ungrateful and childish.

Instead, he sighed. "Right, you let me know if you need anything. Remember, I had to accept a lot of help from Tad to get through school. He sent me gift cards twice a month to help with groceries and he paid for my gas when I drove home."

"I'm okay, Hyrum."

"I know, but if you ever aren't—"

"I'll ask you for help," Livia said, annoyed.

"Good. You like school?"

"Yeah, But...Corvin is here."

"He is?" Hyrum asked.

"Yeah, and some other Caesarean kids."

Hyrum laughed. "The tables have turned! Be nicer to them then they were to you."

"Why should I?" Livia asked.

"Honestly, Liv, a lot of people just need to be taught the right way to help. Imagine if more people in Caesarea knew how to help people that were new. Wouldn't it be a better place?"

"Yes, Hyrum," Livia agreed, impatient.

Except, Livia knew that Corvin should know how to be kind. She didn't understand why his demeanor was so cool around her. Though, she wasn't warm to him either. She didn't see that changing any time soon.

"You feel like I'm lecturing you—"

"It's your default state."

"Just think about it—"

"I'll be nice," Livia said. "But I don't expect to see them much."

"How's your roommate?" Hyrum asked.

Livia spent more time on the phone with Hyrum than she expected. She told him all about Ares, her classes, and her roommate Whitney. The sound of his voice was familiar and comforting. The longer they talked the more her melancholy thawed. When she ended the call there was even a grin on her face to match the warmth in her heart.

Chapter 6

Livia got daring the next morning. She pulled out a beautiful floral dress that she loved but never dared to wear in Caesarea. The sweetheart neckline was a little revealing, but the cap sleeves made the look fairly innocent. The length hit her mid-thigh. It didn't bother Livia but maybe it looked too short?

Livia walked over to Whitney's room and knocked on the door. It opened three seconds later.

"Yeah?" Whitney asked.

"Is this dress too short?" Livia asked.

Whitney looked her over. "No. It's fine. Don't worry about it."

"Thanks," Livia said.

Now, for phase two of her experiment. Livia wore the dress to class. No one gave her strange looks. No one whispered or giggled behind their hands as she passed. It was amazing. Livia felt a sense of freedom and independence that she hadn't felt for a long time. Also, validation. Caesareans were crazy. There was nothing wrong with Livia's clothing style or her strong Taurus house legs.

* * *

"Come on, Livia!" Whitney called, laughter in her voice.

Livia pulled cookies out of the oven. The process of baking had always soothed her. She liked giving other people food. It was her love language. Whitney had a hard test yesterday and Livia wanted to do something nice for her.

Whitney had spent the last several hours getting to know the girls across the hall from them. They sat in the hallway laughing and talking. It was pleasant background noise while she was cooking.

Livia removed the oven mitts and walked out into the hallway. The cookies could wait a bit before going on the cooling racks.

Livia walked out to see the entire hallway lined with girls. Apparently, more than just the across-the-hall neighbors were involved. "What's going on?"

Whitney giggled. "We're having a wall sitting contest."

"Oh," Livia said. "Why?"

"For fun!"

Livia had to figure out a way out of this. She'd win them all without breaking a sweat. After playacting with Oliver, Livia had her fill of pretending to be someone she wasn't. Livia had pretended before Caesarea as she moved through society. At that point, she hadn't actually known about Taurus house so it didn't feel like a deception. Now that Livia knew, there was no way to escape the guilt for taking unfair advantage or being dishonest.

Livia waved Whitney off. "You guys have fun. I'll bring out cookies in five."

Livia returned to the apartment and put the cookies on a cooling rack and started to clean up the kitchen. She shook off the sadness that overtook her. She didn't want to join in the competition in the hallway but a sense of isolation overwhelmed her, knocking her breathless.

Livia would take the cookies out to the girls and she'd feel better. She scooped the cookies off the cooling racks and onto a plate and carried them out to the girls. The satisfaction she usually got from feeding people didn't erase her sadness.

The situation made her remember having a pushup contest in the staff room with one of Justin's officers, a huge Aquila guy named Alexander. He was always razzing her and she'd wanted to stick it to him. She'd won by two pushups after Alexander had collapsed from exhaustion. It had been one of the highlights of her time in Caesarea. It was cathartic to beat him at something but it had been one of the rare times that she'd been completely herself—stubborn, determined, strong, and hellishly tenacious—and then praised and celebrated for it. Why couldn't Caesarea be like that all the time?

* * *

Livia expected to see Corvin again by now, but she hadn't. A full week had passed and each time she left class, she looked for him. Each time she left her dorm room in the morning, she looked for him. Each time she ate at the cafeteria, she looked for him. Another week passed. The novelty of campus life wore off. Livia stopped only looking for Corvin and she started hoping she'd see him. She got on with her roommate and the people in her classes were nice, but she longed to interact with someone who understood the secrets she carried.

Livia didn't know what made her do it exactly—curiosity, mistrust, need. She expected her plan to fail. Corvin had probably pretended to be a student and now that he'd gotten the information he needed, he'd gone back to Caesarea. That's why she hadn't seen him in the past two weeks. Livia arranged to casually walk past room 315 in the Scipio building at 4:15 on a Monday evening.

The door was open and she saw Corvin's face, as he listened to one of his classmates give a presentation. She froze, unable to tear her gaze from his familiar face. He was still here. She didn't know how long she stood there until one of Corvin's classmates—a woman—touched his arm and gestured to Livia in the hallway. Corvin looked startled and his gaze fell on Livia.

Livia unfroze and she ran down the hallway to escape. Corvin came after her, catching her as the elevator opened.

"Wait!" he said. "Livia, hold on."

"No, I'm sorry. I shouldn't have bothered you." She walked onto the elevator. She pushed the button to close the doors faster.

Corvin hesitated a second. Then he leaped into the elevator before the doors shut.

"Corvin!" she shouted in frustration as the elevator jerked downward. "What are you doing?"

Now they were trapped here together.

"Are you okay?" he asked.

"I'm fine," Livia said, pulling herself into the corner of the elevator farthest from him.

"Livia, look at me," he demanded.

She looked up into his face and her frustration evaporated into thin air.

His eyes were piercing, a mix of concern and fear. "Livia, is everything alright?"

"I'm okay," she insisted. "Really, I promise."

"Really?" he asked, studying her face.

"Yes."

"Why are you here, then?"

There was a heavy silence. Livia struggled to come up with an answer that wouldn't make her seem pathetic or like a creepy stalker. "I came to see if you'd lied."

"About what?" he asked, confused.

"Being enrolled here. That you actually weren't here to just…check up on me."

Corvin sighed.

The elevator stopped and the doors opened. Corvin didn't move out of the way. Livia looked past him. "Excuse me."

"We're going to talk," he said, firmly.

"No, we're not," she said.

"You can't just run away." He blocked the elevator door from closing on them.

"I can just shove you," Livia threatened.

"You can," he said, unafraid. "Or we can just talk."

"That's not an incentive to stay," she said.

Frustration crossed his features plain as day, then he inhaled and schooled them. "Please, I'm not making an unreasonable request."

Surprised that he'd shown that much emotion, Livia agreed, "Fine."

"Now," he said, as they left the elevator together. "What is going on?"

Livia thought about running. There wasn't anything keeping her here except her own honesty. Well, also the fact that she liked seeing him. That was a problem, but it was true. She wasn't planning on spilling her guts to Corvin, but she knew that she could. Being around someone with whom that was possible was like finding an oasis in the desert.

"So, I guess…the joke is on me. Right?" Livia said, rubbing the back of her neck, embarrassed. "Hahaha and all that."

Corvin didn't laugh. "Can I do anything for you, Liv?"

"What? No. I'm fine. I'm sorry…you should go back to class. Don't let me bother you."

Corvin shook his head. "You're not a bother. I don't mind seeing you. Next time, let's do it outside our class time."

"Right, that's…"

Corvin tore a piece of paper off a flyer that was on a billboard next to the elevator. He took a pen out of his jacket pocket. He spoke as he wrote. "Here's my personal cell number and my address. Call me. Show up. I don't mind."

Livia accepted the paper in shock. Shouldn't he be annoyed and irritated with her? He hardly ever reacted the way she expected. Part of why she could not like him, she tried to remind herself. "Um, I—"

"Text me?" he encouraged, touching her arm lightly and looking into her eyes. "Then I'll be able to get a hold of you that way."

All the breath fled from Livia's lungs at his touch. It felt so good. Not in that physical way always described in Romance novels where you got tingles running down your spine. Emotionally, though, it helped. There was a relief from the isolation she'd felt. She didn't feel so disconnected from the world, from herself. All of him— his manner, his voice, the way he looked in her eyes—filled a huge crater in her. It scared her but she couldn't deny that even this short interaction with him was good for her.

"Hey," he said, softly. "I know I'm a pest for asking again, but you sure everything is alright, Fabulous?"

Livia laughed at the old nickname. "I think…I'm…I must be homesick, Corvin."

"Yeah," he said. "Is this the first time away from your family?"

"No, I—" Livia cut off. She didn't want to talk about the month she'd been in foster care. She didn't like the tremor that appeared in her voice when she said, "It's just good to see someone that knows me…"

"I'm here," he said. He gave her arm a brief squeeze and released her.

Livia was speechless. First, he was offering emotional support? That was new. Second, she was reacting way too strongly to his presence. She needed to cool it. She wasn't the seventeen-year-old with a crush on the security officer half-a-dozen years older than her anymore. She'd grown past that.

He gave her a friendly grin. "Come hang with us this weekend?"

"Okay, I'll come," Livia agreed, immediately. *No, you twitterpated girl.*

He nodded. "I'll see you then. Call if you need anything. I'm excited to hear how school is going for you."

Livia withdrew back behind the walls she'd constructed for herself. She needed to remember that even if she'd seen Corvin was capable of kindness that he was also kind of a jerk. "Go back to class before you miss something important," she said, in full-on scold mode.

He rolled his eyes and walked away. "See ya, Fabulous."

"Vale, bird-brain," she called back. It was unimaginative to mock him for the meaning of his name, but Livia had to work with what she had.

"Ravens are very intelligent, thank you. But you know that better than me, Auspictrix," he said without stopping.

"You made that word up," she yelled at his back, recognizing that he'd probably called her a bird watcher in Latin. Everyone in Caesarea had learned that about her.

"On the spot!" he called back.

Usually, these types of arrogant wisecracks irritated Livia but she laughed. Livia told herself to walk away but she watched as Corvin got on the elevator. He turned to face her when he pushed the buttons inside the elevator. Before the door shut he imitated a phone with his hand and put it up to the side of his head.

"Call me," he mouthed.

Livia was glad that the elevator door shut before he could see the full flush that heated her cheeks at the reminder to contact him.

Chapter 7

The next day, Felicity sent a second friend request on Tabula. Livia hesitated a fraction and then accepted the request. She hoped she didn't regret this. Not five minutes later she got a direct message inviting her to go on a hike that weekend. Livia wanted to go. She didn't feel safe hiking alone and she might never find anyone else that wanted to go with her. Oliver wasn't the type and Whitney was away on the weekends. The weather would be perfect this weekend and with it being fall who knew when it would snow.

She accepted the invitation. Livia wasn't a hoping person but she hoped this didn't turn on her the way everything else in Caesarea did. With her being mocked or scorned or shunned.

Livia waited at the trailhead prepared with her TARP issue hiking boots—a gift from Justin Aurelius. She'd broken them in on several department training hikes. She smiled. That was a good memory of Caesarea. Livia sighed. She was supposed to stop missing random things about Caesarea by now.

She checked her pack. It had everything she needed: snacks, water, a rain poncho, sunscreen, and a first aid kit. A black SUV pulled into the lot and parked next to her car. Corvin climbed out and popped open the back. He handed Terrance a small pack, Felicity a small pack, and then grabbed his own, twice as large. Corvin grinned when he saw Livia.

"G'afternoon, Liv," he said.

She nodded.

Terrance sidled up to Livia. "How are you doing?"

She nodded. "Good."

"You didn't invite Oliver?" Felicity asked.

Livia frowned. "Was I supposed to?"

"We assumed you would," Terrance said.

"I didn't think he'd enjoy a hike so I didn't ask."

"We decided that even if his job is weird that we like him," Felicity said.

"You do?" Livia asked, confused.

"Yeah, we chatted him up after you left to go study," Terrance said. "Decent guy."

Livia agreed. "I thought so too."

Felicity laughed. "He asked us what happened with Arik."

Livia rolled her eyes. "Really?"

Terrance teased but gently. "I think Oliver likes you."

"Why don't you just tell him?" Felicity asked.

"It's hard to explain," Livia answered.

Terrance and Felicity exchanged a look.

Livia tensed. "What?" she snapped.

"We didn't realize it was complicated," Terrance shrugged.

Livia snorted. "Arik say that?"

"He said you were too different," Terrance said.

"Such bullsh—" Livia bit off her curse. She took a breath. "It doesn't matter. I don't care anymore. Let's hike."

Corvin approached with a map. "Let's decide which trail to take first."

Livia's anger didn't disappear until they had started on the trail. They selected a trail they thought wouldn't be too hard. Felicity was nervous because hiking was out of her comfort zone. Corvin had to reassure her as they set out. Terrance took the lead and Felicity slipped in behind him. Livia waited for Corvin to go before her but he stared her down and gestured with a jerk of his chin.

So, he couldn't even use words, then? Livia huffed and went in front of him.

She wanted to be in the rear so she wasn't stuck in more conversations about Arik. Thankfully, though, neither Felicity or Terrance brought the topic up. Instead, she listened to them talk about non-civ people they thought were hot in their classes.

Livia was quickly bored and occupied herself with studying the vegetation and looking for animals. They were being too loud to see anything good but she saw a few birds—a hawk flying overhead, and a couple of sparrows, even a black-billed magpie.

"Would you make out with Oliver?" Felicity asked.

Livia snapped back into the conversation. "What?"

Okay, she could have not sounded so...offended.

There was a beat of silence.

"So, you don't like him?" Terrance asked.

Livia answered. "Look, I told him I wasn't into dating right now and I meant it. So that'd be kind of cruel if I made out with him."

"So, say it's non-committal," Felicity said.

Livia laughed. "Right. Cause he'd take me seriously after that."

Corvin chuckled behind her.

Terrance took that as an opening. "What about you, Cor? Any hot girls catch your eye?"

"Not that I'm willing to talk about," he said.

"I think if you liked Oliver enough you'd date him," Felicity said looking back at Livia. "You must not click well even if he is a nice guy."

Livia sighed. "I am not interested in dating."

"Did you ever get together with anyone after Arik?" Terrance asked.

"No."

He made a thoughtful sound. "Interesting."

Oh, now she was being analyzed by a Rattus. That was never a good position to be in. Next thing Livia knew he'd either be spewing psychological advice or making drama-filled assumptions to spread to his friends. She almost groaned out loud. Who even knew what type of empath he was? The best defense was an offense.

"When was your last relationship, Terrance?" Livia asked.

He laughed. "You're feisty, Liv. I was together with an Aquila house girl until I came out here. We decided to break up instead of doing a long-distance relationship."

Now Livia felt guilty. "Sorry," she muttered. "That's no fun."

"Yeah, but it was time," Terrance said. "We weren't going to last. She was Patrician class and even though being related to Corvin raises my status I'm plebeian. Plebeian males never marry Patrician females."

"Why not?" Livia asked.

Felicity gasped. "You dated Arik. You had to have known that."

That had been a huge issue in why their relationship ended. Livia was one of the only Patrician class Taurus house members left. The rest of the house were Plebeians. Livia had never grown up with the class distinction and so she'd refused to abide by the rules that made the groups distinct.

"I disagree with it," Livia said. "It makes no sense. It's stupid."

There was silence.

Felicity asked, "So, you did…break all those rules on purpose?"

"Yep," Livia said.

Terrance sucked air into his cheeks. "Wow. Arik must have been… frustrated."

Looking back, Livia hadn't listened to his objections. That would have meant agreeing that they couldn't be together because of arbitrary societal rules. In Livia's mind, she had to prove to him she was willing to break the rules. Then, he'd believe they could stay together but Caesarea had won. Arik had abandoned her.

Except, Livia felt dishonest. She was giving them the impression that she was a rebel instead of an innocent victim of ignorance, but those moments she'd intentionally rebelled were rare. She acted vastly more out of ignorance than outright rebellion. So, she confessed.

"But…that was only some of the time. Like sitting with Arik when I wasn't supposed to at parades and things. I knew where I was supposed to sit. But if I had sat where I was supposed to…I…I didn't know what to do. There were expectations but I don't know what they were. I still don't understand all the rules about clothes? I experimented until people stopped reacting to what I wore. Who knows if they just got tired of talking about it or if I did something right…" Livia laughed.

Terrance stopped walking. "I can't even imagine how hard that was for you. People judge patricians so hard in Caesarea."

"Why didn't Arik teach you—" Felicity looked offended on Livia's behalf.

"There's too much he wouldn't know," Corvin said. "He's plebian and a non-resident. They only visit a few months during the summer."

"But he knew people who knew," Felicity said.

"Arik is not well connected enough," Corvin said. "It would have taken the paterfamilias of Taurus house coming to one of the patres familias of the other houses."

"Why didn't Gaius do that?" Felicity asked.

"We don't know," Corvin said, frustration laced his tone. "Gaius is not good at communicating. He doesn't want to be paterfamilias and it shows in everything he does."

Livia agreed with that. Hyrum tried and picked up a lot of Gaius' slack but sometimes his hands were tied.

"Hyrum tries…" Livia said.

"Hyrum has impressed the patrician class, even earned a lot of our respect but he can't make up for the negligence of his paterfamilias," Corvin said.

Livia sighed. "Hyrum is a saint. I would have given up a long time ago. Lucas thinks they'll break him. At first, I didn't agree. Now, I'm wondering how long it will take to happen. I know that I'm done."

"Wait, you're going Rogue?" Felicity asked.

Livia inhaled and thought about how to answer that. "No." But it wasn't a strong declaration. It wavered with uncertainty because Livia wondered how much difference there was between going non-resident and going rogue. Did one lead to the other? Arik managed to be non-resident but he had people in Caesarea—cousins, aunts and uncles, grandparents. They anchored him there. Livia had some kind co-workers and Hyrum. It hurt not to have a place in the world, to not have a community that would accept her.

"You're the only Patrician family left in Taurus house," Terrance said. "If you go..."

"The house will fall—" Corvin said.

"But...what does that mean?" Felicity asked. "We can't not have Taurus house—"

There was silence.

"Corvin?" Felicity insisted.

"I don't know," he said, softly. "We've talked about raising a plebeian family. It should be simple to do. But they all refuse. We've tried. They're proud of being plebeian and no one wants to deal with the carnage Orcus and Ancus Pius left in their wake."

"Butchers," Livia spat with disgust.

Twenty years ago the Taurus paterfamilias had gone rogue and his younger brother had taken up the reigns of the house. When the elder brother returned, he demanded the position back. The disagreement led to a violent battle that had left Taurus house hollowed out.

"There aren't enough suitable patrician men for all my sisters to marry," Corvin said. "So, it is inevitable in our book that one of them will marry plebeian."

Livia stopped mid-step and turned to look at him. He had five sisters. Understandably, that was a lot of daughters to marry off but was the number of patricians that low? "Are there so few Patricians?"

"We're directly related to most of them," Corvin said. "Which makes a large percentage unsuitable. The patricians of Taurus house slaughtered each other. Hyrum married a plebeian and so did Gaius. Your brother Lucas is the only Taurus patrician left. Rattus house produced more females than males in this generation. Factor in ages, temperament, politics, personality differences and it won't happen. We've been staring down the reality for a long time."

Terrance added, "Yeah. When Hyrum married a plebian the Rattus house patrician women were furious. They thought he should feel obligated to look at them first because they have no other choice."

Corvin sighed. "Yeah, I've been on the receiving end of that ire multiple times. It's pretty much made me swear off dating any of them."

Terrance laughed at this. "Corvin, more than half of them are already your exes! That ship has sailed."

"Fine, sworn off dating them again," Corvin insisted.

Livia stayed silent but she didn't like the catty Rattus house clique either. She'd started referring to them as the malevolence of maidens to Hyrum. She'd expected to be scolded about that but he'd nodded in silent agreement, even adopted the nickname himself.

Felicity laughed. "That seems to be your Modus Operandi. You sure you can follow through on that?"

Livia was glad Corvin was behind her and couldn't see her facial expression. This reputation Corvin had developed was part of the reason her closest Caesarean friend Bella Aurelius wouldn't stop trying to get back together with him. Bella was Justin's oldest daughter and she'd been dumped by Corvin for about a month when Livia came to stay with them. Bella was crazy about Corvin and was convinced he'd take her back eventually.

Corvin had offered to get back together with Bella if she gave up the job that Corvin didn't like. Livia had been livid when she heard this. No boyfriend had the right to dictate where or how his girlfriend earned a living as long as it was respectable work. Livia had spent many a night talking Bella out of giving up the job that she loved and was good at to win Corvin back. Livia had pointed out how controlling it was that Corvin would even ask that. This was the main reason her opinion of him had fallen to such lows. He shouldn't need to make his girlfriend economically insecure to enjoy a relationship with her.

"It's been ages since I've been with anyone, Felicity," Corvin said. "So, I wouldn't say my dating life has a *modus operandi*."

Livia detected irritation in his voice and her anxiety triggered. Corvin seldom expressed emotion in his voice so he must be upset. She suddenly wasn't that pleased to have an irate Corvin at her back. Livia knew it was irrational but her mind started to play through escape scenarios. The next time he tilted his arrogant chin at her she was going to ignore him and take the rear position she'd wanted in the first place. Then she wouldn't be in this ridiculous situation.

Terrance executed a topic change. "Did you guys hear that the library is extending the hours it's open?"

"I did hear that," Felicity said. "Are you going to take advantage of being able to go in at 6 am, Corvin?"

Livia felt whiplash at the friendly way Felicity addressed Corvin. It was like she had no concept of the fact that she'd infuriated him three seconds ago.

Corvin laughed. "I might but I'm pretty sure Terrance won't."

Livia frowned. Wait, he was teasing Terrance now? So, he wasn't angry? Why was Corvin so confusing?

"No, way. I don't get out of bed before eight," Terrance said.

"I will," Felicity confessed. "Mornings are the worst. I get so lonely in my apartment. It will be nice to have a place to go to."

Livia's attention focused on Felicity because that sounded like a serious problem. Livia waited for Felicity to elaborate but the conversation moved forward without addressing it. Felicity didn't seem to mind. It wasn't like Terrance or Corvin were insensitive; it seemed like they'd already discussed it. Livia felt on the outside of their emotional closeness. The random chatting continued until they reached an overlook on the trail.

Livia found a place to sit with a nice view away from the others. She let out a sigh of relief and frustration. Maybe Whitney was wrong about this. Things were the same here as in Caesarea. Livia would always be on the outside of a group. A wave of sadness passed through her and instead of shrugging it off, Livia let it pass through her. The fresh air and the quiet space around her allowed her to do that.

Then Terrance came and sat down next to her. "Hey."

Livia barely managed to keep from jumping to her feet in surprise.

"Hey now," Terrance spoke, soothingly. "I'm only here to chat."

"About what?" she asked.

He considered her with concerned eyes. "Are you okay?"

Livia looked away from him. "I'm fine."

"You got scared back there," he said.

Oh no, was he an *adnotator* like Tavian? *Adnotators* could perceive other emotions by looking at them. Livia tried to remember if Terrance had looked back at her. Maybe he was an *Olfactator*—an empath that could sense emotions by smell. Livia had heard fear was an especially potent stench. "It doesn't matter," Livia said.

"It does matter," Terrance insisted. "What spooked you?"

Livia didn't know how to answer. Rattus were hard to deal with sometimes. It wasn't like you could lie and say they misread your reactions and if you did they got offended.

"I thought Corvin was mad," Livia confessed.

Terrace's expression flashed with confusion. "About what?"

"About Felicity's comment…"

Terrance looked thoughtful. "Oh, right, he was annoyed. That scared you?"

Livia looked away, trying to indicate she wasn't interested in elaborating but he waited. Rattus were so irritating.

"Your silence is saying volumes," Terrance said.

"Can we not have this conversation, please?" Livia snapped. "Some of us aren't interested in dissecting every single emotion we feel."

Terrace's face flashed with hurt. "Some of us would prefer not to experience others' emotions but we don't have a choice. So, excuse me for doing the responsible and humane thing by checking in with you."

Livia sighed and rubbed the back of her neck. She'd insulted him. He made a move to stand. "Wait," Livia said. "I didn't mean to hurt you."

"What did you mean to do then?" he asked.

"I'm…afraid of everyone," Livia confessed.

"Yeah?" Terrance settled back in. "If we're going to interact a lot. That's helpful to know."

Livia sighed. "I guess."

"Is there any way we can make things easier on you?" Terrance asked.

Livia met his gaze. "What are you going to do? Rewrite my history?"

Terrance blew his breath out. "I guess that's fair. But will you give us a chance to get to know you?"

"That's what I'm doing right now, isn't it?" Livia asked.

Terrance grinned. "I'm glad you came."

"Are you?" Livia asked.

"Yeah, Felicity needs people," Terrance looked back at her.

Livia followed his gaze. Felicity was sitting on a rock above Corvin talking a mile a minute. Corvin sat on his haunches and listened to everything she said. He didn't seem to be holding any hard feelings from earlier.

"It's her first time leaving home," Terrance said. "And she's alone. She was too afraid to request a non-civ roommate. She's extremely homesick and Corvin and I spend a lot of time with her but sometimes a woman needs another woman."

Livia studied Terrance's face. He had ridiculous purple hair but his concern for Felicity was genuine.

He turned and caught Livia studying him. He didn't seem to be bothered by that. "Why don't you go chat with her a bit? I'll call Corvin over here and give you some space to get to know each other."

Livia wanted to, but she hesitated. She couldn't hide her fear from him. "You sure she'd want to talk to me? People don't like me—"

Terrance rose to his feet. "Cor, come here, I got a question. I'll send Liv over to chat Felicity up."

So, Livia and Corvin traded places, Livia didn't look at him as they crossed paths.

Livia sat crossed-legged in the spot Corvin left. "Hey."

Felicity smiled stiffly. "How are you?"

"Better than I've been," Livia said. "You?"

Felicity gave a heavy sigh and toyed with her shoelace. "I miss my family."

Livia nodded.

"Do you miss yours?" she asked.

"A little," Livia answered.

"I miss mine so bad it hurts," Felicity put a hand over her heart. "I don't know how I'm going to make it all semester."

"Why not visit?" Livia asked.

"We're planning to," she said.

"When?" Livia asked.

44

"Fall Festival," Felicity said. "Will you come back with us?"

Livia frowned. "I don't know."

"I hope you do," Felicity said.

Livia took a deep breath. "You don't have a roommate."

Felicity shook her head sadly. "No."

Livia smiled. "Well, I met my roommate's lizard before I met her—"

Felicity gasped. "What?"

So then Livia told her all about Ares. It was becoming her favorite story to tell. Felicity laughed in all the right places. Livia cheered up as Felicity told her about the pets she'd had growing up. It was a nice conversation and Livia was surprised when Terrance and Corvin approached.

"We should head back down the trail," Corvin said, his eyes lingered on Livia.

Livia glared at Terrance. What had he told him? Corvin took the lead on the way down and Livia took the rear so she could avoid him. Livia thought she had escaped interacting with Corvin when he interrupted her before she slipped into her car.

He was alone. Terrance and Felicity were in his car. Livia's heart rate sped up. Would he be angry with her?

"Terrance mentioned I offended you?"

Livia snorted. That was the wrong word. "Offended?"

Corvin's head tilted to the side and his eyes narrowed as if he were trying to sort out a puzzle.

"What did I do, Liv? You're angry with me. Let's work it out."

"I'm not angry with you," she snapped.

"Then why are you acting like it?" he asked.

"I'm not angry. I never told Terrance I was angry. You misunderstood somehow."

"What did I misunderstand?" he asked.

"I gotta run, Corvin," Livia said, cutting the conversation short. "See you later."

Livia got in her car and drove away.

Chapter 8

Monday morning Livia got an invitation from Felicity again to do ice cream that weekend. Livia sighed and ignored the message as she got ready. Livia made sure she had the right textbook for her class. Then she slung her bag over her shoulder and walked down to campus.

Oliver waved her over when she walked into the room. Livia went to sit next to him. "How was your weekend?" she asked.

"Funny you ask," he sighed. "I decided to drop out."

Livia's eyes widened. "You did? Why?"

"I got a sponsor for my channel and I decided to make that my job. All this science…it's not me."

"So, I won't see you?" Livia asked, distraught.

Oliver was surprised. "You'd want to see me?"

Well, that was tricky to answer. "Are you staying around the area?"

"No, I'd be going back to California, my home state."

"Right, thanks for being a friend to me," Livia said.

Oliver looked sad. "You aren't going to miss me, are you?"

"A little," Livia said. She liked having him as a friend.

He smiled. "Maybe you can tune into my channel. Call me sometime and let me know what you think?"

"If I ever do, I'll let you know," Livia said.

"I'd like that," he said.

Livia was sad for him. He seemed lonely. "Well, if you ever find yourself back in this area let me know. We'll hang out."

"Thanks," he said. "That means a lot. It will be nice to be back with my family. I miss them."

Then class started, making it hard for Livia to reply.

* * *

Livia dithered over getting ice cream with the Caesarea folks for a few days. Then, that feeling returned. The deep loneliness coupled with the need to connect with someone that understood her. So, she wrote back and agreed to meet up with them. Oliver would fly back to California that Saturday and Whitney planned to spend the weekend with family. Livia didn't want to be alone the entire weekend.

Livia could only describe her feelings about the hangout as apprehensive. Why did Corvin have to confront her at the end of the hike? Why did Terrance have to misrepresent her feelings to him? She didn't imagine it would get better if Corvin knew she'd been afraid of him. She was pretty sure Corvin would be bothered, a lot. He would try to fix it and Livia wasn't certain she wanted that. The status quo between them was familiar. She was fine with that. It didn't need to be fixed.

Livia took a long time getting ready, analyzing every aspect of the way she looked. She ran her mascara wand through her eyelashes one last time. Her anxious brown eyes peered back at her. She attempted to reassure herself. She looked fine. Natural make-up. White shirt, black slacks, dark brown hair pulled back into a sleek ponytail. She was probably dressed too formally for an ice cream shop but she'd rather be too formal than the opposite. People from Caesarea needed to see her as competent and put-together. Livia had to prove to them that she wasn't like her mother.

Livia hated living in her mother's incredibly long, drama-filled, shadow. It made her feel like she had to be perfect. That she could never make mistakes. Sighing heavily, she put away her makeup and grabbed her purse. She'd thought about making up an excuse not to show up. Livia picked through her jewelry to delay the inevitable. She caught sight of the ring Gaius, the current paterfamilias of Taurus house, had given her as a high school graduation gift. An ancient seal ring, the golden band held an oval, onyx stone carved with the image of a Raven. Gaius had told her that it belonged to her grandmother and her mother before her and before her as long as anyone could remember. Livia picked the ring up and slid it over her ring finger. She spoke to it, invoking the spirits of her ancestors, people who were strangers but whom she felt connected to anyway. *Give me courage.*

It was a silly thing, but she didn't feel so alone.

* * *

The ice cream shop was bustling with college kids. She found the three of them sitting in a single booth. The only empty spot was next to Corvin. Livia hesitated.

Corvin stood when he saw her. "Livia."

He lowered his chin respectfully. Livia didn't know if she liked the formal show of respect or not. Sure, it was nice to be acknowledged but it made her acutely aware that he was raised patrician and she most definitely wasn't. He may as well have erected a wall between them for how estranged it made her feel.

There was a silence that stretched heavy between them. Terrance and Felicity watched, curious, waiting. Livia got the sense she was supposed to do something specific in return. She looked back at Corvin and cleared her throat.

"Hi, Corvin, how are you?" she attempted.

A surprised look crossed over Felicity's face and Livia wondered what she had done wrong. Caesarea folk were way too preoccupied with formalities.

Corvin wasn't bothered and turned to Livia and adopted a more relaxed demeanor. "I'm good, Liv. How are you?"

"I'm fine."

"Let's go back to Ratco now that she's here—" Felicity stood. "It'll be easier to chat."

Everyone murmured in agreement. Terrance and Felicity jetted out of their booth seat. They seemed uncomfortable in the crowded ice cream parlor. Only Corvin remained, as if hesitant to move too quickly. She eased closer to him, needing to ask before she went anywhere. "Who is Ratco?"

"It's the codename for the apartment," he said.

"What about getting ice cream?" she asked.

"Do you want some?" he asked.

Livia shook her head. None of the rest of the group was getting ice cream. "No, I'm good."

"I'll pay," Corvin offered, brow furrowing.

"No," Livia's cheeks turned hot. "That's nice, but I won't make the others wait."

"Another time," he said.

Corvin gave her the address to a place fifteen minutes away. Livia pulled up to a little townhouse and found a parking spot labeled visitor and pulled in. She thought about driving away and heading home. There was a high chance that things would only get worse if she went in. She'd committed some kind of blunder when Corvin greeted her. The way Felicity and Terrance had run out of the ice cream parlor made her worry they wanted nothing to do with her.

Livia brushed her thumb over the ring she wore. She took a deep breath. "Courage."

She got out of the car and crossed the parking lot, climbed the steps, and knocked on the door. Terrance smiled when he let her in. "We've been waiting. Come on in."

The first thing Livia saw when she walked in the door was a guitar. It sat propped on a stand next to a stool. Curious, she stared at it.

"It's Corvin's," Terrance said, waving his hand back toward the couches in the front room. "Come in, sit."

He seemed way more relaxed and pleased to see her. Livia wondered at the difference. Livia looked where Terrance gestured. Corvin sat in an armchair. Terrance closed the door behind her and sat next to Felicity on the couch. Livia had a choice between taking the third cushion on the couch or sitting on an empty loveseat. Livia opted to take a seat on the loveseat.

There was a silent moment.

"Did...something..." she looked around at them. She had to gather her courage. "Did I do something wrong?"

Corvin shook his head. "We were the ones that were behaving poorly, expecting you to perform our culture in a public place. I'm sorry."

Livia was confused. "That's why you wanted out of there so fast?"

"Oh," Terrance said. "No, it was just so crowded. As Empaths, that type of environment is difficult to concentrate. Too many emotions."

Livia decided to be blunt. "Are you an *Adnotator*?"

"No, an *Olfactator*, which is worse in that sort of situation. At least *Adnotators* can close their eyes to shut the emotions out. I can't stop smelling."

Livia looked at Felicity.

"I'm an *Auscultatrix*," she admitted.

Livia's eyes narrowed. "I haven't heard that one before."

"I can hear emotions when people speak," she said.

Livia asked, expecting a positive answer. "Even when they imitate a happy tone?"

"Yeah, you can't hide from an empath," Felicity said.

"What was Arik?" Terrance inquired. "If you don't mind us asking—"

"*Gustator*," Livia said.

They both nodded, accepting. Livia wondered if their lack of response should be interpreted negatively. Livia knew *Gustators* were considered useless in Rattus house. You couldn't go around casually tasting people. Status was more determined by familial relationships in Caesarea than by ability, but being a *Gustator* didn't gain Arik any respect.

Livia turned her attention to Corvin. "And you...what are you talking about?"

Corvin sighed. "According to Caesarean custom, You're supposed to tilt your chin up and say my name to invite me to speak to you."

Livia could only think of that as bizarre and she was sure it showed in her expression. "What?"

"Yes," Corvin nodded. "If you lower your chin and say '*Salve*' that is a dismissal."

"What if I don't know the person's name?" Livia asked.

"You lift your chin up and say 'tell me your name.'"

"So, I've been talking to people when they don't want me to and ignoring those that do invite me to speak with them this entire time?" Livia asked.

"It's a Patrician thing," Corvin said. "The plebeians don't stand on formality. With them, you would have been fine as you are."

"Corvin?" Livia couldn't hide her hurt. "Why didn't you tell me this ages ago?"

Corvin winced. "I thought you didn't follow the rules on purpose. I only realized you didn't actually...know. That it wasn't a deliberate choice."

"Who would have told me?" Livia asked.

"Gaius?" Corvin asked.

Livia shook her head. "No."

"I'm so sorry, Liv," Corvin said, running a hand through his hair. "It has been a hard year. A hard two years. So hard, that Justin forced me into this sabbatical. Part of me wonders if he did it on purpose because he knew you'd be here too."

"So, he did ask you to watch out for me?" she asked.

Corvin laughed. "No, he wanted to deny that he'd done it on purpose. He didn't speak a word until I called him to demand answers that first day I saw you on campus."

"What?" Livia gasped.

"He made me apply specifically to this program two days before the deadline. Before, we were negotiating on what my sabbatical would look like. I was going to stay in Caesarea. Then I got accepted and there was no more compromising. He literally kicked me out of Caesarea and said it was for my own good."

"Whoa, really?" Livia asked.

Corvin shrugged as if he didn't know what was going on either.

Livia asked, genuinely concerned, "So, what is Justin plotting?"

"I don't know," Corvin grumbled. "I'm particularly put out with him right now. Did he force you out here too?"

"No," Livia shook her head. "Tavian Hall recommended the school to me. So, I applied. Justin did write my recommendation letter, though. I told him when I got in."

"So you're here of your own free will at least," Corvin said. "That's a relief to know."

"Do you dislike it here?" Livia asked.

"No," Corvin winced. "It's been really good for me."

Livia laughed. "Justin was right?"

"He was so right," Corvin admitted, shaking his head, ruefully.

"That's…pretty hilarious," Livia said.

"Yeah, yeah, everyone else is laughing about it too."

"I'm happy you're happy," Livia said.

Corvin asked, "Are you happy, Livia?"

Livia took a deep breath. "It's…okay? I'm okay. But it's not what I expected."

"How so?" he asked.

"I just thought…it'd be different."

Corvin frowned, concerned. "Is everything okay?"

Livia nodded. "Classes are fine. I like my roommate. No problems."

"Not even with Oliver?" Felicity asked.

"He's left," Livia told her.

"Oh no, what?" Terrance asked.

"He decided to go back to being a twitch player. He got a sponsor and flew back out to California today."

"You sad about that?" Felicity asked.

"A little?" Livia admitted but changed the topic. She gestured to Corvin and then Terrance. "How did you end up rooming together?"

Terrance spoke up. "We're cousins on his maternal side."

Livia looked at Corvin.

"My mom is from Rattus house," Corvin explained. He gestured to Terrance "This is our place. We call it Ratco cause he and Felicity are Rattus and well...I'm Corvin."

"I'm in the dorms," Livia said.

Felicity's eyes widened. "Why did you decide to do that?"

Livia felt her defenses rise at her poorly disguised shock. "They're fine."

"I mean...that must be hard..." Felicity stammered.

"They're fine." Livia glared. She'd had enough of Caesarea's inside vs outside and civ vs non-civ to last an entire lifetime.

Felicity coughed awkwardly to break the tension. "We find it hard cause their out—"

Livia's interrupted. "They're normal people."

Felicity flexed her wrist in an exaggerated circle. "Exactly, so you have to hide who you are all the time. Doesn't that bother you?"

"That's how I grew up," Livia said, realizing as she said it how it would sound to them.

"So, you're okay with that?" Felicity asked, surprised. "You seemed to not enjoy that whole charade with Oliver at the school."

"I...that's...that's the way it is—" Livia said, flustered. She had thought it would be easier. However, Livia was realizing her emotions weren't as straightforward as she'd expected. Caesarea had changed her. She thought getting away, distance, was what she needed. She was starting to wonder if she was wrong.

"We don't consider that very healthy," Felicity said.

Well, this conversation had turned on Livia rather swiftly. She didn't know what to say to that. Everything she'd say would probably make them flag her for mental illness but Livia had lived a difficult life. Having healthy options was a hell of a privilege. She didn't even think like that. If there was food on the table, you didn't ask questions—you ate it. If you were sick, you ignored it—unless you were about to die.

"You're always welcome here," Corvin said, firmly. "You'll usually find at least one of us at home."

Terrance crossed his ankle over his knee. "No big deal."

The show of support touched Livia. She tried to hide it. She brushed her nose and looked at the ground. "I'm fine."

"Why didn't you ask to room with someone?" Felicity asked. "I mean, we could have gotten a place together if you'd posted on the board."

Livia had known about the board. Tavian had told her about it. Just like he'd been the one to mention Cornelia Africana University. It was known in Rattus house as a good place for people from Caesarea to go to college, with its little classically inspired campus and strong humanities emphasis.

"I wanted to feel normal," Livia said. "Like a normal college freshman."

"But we're different from them," Felicity said, confused.

Livia realized Felicity's conception of normal was likely different than hers. She experienced a sense of sharp disorientation as she realized her default definition of normal was shaped by non-civ culture and not by Caesarean expectations. A deep discomfort overwhelmed her as she wondered if she was doing everything all wrong.

"It doesn't matter," Livia said sharply, trying to shake off the sensation.

"But it does," Felicity said with exasperation.

"Stop being so obsessed with how people are different!" Livia stood, an ache tightened her throat. "I won't listen to it anymore."

"Livia may feel more at home in their culture than she feels in our culture," Corvin broke in smoothly. "It's what she is used to."

"She's being unfair," Felicity said. Her eyes shone with a wet sheen.

Had Livia made her cry? Livia tried to figure out if she was close to crying. Was Felicity picking up Livia's emotions? Or had Livia genuinely hurt her? Did Livia need to apologize? Rattus were so complicated.

"Maybe, but getting upset over it will only make the situation worse," Corvin said. "It's okay for two people to feel differently about the same situation."

Felicity huffed and looked away.

Terrance interrupted the spat. "Tell us about your classes, Liv. May I call you that? Liv?"

Livia's hesitated. Unsure of how to fix things. She looked between Terrance and Felicity several times before answering, "Livia. Liv. I don't care."

Felicity turned toward her, conciliatory. "You like your classes? Are they difficult?"

Livia stared at her, annoyed that she appeared so calm. Livia's heart was still pumping heat through her veins. She kept her words as short as possible to avoid hurting Felicity again. "Not too difficult."

"Yeah, piece of cake after Caesarea Academy, right?" Terrance joked.

Everyone laughed, except Livia. She'd already graduated from high school when she came to Caesarea. So she'd never attended Caesarea Academy but rumors about its academic rigor were legendary.

"How many credits are you taking?" Felicity asked.

Livia studied Felicity, surprised at her persistence to continue the conversation. The joke about Caesarea Academy didn't land right but they were still trying. She deliberately took a deep breath before she spoke again. Livia's tension eased a tad and she realized how tense she'd gotten. "Fifteen."

Livia sat back down. Tentatively, they all exchanged information about how their schedules looked. Most of Corvin's classes were late afternoon and early evening. The mornings he spent studying and working out. He ran two miles and did weights in the basement of the townhouse. He still had to maintain department physical fitness standards to transfer over to the academy.

They chatted for over an hour without any more disagreements. They decided to order pizza and keep talking.

Felicity turned to Corvin now the atmosphere was relaxed. "Um, Corvin, I need help with something—"

"What is it?" he asked.

"I'm signed up for the wrong section of math. So, now I need to drop it and add a new one. They're making me submit a form instead of doing it online since it's two weeks into the semester. The online registration closes down after a certain date."

He nodded. "Yeah?"

"So, who do I turn the form into?"

Livia laughed. Not because she thought Felicity was stupid for asking the question but because she'd made the same mistake in Caesarea only in reverse. The forum was a small enclosed place, built underground to hide its existence. Overcrowding could be dangerous so lines were discouraged. That meant most paperwork was handled by Patrons who submitted it on behalf of people to keep public spaces clear. Terrance and Felicity exchanged a look over her laughter—shared disapproval.

Corvin frowned at Livia. "I'm not sure, Felicity. I'd have to look it up."

"You have to turn it in yourself," Livia said.

"I do?" she asked, surprised.

"Yeah," Livia nodded. "Probably in the administration building. You'll have to stand in line."

Felicity's eyes widened. "Oh."

"That's how it is done out here," Livia said. "When I got to Caesarea people got mad at me because I kept showing up to submit forms and papers instead of sending them to my Patron. It was awful the first month. I didn't understand why it didn't work the way it was supposed to."

"Supposed to..." Felicity said.

"Of course, you would manage your own paperwork," Livia said. "Why would you trust someone else too?"

Felicity's chin drew in. "What?"

"It doesn't even bother you does it?" Livia asked.

"Which part?" she asked, eyes looking troubled.

"Trusting people to deal with your papers," Livia said. "Out here, all these people are strangers. You don't know them. It's dangerous for them to have access to your personal information. They can steal your identity."

"What?" she asked in disbelief. "How can anyone steal your identity? Everyone knows..." she stopped. "No one knows me."

She put her hand on her chest and a look of panic filled her face. Crap, Livia hadn't meant to scare her.

"Hey, it's fine," Livia said. "Most people are indifferent. They don't care about you enough to notice you."

This didn't comfort her. It made it worse.

Livia opened her mouth to try and fix it again.

Corvin held up a hand. "Liv, stop. You're making it worse."

Livia frowned. "I'm trying to help."

"I know, but it's not working. Let me, okay?"

"Felicity, what can we do for you right now?" Corvin asked, kindly.

She shook her head.

"Can you tell us what you're thinking?" he asked.

She shook her head again.

"Have you trusted anyone with papers or personal information here?" he asked.

"No," her voice came out quietly. "But...I didn't believe people when they said...people from Caesarea get tricked out here."

"But what Livia said made you realize you could?" Corvin asked.

"Yeah," she said. "What if she hadn't said anything?"

Corvin spoke gently. "But she did and you did the exact right thing by asking questions."

Felicity's face softened. "Right."

"We care about you," Corvin said. "We're here. Livia, Terrance, and Me. If you need anything we can help."

"I didn't realize it'd be so hard," Felicity's eyes filled with tears and she cast a look at Livia. Understanding dawned at that moment. Felicity was so focused on the differences between being civ and non-civ because things were hard for her right now. Livia shutting her down earlier made it impossible for her to talk about what she was struggling with. Struck with guilt Livia made an offer.

"We get out of class about the same time Monday morning," Livia said. "I can walk with you to the admin building. Stand in line next to you."

"You'd do that?" Felicity asked.

Livia nodded. "Yeah."

"That's nice," she said.

Livia shrugged. "It's hard to get used to a new place."

Felicity's tears overflowed.

Livia's guilt quadrupled. She cleared her throat. "I was unfair...earlier."

"How'd you get used to Caesarea?" she asked.

"I didn't," Livia said. "I've moved a lot. Adapted to a lot of places growing up. But Caesarea was...hard."

Felicity's eyes widened. "Are you going to go back?"

Livia hesitated. She thought about being honest. Thought about lying. Thought about her mom. Thought about her brother Hyrum. "I'm trying to figure that out right now."

"Will you go rogue?" she asked, horrified.

Livia sighed. This was the second time Felicity had asked her the question. "That's...I know that's what my mom did. But that'd mean being estranged from Hyrum. I won't do that."

"So, how'd you live there if you hated it?" Felicity asked.

"You hate it here?" Livia asked.

"Well, do you like it?" Felicity asked.

"This is a good place," Livia assured her. "It's a lot safer than lots of the places I've lived. It's beautiful and clean and close to nature. Like Caesarea, it's also very close to nature."

"I never thought of that," Terrance said. "That's true."

"You didn't answer my question. How'd you deal with living in Caesarea, if you hated it?" Felicity insisted.

Livia folded her arms across her stomach. "I don't think my answers are going to be your answers, Felicity."

"Why not?" she asked.

"Well," Livia hesitated. "Have you ever starved? It was better than starving—"

Felicity blinked. "Oh."

Livia looked at the ground. "It was better than a lot of things..."

Livia knew that they all knew her family history. It had come up more than once during Hyrum's political fights with the senate.

"I see," Felicity breathed.

"This is a good place," Livia said, earnestly.

Felicity nodded. "Okay."

Livia said, "Every day will be different. It'll be hard, but good stuff happens along with the bad stuff, usually. That helps."

Felicity laughed. "You're tough."

"I'm Taurus," Livia grinned. It felt good to say it. To own it. Happiness skittered along her skin.

* * *

The pizza had arrived. Livia moved with Terrance into the kitchen. Felicity and Corvin lingered behind. She could hear Corvin's calm voice offering comfort and advice. Livia loaded a paper plate up with Pizza.

Felicity decided not to stay to eat and left the house. Livia tensed, looking between her plate and the door. Should she leave too? Now that her plate was full of food, it'd be weird to walk out. Corvin came into the kitchen. "Everything alright, Liv?"

"Um, we were invited to eat pizza right?" she asked in a small voice.

"Of course," he said. "Please, stay, I got too much for just the two of us."

Livia looked at Terrance with mischief in her smile. "I'm pretty sure you could handle it."

Terrance laughed. Corvin smiled.

Terrance said, "Stay, Liv. It's nice to have a new face around."

"We have the same conversations over and over," Corvin said.

The two of them caveman grunted a conversation about doing chores that made Livia laugh so hard her eyes teared up.

Corvin got himself a plateful of pizza, standing next to Livia at the bar. "Liv, if I may ask a personal question."

Having him so near made her nervous. She didn't know why, but her heart started pounding.

"What question?" she asked.

"Are you engaged?"

She flinched. "What? What made you ask that?"

59

"I was wondering the same thing," Terrance said.

She looked at him bewildered.

"You're wearing a ring," Corvin said.

"Oh, oh," Livia pulled the ring off and put it on the counter in front of her as if it had burned her. "No."

There was silence. Livia explained. "It was a graduation gift from Gaius."

"May I see it?" asked Corvin.

Livia nodded, her throat tight with anxiety.

Corvin plucked the ring up from the counter and inspected it. "Beautiful," he said, quietly. He turned a wry gaze on her. "It's a Raven."

Heat rushed to Livia's cheeks. She didn't want to admit that was part of the reason she'd chosen it. The cool, black stone and the engraved image had appealed to the bird-watcher in her. She tried to shrug like it was nothing. "Gaius said it belonged to my grandmother and her mother and her mother as far back as people can remember," Livia explained.

He turned to her. "The safest place for it is on your finger."

Corvin pulled her hand into his palm and then slid the ring back onto her finger. Livia froze and stopped breathing, as warmth spread in her chest, and a whisper of a pleasant tingle traveled up her arm at his touch.

Livia jerked her hand from his. "That's kind." her voice was short, cold. She tried again. "Of you to say...nice...I—" Thirty seconds ago she knew how to thank someone properly.

"Are you trying to say thank you?" Corvin asked.

"Yes."

"I'm sorry, if...I made you uncomfortable?" he said.

Livia took a deep breath, hating how vulnerable and shaken she felt because of the attraction he'd provoked. Inhaling with him so close was a mistake. It was impossible to ignore his scent. Clean laundry. The smell immediately took Livia back to their first meeting.

"You smell," Livia commented, her mind in another place.

"I do?" Corvin asked, easing back.

"It's the same smell from the night we met—"

Corvin stopped moving backward and tilted his head to the side. "Does that bother you, Liv?"

"I don't know," she said. "You kept me safe but—"

"You were hurt," he said. "Does it upset you to remember?"

Livia closed her eyes and shook her head. She stepped back from him. "I'm alright now."

To prove her point she took a big bite of her pizza. Corvin continued to watch her. "We can talk about it," he said.

"Nope." Livia took another bite.

"Well, you're eating," he said. "That's a sign you're not too upset."

Livia remembered being unable to eat the night they first met. Not until after midnight when he'd offered her dark chocolate that Arik had told him was her favorite. Then he'd sat with her through the entire night, as she had awful nightmares. He hadn't complained when her terror had made her cling to him. When she'd pressed her face into his back and flung her arms over his shoulders he remained still as a rock and let her hold him.

Suddenly, Livia wanted to cry. That Corvin was different from the Corvin she'd met in Caesarea. She missed that Corvin. She sometimes wondered if she'd imagined him, and that hurt her heart.

Terrance had stilled and watched them with concern on his face.

"I'm fine," she told him. But her appetite had disappeared. She took a bite and couldn't swallow it. She grabbed a napkin and spat into it.

"Liv," Corvin said. "Why don't—"

"I'm going to go," Livia flashed a smile. "Nice night. Thanks for the invite."

Then she fled. She grabbed her purse, pulled out her keys, and slipped out the front door.

Chapter 9

Livia met Felicity at the student center after lunch. Felicity looked right past Livia. Livia had to wave and call out her name before Felicity recognized her. She looked startled and walked toward her.

"I didn't expect to see you dressed so casually," she said, embarrassed.

Too late, Livia realized she hadn't even thought about dressing up. Something she never neglected to do in Caesarea. She was in jeans, a battered tee, and a pair of flimsy sneakers.

"Oh, um," Livia didn't know how to respond. Saying I forgot I needed to impress you would probably backfire on her.

"Patricians never wear sneakers," Felicity said. "Did you know that?"

"No." Livia had adapted to wearing only ballet flats in Caesarea, though.

"Most girls wear heels," Felicity said. "It's a big deal you only wear flats."

Livia had noticed but she'd always worked on her feet and didn't own a pair. Not only were heels expensive but they were the least useful shoe in existence. She wasn't about to parade around in a product that was a waste of her hard-earned money.

"I hate heels," Livia said.

Felicity smiled. "Well, the Lupus house females were fans. They stopped wearing heels all summer long. It was their way of showing support after that breakup with Arik."

Livia's eyes widened. "What?"

Felicity nodded. "I had this whole talk with Corvin after the hike about how not knowing how the patricians communicate via fashion probably meant you missed all their shows of support."

"They supported me?" Livia hated the emotion that crept into her voice. She cleared her throat and shook her head. Though, the ritual was useless with an empath. Livia sighed.

"You didn't notice," Felicity confirmed.

"No."

Felicity looked sad. "I'm sorry, you felt so alone."

"Right," Livia nodded. She could tell Felicity was absorbing her emotions and she didn't want that. She decided to change the subject.

Livia pointed. "Now, the admin building is right over there. Do you have your papers?"

Felicity nodded.

"Let's go."

They wandered around in the building a bit before they found the office they needed in the basement. Felicity looked around the corners with trepidation. "There's no security," she said, concerned.

"There doesn't need to be," Livia said. "I was freaked out for weeks in Caesarea because there are so many guards everywhere. Constantly felt like I was in danger."

"But the guards keep you safe," Felicity said.

"There are no guards out here unless there is a reason for them," Livia said. "No guards, safe place."

"But...guards prevent bad stuff from happening. It's better to be safe and have them there than be sorry. Also, cause Taurus have super strength and Aquila super speed, way more can go wrong faster," Felicity argued.

Livia nodded. "Yeah, but it took me a while to figure out that basic assumptions about security are different in Caesarea. Justin and I had this epic talk about it when I started to refuse to leave the house. He didn't understand why I felt unsafe when there were security personnel around all the time."

"But…I feel unsafe cause there are no guards anywhere," Felicity said.

Livia nodded. "If you're from Caesarea, yeah, it'd feel weird. But I didn't grow up there so it was a shift in mindset, definitely."

Felicity sighed. "Do you like it better without the guards?"

"Oh yeah," Livia said. "I can relax out here. Sort of…"

"Sort of?" Felicity asked.

They waited in line and Livia looked around. "There was a freedom in everyone knowing my House. Here, I have to hide it."

"Yeah," Felicity said. "That is harder than I expected too. I was warned and everything but—"

"Me too," Livia agreed.

They smiled at each other. They didn't have to say anything else. It was nice for both of them to be around someone who understood. Felicity finished her business and they left the building together.

"Are you coming to Ratco again this Saturday?" Felicity asked.

"Probably," Livia said. Though, she thought about not going to avoid Corvin. She was still mortified over how she'd left last Saturday. She dreaded seeing him.

"Good," Felicity said relieved. "I like Corvin and Terrance but it is nice to have another girl around."

"They get into locker room talk?" Livia asked.

Felicity looked surprised. "No, nothing like that. Corvin would shut that down so fast."

Livia frowned. "Then what's wrong with them?"

Felicity sighed. "They're so…they're family. So, I don't feel like I belong there. Like I'm a third wheel. But if you're there I don't feel so…different."

"Like an outsider?" Livia asked.

"Yeah," Felicity said. "And I feel like that all the time here—"

"I know how that feels," Livia said.

Felicity looked at her surprised. "You do, huh? I'm so sorry. I wish I'd done more to help people that were new to Caesarea now. This feeling is awful."

"I'll come," Livia promised her.

The rest of Livia's week flew by faster than she expected. Then Thursday night Corvin texted her. She hadn't known he had her number this entire time.

He wrote: Liv, you busy tomorrow night?

Livia: Why?

If he asked her on a date…that'd be…a no.

Corvin: I need help.

Livia: With what?

Corvin: Our fridge is broken and I need to move it to fix it.

Livia: You need help fixing your fridge?

Corvin: Yes.

Well, she didn't expect this but part of her liked being able to make her awkwardness up to him. Also, it'd be a trial run to see if she could do Saturday or not. So she agreed.

Corvin answered the door. Livia's gut lurched when she saw his face. She took a step back and was going to run away. Then Corvin smiled.

It was the smile she remembered pre-Caesarea. There was something open in his face, his eyes, that drew her in. "Corvin?" she asked, stupidly.

"Come on in, Liv," he said.

There was an inflection in his voice. That was different.

Livia walked through the front door. She debated on saying something. Then decided to keep her mouth shut. She was here to make up for telling him he smelled and then running away.

Livia followed Corvin into the kitchen. There was a laptop with youtube videos pulled up on it, the owner's manual, a handful of tools, a notebook full of notes.

"What's wrong?" Livia asked.

"Our ice maker isn't working," he said, turning to face her. A lush black curl hung across his eyebrow, not quite in his eye but close enough that Livia wanted to brush it back. Her hand clenched into a fist.

No. Livia scolded herself not to think like that

"You're not going to call someone to fix it?" she eyed him. He was rich enough to do that.

"I want to try it this way first," he said. "I need to get to the back of it to check the lines..."

Livia looked around, mostly to escape his direct gaze. It was giving her butterflies. "Where's Terrance?"

"He's taking a nap. Class was rough on him today."

"Is he okay?" Livia asked.

"Yeah," Corvin said. "It's an empath hangover. He'll recover after some alone time."

"Something went wrong?" Livia asked, tentatively.

"They were doing group presentations in front of the class," Corvin explained.

"Oh." Livia immediately understood. Speaking in front of people terrified her too.

Livia and Corvin worked together to pull the fridge out from the wall. Her Taurus strength made the work smooth and easy. She tensed when Corvin sidled next to her, but she noticed that he smelled different. A sharp lemon scent and lavender. She studied him, puzzled.

"What's wrong?" he asked.

"You..." Livia hesitated to bring it up. "Nothing."

"Do I smell different?" he teased.

Livia's face flamed red. "I'm sorry about that."

He laughed. "I hoped the change would help?"

It was weird, but it did. Also, what a thoughtful thing to do. Livia turned away from him as her attraction to him flared. "Whatever. There's enough space for one of us to go back there. Is it going to be me or you?"

"I'll go," he said.

Corvin slid behind the fridge and fiddled around for a bit. "It looks like the hose is fine. That's not the problem."

After a great deal more muttering and puttering around Corvin determined that they needed to replace the condenser motor. He slid out from behind the fridge and strode over to the laptop. He typed and scrolled silently until he found the information he needed.

"Okay, they have the part in stock at the hardware store on main. You up for coming along?" He closed the laptop and looked at her.

Livia nodded. "Sure."

They hopped in the car together. They had pulled out of the lot and stopped at a light before it hit her. Livia was completely alone with Corvin. A heaviness settled in Livia's stomach, it wasn't fear of him exactly. She was afraid that she was doing the wrong thing.

"You okay, Liv?" Corvin asked, softly.

She didn't answer.

"Liv," Corvin said with an edge to his tone. "What's wrong?"

"This has never happened," she squeaked.

"What?" he asked.

She gestured between them. "We're...we're alone."

"We've been alone for over an hour. Are you scared I'm not taking you where I said I would?"

"No, I'm scared Justin is going to find out," Livia said, on a panicked inhale.

Corvin laughed. "Liv, he's not our boss out here."

"Right, he can't fire me," Livia said, exhaling.

"No, he can't," Corvin said. "Because you don't even work for him anymore."

"And you're not...you're not my supervisor."

"I never was really—" Corvin said, confused.

"But you had rank," Livia said.

"True," Corvin said. "But all those ranks and responsibilities I had in Caesarea mean nothing out here."

Livia's heart rate slowed. "Right. You're just Corvin."

"I'm just Corvin," he said.

Livia honestly didn't know what just Corvin was like.

"I'm just Livia," she said.

"Nice to meet you," Corvin quipped.

But the joke felt appropriate. It did feel a little like they were meeting for the first time. She laughed.

"We're okay," Corvin reassured her. "No one is getting fired for picking up a refrigerator part, okay?"

Livia nodded, relaxing into her seat.

"How about music?" Corvin asked.

"Please," Livia agreed.

Corvin looked over at her. "What do you want to listen to?"

She shrugged. "Your car, you choose."

"It's folksy country stuff—"

"I don't care," Livia said. "It'll be interesting to listen to something new."

Corvin turned the music on and turned it up. "What do you think?"

"Give me a minute." Livia gave him a hesitant look.

"What?"

She was nervous to let down her guard around him. "I'm going to listen."

"Go for it," Corvin said, looking the other way so he could check for a car before he turned right.

Livia took a deep breath and closed her eyes. She relaxed into her seat and tried not to think of anything but the music. Corvin remained quiet. That was nice. Arik always talked when she tried to listen. To him, music was only noise.

It took a while for Livia to relax enough to feel the music and she decided she liked the way it danced inside her head. Slow, yet still upbeat. The music was light and happy, not the usual dark and heavy stuff that dominated Livia's playlist. She opened her eyes.

Corvin was looking ahead to adjust for traffic so he could turn into the parking lot of the hardware store.

"It's nice," Livia said. "Not my usual, but refreshing."

Corvin grinned. "Glad you were willing to give it a chance, Liv. What's your usual?"

'Just' Corvin smiled a lot more than Caesarea Corvin and he also was way less tense. His voice was less clipped and more mellow. The change was interesting. While they wandered through the store Livia and Corvin had a detailed conversation about their music preferences. She enjoyed their conversation but wondered the entire time why it had taken them an entire year to have it. The longer they talked, the more apparent it became that they both had a voracious appetite for music. Corvin knew most of the bands she named, even some of the more obscure ones. When she challenged him he'd quote a lyric or hum a few bars. He was like a musical encyclopedia.

"How do you know all this?" she demanded on the way home.

"I'm Lupus, Liv," he said. "I remember things. Also, I really like music."

"Me too," she confessed. "It...comforts me."

"Yeah," he nodded. "Music is good for that."

"Sometimes...it's the only thing that does," she said.

"I'm glad you have something that does that for you," Corvin said.

Livia looked out the window, feeling vulnerable at having confessed something so personal to him. She waited for him to make himself vulnerable as well, to show her that her emotional risk was reciprocal but he didn't say anything else. The sting bit deeper the longer the silence went on.

Livia was glad when she was able to escape the car. She wanted this whole thing to be over. She felt embarrassed for having confided even the least bit in Corvin. He was only interested in being polite to her. She shouldn't have opened herself up to him. She needed to remember that he wasn't supportive of Bella so it was likely he'd treat her the same way. Pursuing her attraction to Corvin Tullius would be an epic mistake. She couldn't forget that.

Corvin put the part on the counter and pulled up a video about changing the condenser motor on his computer. "This shouldn't be too hard, Liv."

She nodded, not speaking.

They watched the video together. Corvin took the condenser motor out of its package. "Let's give this a whirl, huh?"

"Sure," Livia said.

"Can I get you anything, Liv? We have some drinks in the fridge. Dr. Pepper? Coke?" Corvin asked.

"No," she said, a touch too sharp.

Corvin hesitated a fraction, eyes searching her face. Then pulled out a coke from the fridge and opened it and took a drink. "It's not a big deal if you want one."

"No, thank you," Livia said again.

His eyes narrowed the slightest bit but he screwed the cap back on his drink and slipped behind the fridge with the motor in hand.

"Corvin," Livia said sharply. "Unplug the fridge!"

"Oh, right," his voice muffled behind the fridge. "Thanks, Liv!"

The whirring of the fridge silenced. Livia rolled her eyes. Good thing she was here to keep him from electrocuting himself.

"I think that's it," he said, several moments later.

"Great," Livia said, relieved she could be done being around him now.

The whirring of the fridge started again. "Let's push this fridge back into place."

"Right," Livia agreed.

They pushed together. After a few slight adjustments, the fridge was black in place.

"Thank you, Liv," Corvin said, sincerely. "I appreciate your help."

She nodded and grabbed her purse and keys from the counter.

"Will I see you tomorrow?" he asked, trying to catch her gaze.

She shrugged, refusing to look at him. "Maybe. I might need to study."

"Is everything...alright?" he asked, stepping closer.

Livia drew back one step for each one he advanced. Corvin stopped. "Liv—"

"See you, Corvin," she said.

"Liv? What did I do?" he asked.

"Nothing," she said.

Corvin's eyes narrowed. "Tell me why you're upset with me."

Livia turned and strode toward the front door. Corvin's hand pressed against the door as she turned the knob. Livia wanted to jerk it open and send him sprawling, heavens knew she could, but she'd spent her entire life being careful about giving into such petty feelings. It was easier to school her impulses than it was to give into them.

"Corvin," Livia ground out. "Stop putting yourself in this situation."

"What situation?" he asked.

Livia jerked the door open easily, but it was a slow, controlled movement, not an impulsive angry one. "The one where I have to show you that you

70

can't stand in my way."

She slipped out the door without further fuss and pulled it shut behind her. She could feel him tug on it from the inside. She held it closed until he gave up. Then released the door and walked toward her car. Corvin opened the door when she was halfway to her car. He stood there, watching her.

It shouldn't satisfy her so much to see the anger etched into his expression. "Livia," he snapped. "If you're angry at me for some reason just *tell me*, don't play these stupid games."

"Don't try to trap me ever again, Corvin Tullius. I can't promise the third time that I'll choose to control my temper."

"I didn't trap—"

"Didn't you?" Livia demanded.

He took a deep breath. "Okay, I didn't want you to run away like you did last time. I don't like it that I make you feel that way. Tell me what I can do to change that, Livia."

He seemed genuinely upset and Livia felt vindicated. She'd showed emotion, he'd showed emotion. It felt equal. Satisfying. It also felt childish and ridiculous. Was she in elementary school?

"I don't want to tell you what to do," she said.

He looked frustrated. "You just did. Rule one: Don't trap you."

"I like that rule." Livia smiled.

Corvin sighed but a corner of his mouth turned up. "What else did I do to make you angry?"

Her smile disappeared. "I wasn't angry."

Corvin's expression fell. "I hurt you."

Livia was frustrated because she could feel her expression betraying the truth of his words. She didn't want that. "I don't have time for this, Corvin," she snapped and stomped to her car.

He didn't move. Didn't try to stop her or call her back.

Livia opened the door, started the engine, and pulled away. She didn't like the fact that this was the third time she'd run away from him this way. Why did she get so irrational when she was around him? So, he didn't respond to her emotional confession the way she expected. Why did that have to be such a big deal to her? With any other person it wouldn't even phase her. Why was Corvin this weird exception?

Chapter 10

Whitney was starting to be the person that Livia went to for relationship advice. Whitney was crocheting on the couch when Livia came into the living room and lay on the floor in front of her.

"What's going on, Liv?" she asked.

"I have a problem with this guy—"

"Oliver?"

"No, this is a new guy," Livia said.

Whitney made an intrigued noise. "Go on."

"I know him from work back home—"

"Oh, you ran into him at that library service project, didn't you?"

"Yeah," Livia said, surprised she remembered.

"So, what's the problem?"

Livia took a deep breath. She couldn't tell Whitney all the details. She'd spent three days trying to figure out how to navigate this conversation without spilling anything she shouldn't.

"I've had a crush on him for—" since I was seventeen "—a while but I know he's all wrong for me."

"How do you know that?" Whitney asked.

"He dated one of my friends back home and he didn't treat her very well—"

"Why? What did he do?" Whitney asked.

Livia sighed. "She got this job she was really excited about and good at and he asked her to quit because he didn't like it."

"Oh," Whitney sounded, concerned. "Do you know the reason why he didn't like it?"

Livia paused. "No. It's not like I interrogated him about it."

"Well, you can't be upset unless you know the reason. What if they were asking her to do unsafe things or the person she was working for was a jerk or something?"

Livia picked at the carpet anxiously. "Here's the thing. I can't ask him why he objected to her job."

"Why not?" Whitney asked.

"I don't know how to bring it up—" Livia said.

"Just bring it up," Whitney said.

Livia shook her head. "We're not that close. That's the thing. We're not close and that won't change so I need to stop liking him."

Whitney sighed. "You're not going to like my advice."

"What is it?" Livia asked.

"There are two ways to get over a person," Whitney said. "One, you date other people until you find someone you like better—"

Livia let that sink in and her heart sank. You didn't find many people better than Corvin—good family, financially stable, smart, professional, hard-working, community-minded. The boys in the general population wouldn't catch up for years. Livia had time, though, she could wait.

Whitney continued. "Second, you tell them you like them and it either works out or it doesn't."

Livia frowned. "I don't like that."

"Why not?" Whitney asked.

Livia turned toward Whitney. "What if it works out?"

Whitney laughed. "Then great! Right?"

"This is bad advice." Livia pulled herself into a sitting position and stood up.

"Wait, what's his name?"

"I'm not telling you—" Livia said, walking away.

Whitney laughed again. "Come on!"

"No. You already know too much."

* * *

Livia struggled to decide to go mingle with the Caesareans that weekend. Her little spat with Corvin left her discouraged. How long was he going to put up with her attitude? She was emotionally self-aware enough to know that she needed to interact with other people to ward off one of the depressive spirals she was prone to, but she couldn't expect the others to like her if she kept fighting with Corvin.

Were things so bad with Corvin that she shouldn't go? He hadn't deliberately done anything rude or mean. He'd even changed how he smelled for her. Shouldn't that count for something? In the end, it was the smell thing that made up her mind. He'd made an honest effort. She couldn't snub him because he didn't act the way she wanted him to right when she wanted.

Livia made a batch of cookies and headed over to Ratco. Just having people to give food to improved her mood dramatically. Terrance lit up when he opened the door and saw her. "Hey, we weren't sure you were coming! Come in!"

"I brought cookies," Livia said.

The Caesarean's made a big deal out of this. Livia had a reputation for making good cookies. She'd started working at a catering company when she was 14 and at 15 had moved back to the kitchens on the desert team. Then she'd worked at a bakery for a while before she moved to Caesarea. Livia was pro at baking and it had become her trademark way to apologize to people. Everyone in Justin's department knew this about her and found amusement in it.

Corvin's eyes twinkled when he saw the plate of cookies. He leaned in close so only she could hear. "Are these the famous apology cookies?

Livia's cheeks warmed. "I, um, maybe—"

He tilted his head. "Maybe?"

"I'm sorry," Livia squeaked.

He grinned. "We're good. Thank you for the cookies."

Livia relaxed. "Is the fridge working?"

"Yes," he grinned. "Mission accomplished. Thank you for helping me out."

Livia nodded. "No problem."

Corvin stepped back.

The evening was full of lightheartedness and fun. No serious talk came up to Livia's surprise. They all laughed and teased each other as they played card games. It was a good evening and Livia enjoyed it fully, refusing to think about her past or her future. This was one of the good times that made the bad stuff bearable.

Livia walked into the fall night air grinning, still alight with happiness from the evening. She hopped into her car and tried to start it. All Livia got was a clicking sound.

Livia groaned. "No, come on, I replaced your battery earlier this year."

Livia took a deep breath and tried again. Nothing. Livia could not afford another repair bill. Maybe she'd forgotten to turn her lights off and needed a jump. She got out of the car and walked back toward Corvin's place. Felicity had already taken off. Livia got to the door and lifted her hand to knock when a sound made her freeze.

Guitar music. Someone was playing.

Livia huddled closer to the door to listen. She didn't realize how long she had stood there listening until someone walked out the door the next house over and looked at her. Livia didn't want to look like a burglar so she knocked—too hard.

Her face heated. The person walked away without a word and got in a car. The guitar music stopped. Footsteps. The sound of the door unlocking. Corvin's face appeared. "Liv?"

"Hey, my car won't start."

"Oh," he said. "Let me grab a flashlight and a jacket. I'll be out in a sec."

Livia waited on the lawn. Corvin came out a moment later with a flashlight clutched in one palm, still threading his arms through his jacket sleeves.

"Has it been giving you a lot of problems lately?" he asked.

Livia sighed. "One of the belts snapped this summer. I had to pay to repair some of the stuff it broke too. It was…a lot of money."

"Alright, what do you think it is?"

"The battery," she said.

"Did you leave your lights on?" he asked.

"I don't remember doing that, but I must have because it won't start."

Corvin's expression didn't change. "Let's see what we got."

Corvin's flashlight traveled over the car. "How old is it, Liv? It's a Honda Prelude. They don't even make that model anymore."

"It's a 2000."

Corvin made a clicking noise. "Did the mechanic give you a hassle about replacing parts?"

"No."

"Well, let's hope that if we got a serious problem on our hands they don't charge you extra because the parts are hard to find."

Livia sighed. "Probably just the battery."

Corvin held out his palm. "May I try to start it?"

Livia handed over her keys.

Corvin tried to turn the engine over and got the same odd clicking noise. He winced. "That's not a dead battery noise…but it's fairly easy to check…"

He rotated the key a notch back. Then he tried the interior lights. They turned on. He tried the radio. It turned on. He tried the headlights. They turned on.

Corvin sighed. "I mean, we can run to Walmart in my car and get a meter to be completely sure, but I think it's something to do with your starter. Maybe the engine."

Corvin turned the car off and slipped out of the car and closed the door and handed the keys back to her. "Why don't you let me drive you home tonight? We can deal with it in the morning."

"I need this car tomorrow," Livia groaned. She had errands to run.

"Want to run out and get a meter?" he asked.

Livia sighed. "We should make sure before we call a tow, right? That will be expensive."

"It will be alright, Liv." Corvin put a hand on her arm. "We'll figure it all out."

Livia's mood sunk like a sputtering balloon. This was an awful way to end a good night.

"Let me run in and get my keys and check in with Terrance," Corvin said.

Terrance ended up coming with them. He slid into the back seat. "Thanks for letting me come, Corvin. I've needed to pick a few things up."

"No problem," Corvin said.

"I don't have a car so I bum off Corvin whenever I get the chance," Terrance grinned.

Livia didn't respond and only nodded. She was looking out the passenger window trying to talk herself out of crying.

"You alright, Liv?" Corvin asked, softly.

She nodded again. Too afraid she'd cry if she spoke.

"Hey, if it's about money. We can work something out," Corvin said. "There's stuff that needs to be done around the townhouse, like the fridge. I'd pay you."

Livia didn't respond. She had no intention of doing that. Ever. She'd get a real job before she ever relied on Corvin for money.

"No offense, Corvin, but I'm not helpless. I can get a real job."

He was silent a moment. "I'm offering help, Liv, not an opinion of your abilities."

"Right," Livia looked out the window and ignored him. "Of course not."

"You don't mean that," he said.

Livia's gaze snapped back toward him. "What?"

Corvin took a deep breath and said calmly. "I assume you think that I hold a negative opinion of you—"

Livia laughed. "Of course you do."

"I don't," he said.

Livia shook her head. "You're Caesarean of course you do. I'll never be good enough for you."

"You are good enough—' Corvin insisted.

Livia laughed in sheer disbelief. "You expect me to believe that?"

"Why wouldn't you?" Corvin asked.

Livia turned to look out the window again. "Let's drop it."

Corvin sighed. "Do you know what bothers me the most? You seem to not trust me anymore, Livia."

Livia snorted. "I'm not sure I ever did."

"You did," Corvin said.

She turned to snap at him. "Then I never should have."

Pain flashed across Corvin's features. "Why do you say that, Livia?"

"Cause I've watched you this past year and…" Livia suddenly halted, realizing what she was about to say.

"And what?" he pressed.

Livia turned forward, stiff. "It's not important."

"So, it should be easy to tell him then," Terrance interjected easily from the back. "No big deal."

"No—" Livia said.

"If it's this hard, that means it's something significant—" Corvin infused his voice with an air of seriousness.

"It's not, I—" Livia's heart thudded. This was getting all turned around on her.

"Then tell me," Corvin pressed.

Livia broke. "I think you pretended to be a certain person when I first met you, but you're not that person. You pretended to be another person at work, but I don't know if you're that person either. So, how am I supposed to trust you, Corvin?"

Corvin sighed. "I'm not going to deny that you're right. Cause you're right. I pretend a lot. But don't you pretend?"

"No," Livia said.

"So, why did you start wearing business casual clothes when you moved to Caesarea?" Corvin asked. "That's not how you dressed when I met you. That's not how you're dressed now…"

"There's a reason I do that—"

"So, you assume there are not reasons why I act the way I do?" Corvin asked.

"I don't understand them—"

"That doesn't mean my reasons aren't valid," Corvin said, angry now. "But I get you're upset. You're not the first person to end a relationship over this issue."

Livia leaned across the space between them and spoke with a fury she didn't know was inside her. "Corvin, we don't have a relationship to end!"

He flinched. Livia didn't blame him. She was frightened of herself. She drew back against the door and looked out the window, wrapping her arms around herself. She was shaking and she didn't like it. She wished she could escape. "Don't expect," she said in a shaky voice. "That you can ignore me, avoid me, and patronize me for an entire year and still call yourself my friend. That you can still have my trust. Your actions speak louder than a few compassionate words, Corvin Tullius. You showed me who you are."

"That is unfair," Terrance cried. "You—"

"Terrance," Corvin cut him off. Livia had never heard him sound sterner.

"Corvin, she—"

"Terrance," Corvin raised his voice this time.

Livia flinched, her stomach turning.

Corvin looked at her and almost whispered. "Thank you for trying to defend me, Terrance. But I'd like to do this my way."

"Livia," he spoke her name gently. "I'm sorry that I hurt you. I never wanted that. Can you believe that?"

"I don't know," she whispered.

"Okay," he said, simply.

Livia hugged herself, feeling awful, waiting for him to say what he should say. She had no reason to expect that he should be her friend. He didn't have any responsibility for her. She tried not to cry. "I'm sorry, Corvin. I'm so sorry."

"What are you sorry for?" he asked, low-toned and gentle.

"I don't deserve to have you for a friend. I understand that. I'm too...I'm an outsider, my family is so...broken, I'm poor, I'm young, I'm a girl. Why would you ever want to be my friend? I don't have a right to be so angry, to have expectations."

Corvin was silent. Livia chanced a glance at him. His lips were pressed together, there was a sheen in his eyes.

"I'm so sorry," she whispered again. "I'm so sorry."

"Please, stop apologizing, Liv," he said. "I've been an idiot. If you'll forgive me, we can start over. We're both students at the same university. We come from the same community and we can be friends."

"No. I won't be your friend here and then have you...do that thing. That thing where you change in Caesarea. I don't want to be friends if that's what I'm getting into. You have to be my friend in every place and in front of anybody, Corvin."

He took a deep breath. "Okay. I will agree to that."

"You will?"

"Yeah, yeah, I will," he said.

"I don't believe you," she said.

"I know you won't. Not until I prove it to you, but I'm willing to do that."

"Are you?" she asked.

"Yeah," he said.

"Why?" Livia asked.

Corvin pulled into a parking spot. He was silent for a moment, hands moving on the steering wheel. "Because...you've always made me want to be a better person, Livia. I like that."

"You like that?"

"Yeah, I do."

Livia shook her head at him. "No, you don't. Who would like that?"

He laughed. "I do, trust me."

"We've established I don't trust you."

He laughed again.

"Seriously," Livia opened her car door. "I'd rather we agree not to be friends."

"Why?" Corvin looked insulted.

"It's easier."

"But not as fun," he teased.

"You think me yelling at you is fun?" Livia asked.

He grinned. "Do you?"

"No!" Livia got out of the car and slammed the door. She flinched. She'd shut it way too hard and made a huge sound. Since it was metal she didn't think she could hurt it. Corvin got out and she met his eyes with apprehension, worried he'd be angry.

"That's why you're the perfect friend," Corvin said over the roof of the car, continuing their conversation as if a Taurus slammed his car door every day.

"No," Livia said. "I'm not doing this."

"Why not?" he asked.

"You're going to fake me out," she said. *Also, you make me slam car doors, and cafeteria doors, and even house doors.*

"I'm a lot of things, Liv, but a flake isn't one of them," he said.

Livia looked to Terrance. Maybe he would discourage Corvin. No true Caesarean would approve of her hanging out with Corvin.

He shrugged. "I have been disinvited from this conversation."

Well, he was no help.

"Nope," Livia said. "Not friends."

"Okay, trial period? Thinking about being friends?" Corvin gave her a pleading look.

"I didn't even know you were capable of making that facial expression," she said.

Corvin doubled down. "Please?"

"I will think about thinking about being friends," Livia said.

Corvin laughed and so did Terrance.

"No promises," Livia warned.

"I'll take it," Corvin said. "Miss thinking-about-thinking-about-being my friend."

"Now, you're mocking me," Livia drawled. "Nice start, Corvin."

"Never promised to be a perfect friend, just a reliable one," he said.

Livia glared at him. "What is even your definition of being a good friend anyway?"

"I'll think about it and get back to you."

"No, I'm not into that," Livia said. "Tell me now, gut feeling, without thinking about it. What does a good friend do?"

"Keeps your secrets," he said, raising an eyebrow. "You?"

"Won't ever lie to you," Livia said. "Not even to protect you."

Terrance interjected in a sardonic tone. "Hmm, you both sound like you've been betrayed."

Livia looked at Corvin with surprise, realizing. He looked away.

"Let's get that meter," he said, stalking away.

Chapter 11

Corvin wouldn't look at her. Livia was okay with that. He was acting like a relatable human for once. He sighed as he leaned over her car battery.

"Liv, it isn't the battery. It's fine."

"So…" Livia drawled.

"It's something else, which means…"

"Lots of money," she said.

"That too," he laughed. "What do you want to do here?"

He finally looked at her.

Livia rubbed her forehead.

Corvin wiped his hands off on his jeans. "I don't think the car is worth fixing, Liv. If it's an engine…the car is over twenty years old. You're throwing money away."

Tears pricked Livia's eyes.

"I'm sorry," Corvin said. "But the best advice I have for you is to trade it in and buy a new car."

There were very few things that Livia was impractical about, unfortunately, her car was one of them. She knew Corvin was right, but her emotions did not agree. Her heart hurt, her stomach twisted, her mouth went dry as ash. She had to reach over and place her hand on the car to stay standing. It was her car. Corvin had no concept of how hard she'd had to work to earn the money to buy it. The amount of work she had to do to keep it. Buying this car had been a huge turning point in her life. She'd proved to herself that her hard work could affect her situation. It gave her independence, pride, opportunity, security, and a space that belonged only to her. Livia didn't want to know what kind of person she was without this car.

Corvin realized she was struggling. He stepped close, placed a hand along her arm. "Hey, hey, it's a bad time of night to make decisions. Why don't you let me drive you home? We can figure it out tomorrow or Monday morning."

Livia couldn't protest. She let Corvin lead her to his car, open the door, help her inside. Things she normally wouldn't allow. Terrance hopped in the back, while Corvin went around.

"Liv, you alright?" Terrance asked.

Livia made some kind of vague noise.

Corvin slid into the car. "Alright, I'm going to need your address."

Livia didn't move.

"Liv," Corvin insisted.

She felt like she was moving through molasses as she reached for her phone. She looked at the screen, numbly. Time passed, empty, silent, heavy.

Corvin's fingers brushed her face. "Livia, look at me."

She did.

"It's going to be okay," he whispered. "I'll call Justin and Hyrum tonight after I drop you off. We'll figure something out together, alright? We'll make this a team project."

Tears welled in Livia's eyes. "It's my car."

He nodded. "You're attached to it."

"My car," with a hint of a wail in her tone.

"It means a lot to you," Corvin said, running his thumb over a tear that ran down her cheek.

Livia broke. She tilted her head forward and sobbed.

Corvin rested his hand on the top of her head. "Liv, hun, it will be alright."

She reached out for him then drew herself back. "Wait, no."

"Hey, no big deal," he said. "It's alright."

He reached out and grabbed her hand and placed it on his shoulder. "I'm okay with this if you are..."

She nodded and clutched at his shoulder. Corvin rested his hand over hers on his shoulder. Then he wrapped his other hand around the back of her head to guide her forehead to his other shoulder.

Livia was so shocked by his tenderness that her sobs stopped. His thumb brushed feather-light across the tops of her knuckles. His hand moved in her hair, caressing in a comforting motion. There was something so overwhelming about this physical kindness. There was a relief that she could be treated such and awe that Corvin would think her deserving. Then there was the grief that she'd experienced so little of something so healing. Livia's sobs returned on a tidal wave of bittersweet emotions. She'd wondered if she'd fare better pulling away, but she couldn't bring herself to do it.

She wanted to be close to this version of Corvin. She'd recognized from the first the depth of his compassion, the deep tenderness of his spirit. This was the Corvin she recognized. The one she trusted. He still existed.

She didn't know how much time had passed until her sobs ran out. She laid her cheek on Corvin's Lemon and Lavender scented shoulder and closed her swollen eyes.

"I don't usually do this to people," she whispered.

"Cry on them?" Corvin asked.

"Hmm," she agreed.

"You should try it more often," he teased.

Livia shook her head and pulled back. "I should go home."

"Tell me your address." Corvin released her slowly as if she might break.

Livia almost mocked him. Did he think a hug was going to break her? That was laughable. Resolve filled Livia. She wasn't going to let this car thing get the best of her. She'd figure out how to manage. She always had. She always would.

###

The next morning before Livia even got out of bed Justin texted her. She squinted at the phone and read what he wrote.

Justin: *Corvin called late last night. Let me know what you need and we'll work things out.*

Livia wondered if Corvin had called Hyrum too. If he had she was surprised that Justin had beat Hyrum to contacting her. As if thinking of her brother summoned him, the phone lit up with his name. She answered the call.

"Hyrum," Livia said, bracing herself.

"You need to get rid of that car," he said. "Corvin called me last night and I know the car is special to you, Livia. But you've already spent a thousand dollars on it this year alone and do you know how much an engine costs to replace?"

"Hyrum."

"I have extra cars sitting in my garage! Sitting there, Livia. It's wasteful. I feel sick inside when I think about you out there with that piece of a crap car when I have more than I need. It's…immoral. Stop being stubborn and let me send you out a decent car."

"Fine," Livia said.

"Like it's not…wait? What?" Hyrum stopped his furious tirade.

"Send me the car," Livia said.

"Oh. Okay. Gaius is gone again. So, I have to stay around here but maybe someone is coming out that way and can drive it to you. I will call you back this afternoon."

Livia texted Justin. *Everything is fine. I am going back to sleep.*

Livia switched off her phone, turned over in her bed, and enjoyed sleeping in on her Sunday morning. When she turned on her phone late afternoon she had messages from Corvin, Hyrum, and Justin that said she should call them. She would call Hyrum and ignore Corvin and Justin.

"Liv," Hyrum said. "Great news! The Halls are going to use fall break to give Tan a tour of Cornelia Africana College. She's thinking about applying there next year. They want to spend a weekend here with family and then they'll drive one of my cars out there instead of having to rent one."

"Oh, that's a really good solution," Livia was a little surprised it wasn't harder. "So, I'll have to go for three weeks without a car."

"Yeah," Hyrum said. "That alright?"

"Yes. I'll figure it out," Livia said. "And there are people around here. Corvin. My roommate."

"Okay, good. We're good."

"What do I do with my old car?" Livia asked.

"You decide," Hyrum said. "I don't care. Sell it. Give it away. Whatever."

Livia said goodbye to Hyrum. It was time to figure out how she was going to get her Sunday groceries. Whitney always went home on Saturday night and came back Sunday evening. So asking her was out and Livia didn't want to rely on Corvin too much. Only if she had to. So she looked up bus schedules. There was a stop about a half-mile from her dorm. It stopped right in front of a grocery store. If she hurried through the shower, she could make the three o'clock bus. Then return on the last bus at six o'clock that evening.

Livia got to the bus stop five minutes early. She got on and found an empty seat. She didn't know the area very well yet and so paid careful attention to their route as they drove. They pulled onto a freeway that she'd never been on before. After about ten minutes they exited off and wound their way through a separate part of town she hadn't known about.

The houses were older, run-down in this area. The streets were dirtier and shabby-looking. Livia saw signs that it was an area that struggled with poverty and a little bit of trepidation filled her. Maybe Livia should have asked Whitney if this was a safe part of town before she did this. Livia had grown up in such neighborhoods. She knew that most people minded their own business but she'd always had her family nearby if she needed help.

Livia knew she could win a fight, but she feared hurting someone or having her powers discovered. If she didn't keep a low profile, she risked getting punished by the Senate.

The area around the grocery store looked much better. The mix of cars in the parking lot showed that affluent and poor mingled together in the area. Livia went in and found the store incredibly busy. The lines at the registers spilled over into the aisles. The grocery store was unfamiliar. She had to backtrack through the aisles to find the things she needed. It took much longer than she predicted to find the things she needed. She had twenty minutes to get back to the bus on time when she got in line. After a solid five minutes of not budging, Livia switched to another line.

Thankfully it moved faster. She looked at her watch, as the cashier rang up the woman in front of her. She was pawing through an envelope for coupons. Livia's heart started to beat harder. She did not like cutting things this close. The woman's credit card was declined. She laughed and opened her wallet. She pawed through it and scrounged up the cash, bill by bill to pay her total.

"Please, hurry," Livia told the cashier when she started her groceries. "I need to catch the bus in seven minutes."

The cashier gave her a vacant look and didn't hurry one bit. Livia thought about running and leaving the food on the belt for the cashier to clean up. But she didn't want to go through this ordeal all over again.

Livia feared if she urged the cashier to hurry again she would go slower. She kept her silence, though, she was giving the woman quite a tirade in her head. Livia paid, gathered her bags, and sprinted out the door to see the bus taking off—two minutes early. She'd missed it.

Livia cursed. Then she panicked. What was she going to do? She could try and remember the route they took here to get home. Except, she didn't think walking with grocery bags along the side of the freeway in the dark was a good idea. She could hear Hyrum's voice in her head saying, "People get killed that way, Livia." That was only the start of the trouble she could get into.

Oh, how she wished she could call Hyrum to pick her up right now. She knew he'd drop whatever he was doing in an instant to come to pick her up. She thought of Corvin. She might be able to call Corvin.

She hated it. But she pulled out her phone and she called him. He didn't answer. Livia's lungs pinched and her heart raced. Wha—

Her phone rang. Corvin was calling back.

She answered. He spoke before she could say anything.

"Hey Liv, sorry I missed your call the first time around. What's up?"

Sudden anxiety struck her, making it hard to speak. She was sure once she explained Corvin would rail at her and tell her how stupid she was. She swallowed hard. "I'm stuck," she whispered.

"You're what?" Corvin asked.

Livia was terrified to explain what she'd done. He would call her stupid and annoying and take back his offers to be her friend. Livia took a deep breath and tried to talk herself out of her fear. Corvin wasn't her mother. He was TARP. Justin had trained all his officers to never behave like that.

"I'm stuck," Livia managed.

"Where?"

"At a grocery store."

"How'd you get there?" he asked.

"I took a b-bus, but I miss-missed the last one. It's not safe to walk—"

Corvin interrupted. "Okay, I'm on my way. Which grocery store? What address?"

Livia managed to explain where she was to him.

"Liv, what are you doing way over there?" Corvin asked.

Livia's entire body flushed with heat. Here it came. The tirade. She closed her eyes and didn't answer, waiting to ride it out.

"Okay, I'm coming. Don't move. Stay there. Understand?" Corvin waited for her to answer.

"Yes," she answered.

Chapter 12

Livia wished Corvin had yelled at her. It was torture imagining all the awful things he'd say when he finally got here. She was a screwup. She shouldn't be living on her own. What if he hadn't been around to help her? She'd be in real trouble then and maybe next time he wouldn't come so he could teach her a lesson about being less stupid.

When Corvin pulled up to the curb all her muscles were in tight knots. Corvin was out of the car the second he parked.

"You okay?" he asked.

She nodded.

"You sure?"

She nodded again.

He stepped close and bent toward her. "You look scared," he spoke softly. "Did something happen?"

Livia shook her head.

He met her eyes and said, sincerely. "I'm so glad you called."

Corvin helped her put her groceries in the trunk then opened the door for her to get in the back seat. Livia slipped in. Corvin shut the door and walked around the back of the car.

Terrance was in the front seat. "Looks like a rough area around here, Liv. You have any problems?"

"No," Livia said.

Corvin got in the car. "Let's head home."

Terrance made a silent gesture at him. Corvin nodded. Livia wondered about the interaction but was too concerned about getting yelled at to say anything.

Corvin broke the silence. "Liv, did you hear from Justin yet?"

"We texted."

"What did he say?" Corvin said, casually.

"I'm supposed to call him."

"Why haven't you?" Corvin asked.

Livia flinched. This innocent-sounding interrogation would be the start of the verbal abuse. Livia answered as monotone as possible. "Hyrum arranged for friends to drive out one of his cars three weeks from now."

To Livia's confusion, Corvin's voice didn't sound scolding in the least. "Let Justin know that. He's worried about you."

"You shouldn't have called him at midnight," she snapped.

Livia gasped at her audacity and went rigid in her seat. This was the wrong time to bring that up. She closed her eyes and waited for him to scream at her.

"You...alright, Liv?" Corvin sounded puzzled.

She didn't answer.

"Hey, are you in pain?" he asked. "Did someone hurt you?"

"No."

"Did anything else happen?"

"No."

Terrance looked back at her. "I know you're scared, Liv," he said, low, quiet.

Heat rushed to Livia's cheeks. That must have been what that silent conversation earlier was about.

"Talk to us, Liv," Corvin encouraged. "Justin didn't sound upset did he?"

"No," she said.

"Hmm," Corvin said. Then he went quiet. Livia didn't say anything and he didn't say anything until they reached her apartment.

Corvin and Terrance helped her carry her groceries inside in silence.

Livia expected them to go away, but they lingered. Corvin studied her. He approached. He lifted a hand to touch her.

Livia flinched away.

Corvin looked surprised. "Is it me? Are you frightened of me?"

Livia didn't answer. Corvin strode across the room and sat down. "I'd like to know why."

Livia looked at Terrance who was looking confused.

Livia swallowed. "I made…a mistake…"

"And?" Corvin asked. "What usually happens when you make a mistake?"

"Depends on the person," Livia whispered.

"Livia," Corvin said. "I am not your mother. I am not your father. I am not Hyrum. I am Corvin. I have my hang-ups but I tend to let go of most things pretty easily."

"Are you…mad…at me?" she asked, eyes lowered to the floor.

"No," he shook his head. The look in his eyes was bewildered. "I was never mad at you. You did your best to be resourceful and independent. I wouldn't call that a mistake."

"But something might have happened," Livia choked. "I was stupid."

Corvin inhaled and his head tilted to the right, considering. "But you went out and got information and can make better decisions now based on that information. That's how life works, Livia. You have to take risks or you never learn, and a life in which you never learn anything isn't worth living."

"So, you don't think…I'm bad?" Livia asked.

"Bad? No. I'd rather you not take the bus out there again, but if you do, bring someone with you and do it in the morning. You'll be fine." His tone didn't change but Livia trembled. She was afraid he'd rage at her the second she made the wrong move.

"Okay," Livia whispered.

"Do you want to come grocery shopping with us next Sunday?"

Livia hesitated. "I don't want to bother—"

"It's not a bother," he insisted. "Your safety matters to me, Livia. I'm more bothered that you felt unsafe for twenty minutes than I ever will be by you asking for my help."

"Okay," she whispered. "Thank you for picking me up Corvin."

"Glad to be around to help, Livia," he said. "Call us if you need anything else, alright?"

Livia blinked. He wasn't going to yell at her. She took a deep breath and the knots in her stomach eased. She could feel her features smooth and the tension across her brow disappeared.

She nodded. "I will."

Corvin dipped his head in response. "Good. Text me if you want to join us to get groceries next Sunday."

"I will."

Corvin stood up. "See you Saturday, right?"

Livia nodded again.

"Call me if you need a ride to Ratco."

* * *

Livia called Justin that evening. He answered on the third ring. "Livia, I've been anxious to hear from you."

"I'm sorry—"

"You must be overwhelmed," he said. "I understand, but it is nice to finally communicate directly. What can I do to help, Livia?"

"Hyrum arranged for one of Quin's old cars to be sent out here—"

"Is he asking you to pay for it?" Justin asked.

"No, he's giving it to me," Livia said.

"That's nice."

"Yeah, but I don't know what to do with my old car. It's stuck in Corvin's parking lot—"

"I know someone that might want it here. Will you let me get back to you on that?" Justin asked.

"Yes," Livia said with relief. "That would help loads."

"How is school?" Justin asked.

"It's good."

"Corvin reports that aside from the car breaking down you've been doing well."

Livia asked, trying to ignore how much it hurt that Justin didn't trust her. "Did you send him here to watch over me?"

"That's only fifty percent of the reason," Justin answered. "I did worry about you."

"What's the other fifty?" Livia asked, surprised by his honesty.

"I sent him there so you could watch over him."

"What? Justin! I'm not—I can't—" Livia exchanged verbal protest for a heavy sigh.

"You can't what?" he asked.

"I'm not close to Corvin," Livia answered. "I can't watch over him for you."

"Why not get closer to him then?"

"Justin!" Livia cried, scandalized.

He laughed. "What?"

"This is not funny," she snapped.

"Tell me how he is, Livia," Justin said. "Is he okay?"

"He seems fine," Livia answered. "I only see him once a week. I don't know."

"Does he seem happy when you see him?" Justin asked.

Livia thought. "Not at first but he's been more relaxed recently. He said he likes it here once."

"That's good news. Is he dating?" Justin asked.

Livia started to feel guilty about this whole interrogation. "I don't like this, Justin. You can't expect me to be your little snitch. If Corvin is dating someone he can tell you himself."

Justin laughed.

"I'm being serious. I'm not a gossip and I'm not going along with this stupid plan of yours."

"I'm surprised but also pleased by this response," Justin said. "I had no idea you'd react this way."

"Well, stop being pleased because I'm a hair away from never speaking to you again." Livia didn't like feeling like Justin's lab experiment.

"Alright, Livia, we won't talk about Corvin unless you bring it up. If anything concerns you, please let me know."

Livia groaned. "What have you been asking him about me?"

"You can ask him that," Justin said.

"Right, 'cause it'd be too easy for you to answer the question while I have you on the phone," Livia said, sarcastically.

Justin laughed heartily again. "I have no pangs of conscience over obtaining information covertly, Livia. If I did, I wouldn't have lasted in this line of work. How's Oliver, by the way?"

"He moved," Livia growled. Why would Corvin tell him about that?

"Well, that doesn't mean you can't contact him," Justin said.

"Why is this a big deal?" Livia demanded.

"It's not a big deal," Justin said. "It's just interesting. You have people who are interested in what happens to you. Does that have to be a bad thing?"

Justin was starting to sound way too much like a parent now. Livia rolled her eyes. "I gotta go, Justin."

"I'll get back to you about the car by this evening," he said.

Livia ended their conversation. She closed her eyes, exhausted. Why did everything have to get complicated? Because whether she liked it or not, she now felt obligated to keep an eye out for Corvin. She had to wonder did Justin calculate that? Did he know her psychology that well? Did he know that Livia liked Corvin? Was he matchmaking? Or was he trying to keep an eye on one of his agents? Justin said to let him know if anything concerned her? What did he think Corvin was going to get up to?

Chapter 13

L ivia opted to ask her roommate Whitney for help before she left to go home for the weekend. So, on Friday they hopped into her car and headed to the store. It was a beautiful fall day and Livia updated Whitney about her last shopping adventure as they drove.

"I know what part of town you're talking about," she said. "It's safer to stay on this side of the freeway. How do you know this Corvin guy?" she asked.

"He's from back home," Livia said. "We have a little group of us that meet on Saturday nights."

"Oh, so, you hang out while I'm away?" she asked. "That makes me feel better. Sometimes I worry about leaving you alone."

"No, I'm fine really. I like to be alone sometimes."

Livia actually liked having the apartment to herself for long periods. It made her feel like she was in charge and could do whatever she wanted and that was more healing than she'd probably admit to anyone.

"What did you do with the old car?" Whitney asked.

"A friend from back home, Justin, knew a guy that wanted it. He said he'd arrange for it to be towed and transported and give me $200 for it."

"Are you happy with that?" she asked.

"Yeah, it was a more than fair deal. It would have cost more to tow to the scrapyard than what the car was worth. So…"

"And your brother is sending a new car two weeks from now?"

"Yeah, some more friends from home are driving it over."

"Which friends are these?" Whitney asked.

"Tavian and Adrian, Arik and Tan," Livia said.

"Oh, those twins and your ex. Well, that should be a drama fest, right?"

Livia sighed. "I hope not."

"Are you dreading seeing him?" Whitney asked.

"Not dreading...sometimes he can be easy to be around. I just hope he doesn't do one of those little sulks he gets into. I mean, it's only three days, right? He can't do that much damage."

Whitney laughed. "Hopefully not."

Whitney and Livia talked as they walked. They bought the groceries and loaded them into the car and drove home.

* * *

Livia walked up to Corvin and Terrance's door and knocked. Corvin answered and invited her in. Livia turned to wave to Whitney before she stepped in.

"Who is that?" Corvin asked.

"My roommate," Livia answered. "She drove me over."

Corvin waved at Whitney too. Whitney didn't drive off immediately and waved back. Corvin approached her car and Whitney rolled down the window.

"You're good to drive her back home?" Whitney asked. "She told me she'd be fine..."

"Yeah, I'll make sure she gets home at a decent hour," Corvin said, easily.

"Okay, good. You Corvin?" She asked.

"Yeah, and you're the famous roommate that owns a bearded dragon," Corvin teased.

Whitney laughed. "You're invited to come to meet him anytime."

"Thanks. It was nice to meet you."

"You too," Whitney said. "Gotta go."

Whitney rolled up the window and backed out. Corvin returned to Livia. "You talked to her?" Livia asked.

"Yeah, you can tell a lot about a person from your first impression—"

"And—" Livia drawled.

"What?" Corvin looked at her.

"What did you learn?"

"I liked that she didn't leave until she'd confirmed I wouldn't be inconvenienced by driving you home. So we can rule out her being a psychopath. She's willing to let me into your apartment so that means she's friendly and curious about people. She guessed my name so that means you *talk* about me—"

Corvin wiggled his eyebrows. Since when did he do things like that? Livia sputtered. "Do not!"

Corvin grinned at her. "Teasing, Liv."

"Speaking about talking about people," Livia glared at him. "Have you talked to Justin lately?"

"Yesterday," he said.

"You told him about Oliver!" Livia snapped.

"I did," he said, shamelessly. "Let's continue this conversation inside."

As soon as the door closed behind them Livia whirled on him. "Why did you mention it?"

"Why shouldn't I?" Corvin asked.

"We aren't dating," Livia said. "So, it's insignificant."

Corvin shook his head. "It showed you were making friends here and settling in. It wasn't insignificant."

Livia frowned. "What else does he ask you about me?"

Corvin's face creased with concern. "Are you upset about something, Liv?"

Livia sunk onto the couch and crossed her arms across her chest. "He's spying on us both."

Corvin laughed. "Explain."

"I asked him if he sent you here to watch over me," Livia muttered.

Corvin grunted. "What did he say?"

"That was only fifty percent of the reason why you were here—"

Corvin's eyes widened. "He was that transparent with you? That's impressive."

"The other fifty percent of the reason why you're here is so I can watch over you—" Livia growled.

Corvin's lips pursed as if he were trying not to smile. "You don't like that?"

Livia huffed and tried to act nonchalant, but she couldn't mask the worry that came out in her tone. "Are you okay?"

Corvin laughed. "I'm fine."

"You sure?" Livia insisted.

Corvin lowered himself into the armchair across from her. "You can tell Justin everything is fine here."

Livia furrowed her brow. "But is it? Really?"

"Yes," Corvin nodded. "I miss my family but it's been a nice break."

"Your classes aren't stressing you out?" Livia asked.

"No."

"You lonely?" she asked, hesitantly.

"No more than usual," he smiled.

"You're usually lonely?" Livia asked, curious.

Corvin shrugged. "Mostly romantically. I don't like being single."

"Justin asked me if you were dating anyone—" Livia said.

"What did you tell him?" Corvin folded his hands over his belly and settled more firmly into the armchair.

"That if he wanted to know something like that he'd have to ask you himself—"

Corvin gasped. "No!"

"Yes! I'm not a gossip or a snitch," she said.

Corvin tried to contain his laughter by putting a hand over his mouth and failed. After he'd contained himself he scolded her. "Livia, you're not supposed to talk to your patron like that!"

"I'm not turning into his spy—"

"Livia, he'll think we're dating if you talk like that," Corvin said. "You don't show more loyalty to me than to Justin if you don't want rumors to spread."

"So, you're just fine with me telling him whatever I want about you?" Livia demanded.

"As long as it's honest," Corvin said.

"You don't have a problem with him invading your privacy?" Livia asked.

Corvin looked so confused that Livia put a hand over her eyes and sighed. "Let me guess. Not a Caesarean thing, right?"

"I mean, it's Justin," Corvin said, splaying his hands out. "The man is one of my best friends and knows all my secrets. There's no point in hiding anything from him—"

"Then why does he need me to watch out for you at all, then?" Livia demanded.

"Cause he wishes he were here to do it himself," Corvin said. "Patrons often ask clients to do things that they can't do themselves. That's how the system works."

Livia sighed.

Terrance came out of the kitchen with chips and salsa. "So, what's this I hear about you and Livia dating, Corvin?"

"No!" Livia rounded on him and pointed a threatening finger. "Don't you dare! That's how those stupid rumors start. That's the last thing I need people to start in on."

Terrance adopted an innocent expression. "All I heard is that Justin thinks you're dating now?"

"Cause she said she wouldn't snitch on me or answer the question if I was dating anyone," Corvin said, heaving out a huge sigh.

Terrance's mouth popped into a huge 'O.' "Well, we're lucky the Aurelians have tight lips, then." He turned on Livia with a look of disbelief. "What possessed you to talk to your patron that way?"

Livia rubbed her temples. "You Caesareans are going to make me lose my damn mind."

To her surprise, both Corvin and Terrance laughed.

Terrance turned to Corvin. "So, are you going to call and explain or let him think you're secretly dating?"

"I better call," Corvin shook his head. "I'll do it later. Justin is busy inducting two recruits tonight."

"Where's Felicity?" Livia asked.

"She's gonna be late," Terrance answered. "She's on a date."

It was Livia's turn to be surprised. "A non-civ?"

Terrance nodded. "She'll be here to report in about a half-hour."

That left Livia here alone with Terrance and Corvin and that suddenly made her anxious. She ran her hand up and down her arm and tried to think of something useful to do.

Corvin's eyes narrowed in on her soothing gesture. "What are you thinking, Liv?"

Livia sighed. "We should do something…"

"Watch a movie?" Terrance suggested.

"Felicity would miss part of it," Livia said. She didn't want to watch a movie either. She wanted to do something with her hands.

"Liv, what do you want to do?" Corvin asked.

"Can I—" she hesitated. She felt uncomfortable asking to use their kitchen and their supplies. "Can I bake you some cookies? I mean, if you have supplies on hand?"

"Really?" Terrance asked. "Cause that sounds amazing!"

Relief flowed through Livia. "Yeah, let's do it!"

So, they inspected the kitchen and didn't find any brown sugar or chocolate chips so they had to settle for sugar cookies, but that wasn't a problem for Livia.

Livia mixed the ingredients while Terrance and Corvin sat on barstools and watched. They offered to help a few times but she turned them down.

About halfway through the process, Terrance commented. "This is kind of fascinating to watch."

Corvin chuckled. "She transformed before our very eyes, didn't she?"

"Yeah, also, why is it so darn relaxing to her?" Terrance asked.

"I think it's tactile," Corvin said. "The way she presses her entire palm against the curve of the bowl. She rolls the cold eggs back and forth across her palm before she breaks them. The way she taps the bottom of the measuring cups on her palm to level them—"

"Yeah, but there's like this timing in her head. It's like a dance..." Terrance said.

Livia froze, self-conscious. "Um...I—"

"You feeling alright, Liv?" Corvin asked. "Taurus get tactile sensory cravings when they get too worn out."

Livia looked up and met his eyes, confused. "We do?"

"You must be tired," Corvin repeated.

"I had a couple of tests this week," Livia admitted.

"Did you study a lot?" he asked. "Stay up late?"

"A couple of nights..." Livia said. "But I don't feel tired—"

Corvin smiled. "You're Taurus, Liv, you won't feel tired until you're ready to pass out."

"What does that mean? Tactile sensory cravings?" Livia asked.

"Means your body wants touch to compensate for something it's lacking," he said. "In this case probably a good night's sleep."

"What if I don't want to touch at all?" Livia asked, quietly.

"Often happens when Taurus get too hot or too stressed," Corvin said.

Livia sighed. "You are kidding me—"

"No, but I'm not Taurus. What I've heard could be wrong..." Corvin said.

Livia started baking again. "No, that just would have been nice to know...
"

Terrance and Corvin exchanged a startled look. Livia started shaping dough balls between her palms.

Corvin leaned forward and rested his elbows on the counter. "Yeah, uh, my uncle Marcus complains a lot—he's a doctor—that Taurus women ignore how tired they are and make themselves chronically ill because they ignore what their body needs. So, if you're feeling like you just can't resist touching something, you might want to curl up around a pillow and take a nap instead of...is this what you usually do? Bake?"

"Yep," Livia answered.

She was frustrated. First, why hadn't her mom told her? But Livia was used to being disappointed by her mother so this wasn't a surprise. Gaius, though, he should have said something, but he probably didn't know that she didn't know. So, it took Corvin observing her and doing his irritating people analysis thing for her to figure it out.

Livia lined the cookie sheets with dough balls in silence and then slipped two pans in the oven to bake. She went to the sink to wash her hands. She was surprised when Corvin's hand shot out and adjusted the faucet. "That's hot!" he barked.

Livia looked at him in surprise. Livia swallowed as the surprise turned to fear. Was he angry at her?

He froze and looked instantly sheepish. "Sorry, Liv, I-I have too many little sisters. Reflex."

His fingers passed through the water. "That's nice and cold. It will feel good."

He stepped away and looked across the room. He acted almost embarrassed. Interesting.

Livia ran her hands under the water. To her surprise, the water did feel really good. She didn't realize that tension had built up in her forearms and wrists. The cold water washed it all away.

"Is that also a Taurus thing?" Livia asked, quietly.

"Yep," Corvin answered.

"Thanks," Livia said.

"No problem, Liv," Corvin said.

The doorbell rang and Corvin left to answer it.

Livia looked at Terrance.

He smiled at her. "You okay?"

"I thought he was mad at me," Livia whispered.

Terrance shrugged one shoulder. "Nah, he just got protective. Hard not to be when you don't know basic things about taking care of yourself."

Livia's cheeks reddened. "I can take care of myself."

"I don't doubt that you can keep yourself alive, Livia. I think you're real good at that but I don't think you're good at being kind to yourself."

Livia frowned. "Why does that matter?"

Terrance sighed. "It'll catch up to you sooner or later. Taurus women are notorious for it. Taurus men get violent when they're pushed too far and the consequences of that are really severe so they take care of themselves. Taurus women tend to internalize and the result of that is a lot of mental illness. That, unfortunately, causes dysfunctional families and negative patterns get passed on…" Terrance sighed. "It was a huge problem in the collapse of the Patrician families of Taurus house. Taurus women just can't push themselves the same way Rattus, Aquila, and Lupus women can. They're meant to sprint, not run marathons, and the culture even just a generation ago refused to acknowledge that. We know better now but…" Terrance's eyes filled with tears. "We lost a lot of them before we learned that."

Livia inhaled sharply. "That…makes a lot of sense with what happened with…my mother. She couldn't stay and survive—"

"Those parts of Caesarea are still around," Terrance admitted. "But there are pockets now, there are people and places that will help you. TARP does amazing work with Taurus and so does Corvin's uncle Dr. Tullius. His work has saved a lot of them."

Livia nodded.

"Livia," Terrance said, intently. "You are in such a crucial position right now. Your foremothers aren't there to tell you what to do and that's awful but it's also a gift. You're free from the traditions that harmed them. You have to find the courage to make new traditions. Healthy traditions that will protect you and your daughters and their daughters. You can create a new culture."

Terrace's passionate speech was interrupted by an enthusiastic Felicity coming into the kitchen. She told them about her date while they ate sugar cookies hot out of the oven. Corvin didn't let Livia clean up the kitchen and insisted that he would take care of it later. Felicity was too worn out to stay for long and left only a few minutes after their cookie binge.

Livia looked to Corvin.

"You ready to head home, Liv?" he asked.

Livia nodded. "It's still early but…"

"That's alright," he said. "I think you need the extra rest."

Terrance pulled Livia into a tight hug. "See you next weekend. Be kind to yourself."

Livia closed her eyes and didn't let go of him immediately. The hug felt good, something that didn't happen frequently.

Terrance laughed. "You're Taurus tired."

"What's that mean?" Livia asked.

"Extra cuddly," Corvin said. "Come on. You need sleep, Liv."

Livia did get in random moods where she'd want Arik to hold her forever. Those moments seemed random and unpredictable but now she knew they were provoked by exhaustion.

After Livia and Corvin got in the car she asked, "Does everyone in Caesarea know about Taurus…tired?"

"No," Corvin said. "It's actually weird that more people don't know. Taurus aren't well understood. Partially because it was taboo to talk about a lot of things—"

"Mental illness," Livia said.

Corvin looked at her in surprise.

"Terrance told me," she said.

"Yeah, and intimacy," Corvin said. "Taurus are often seen as invulnerable because they are so strong and so tough but they're fairly sensitive."

"I don't think Arik knew," Livia said.

Corvin sighed. "That's not surprising to me. I don't know that I would know if I didn't have certain people in my life—Justin and Flavia are very open about it. My Aunt Garnet had a very difficult time managing chronic pain and her marriage relationship. She begged Uncle Lucius to divorce her for about five years. She said it would be better if she were alone forever. It was hard to watch."

"They didn't divorce," Livia said. "Right?"

"Right," Corvin nodded. "Uncle Lucius worked through it with her and it got better. They live a really quiet, almost reclusive life out on a ranch. They're happy and content."

"Sometimes…" Livia hesitated. She shook her head. She'd learned not to do this already. No confessions. Corvin wasn't interested.

"Sometimes what, Liv?" Corvin asked, quietly.

106

She laughed. "It's alright. You don't have to listen."

"I'd like to listen, Liv," Corvin said.

Livia didn't say anything until they were pulling into her apartment. "Sometimes I feel that way," she confessed. "Like it's better to live alone. Forever."

Corvin spoke quietly. "Often, Liv?"

"Not as much as I used to—" she said. "It's been…a while. This place must be good for me."

"It usually happens when life becomes too difficult to deal with," Corvin said. He reached over and pulled her hand into his and squeezed it. "If you ever feel that way again, you can come to tell me about it, okay?"

Livia laughed. She liked the feel of his hand holding hers. That somehow eclipsed everything else.

"What's funny?" Corvin asked.

"That feels ridiculously good," she answered.

Corvin smiled and squeezed her hand again. "This?"

Livia laughed again.

"You're so tired, Livia," he said, gently. "Promise me you'll go in and sleep?"

"I promise, Corvin."

He released her hand. Livia stifled a groan of disappointment. She pulled herself out of the car and waved. Corvin waved back and started to pull out of the parking lot. She went into the apartment and ate a peanut butter and jelly sandwich and then went to bed.

Chapter 14

L ivia twisted her Raven ring around her finger and peered anxiously out her window. The Halls would be here in less than an hour and she couldn't stand the wait.

"I think you like-like Tavian," Whitney teased.

Livia tossed a glare at her. "Hush, you."

"You get this soft look on your face every time you talk about him."

That's cause Livia worried about him. Everyone in Rattus house could sense emotions, but Tavian was an *adnotator,* someone who could discern emotions by sight. Livia had seen the toll it could take on him. Adrian could sense emotions through touch—a *tactor.* Since he could control who he touched the majority of the time, being an empath wasn't nearly as draining on him. Adrian was completely different than Tavian as a result—less empathetic, careless to a fault, and impatient.

"You'll understand when you meet them," Livia said, pacing across the spotlessly clean kitchen.

"Does he know Corvin is the competition?" Whitney asked.

Livia turned, surprised. "What?"

"You like Corvin," Whitney said.

"No...why do you think that?" Livia asked.

Whitney shook her head. "One, you can tell. Two, you told me yourself."

"I did?"

"He's your work crush," she said.

Livia pouted. "You're sworn to secrecy!"

"Why not tell him?" she asked. "He's cute. He's nice. I'd date him."

Livia glared at her.

"You're gonna miss your chance," she said

Livia huffed. Whitney figured it out. Livia wasn't careful enough. But she worried. Could everyone tell? Was she transparent to everyone? She wanted to stop liking Corvin. They'd adopted a more friendly relationship the past couple of weeks. There were no more slammed doors or dramatic stomp offs on Livia's part. She was embarrassed to admit it, but that conversation with Corvin about Taurus needing sleep had been pivotal in managing so many negative emotions. The first week she was ready to give up on the whole experiment because she was sleeping way too much. Then Monday hit and she felt like a whole new person.

She could concentrate better in class. She was more social with her classmates, and she didn't feel like people were judging her as much. Instead of spending a lot of energy battling dark thoughts, she was able to focus more on people's little dramas. She encouraged Felicity in her attempts to adjust to life outside Caesarea. She congratulated Corvin when he turned in a huge project. She checked in with Terrance when he'd had a long day.

Livia didn't recognize herself and she liked it. She started scheduling time to sleep. She said no to late-night movies and any activities after 10:00. Whitney was kind of annoyed with her about it and this was the first time they'd had a real conversation in three days.

Still, Livia's attraction to Corvin being obvious stressed her out. Corvin Tullius was the son of Lars Tullius, the paterfamilias of Lupus house. Corvin would be paterfamilias of the largest house in Caesarea eventually. He had a large loving, tight-knit family, who were all well off and multi-talented. There was no way they would consider her anywhere near qualified to be materfamilias one day. And if by some miracle they did, Livia wouldn't consider herself capable of filling that role.

Livia's life had been too different from Corvin's. It would never be possible to overcome the differences in their life experiences. Though, that was small compared to what Livia really feared. What if she was just like her mother? She saw the parallels. A young girl with a rough home life falls in love with the richest, most well-connected, and prominent guy in Caesarea. Was Livia that shallow? Was she that desperate? She wanted a better life for herself and her children than what her mother had. That meant making different decisions. Corvin was a little too close to the type of man her mother had chosen the first time around, and they'll all paid dearly for that. Livia needed a guy that was safe, boring, predictable. Corvin was not that guy. Again, she needed to stop liking him. He was too complicated, too confusing, too powerful, too all the things that made a man terrifying.

A knock sounded on the door.

"They're here!" Livia cried.

She ran to the door and threw it open. Tan immediately tackled her in a hug. Livia hugged her fiercely back. "Tan! I missed you!"

"Livia, that's too tight." She laughed.

Livia released her instantly. "Sorry."

Tan only grinned and stepped aside so Adrian could pull her into a hug too. She ignored the fact his hug was too tight. "Liv!"

"Adrian," she grunted. He let her go.

Tavian smiled at her. "In a mood for a hug, Liv?"

"Yeah," she said. She loved that he asked. She pulled him close, more gentle. Tavian tugged her into a perfect hug. His arms encircled her with just the right amount of pressure and pulled away at the exact right time. This guy put her soul at ease.

Then there was Arik.

Ooo, she'd forgotten how nice it could be to look at him. Adrian and Tavian were fine, no doubt, but Arik was make-you-forget-your-own-name handsome. His dark brown eyes were crowned with an expressive forehead that puckered in the most heart-wrenching way when he frowned. His lips were so perfect it was almost unbelievable that they weren't sculpted by an artist. Arik was flawless—at least when it came to looks. The other things, the more important things—like loyalty, consistency, and fortitude, weren't his forte.

"Liv," he said, reaching out for half a hug.

"Hey," she said, trying to smile in a way that was friendly but not I-still-like-you friendly. She pulled away from him quickly and introduced them all to her roommate Whitney, whose eyes were huge. She seemed a little awestruck and Livia tried to tease her out of it a bit and failed.

The Halls were amused, immensely, and they retreated to the parking lot to show her the car.

"Sorry, bout that, guys. She's usually more down to earth," Livia said.

They laughed about it.

"Not every day you see three hunks," Tan said.

"Three sexy hunks," Arik said.

"Served straight up to your door," Adrian joked.

Livia exchanged a mutual eye-roll with Tavian. They operated on the same bs-detecting-wavelength, thankfully.

They handed over the keys and Livia made them all smoosh in so she could take the car for a drive. "Who's hungry?" she asked.

They all chimed in for food. So, Livia drove them to the best hamburger and fries place in town. They caught up over dinner and then Livia drove them to their motel and drove herself home.

* * *

The next morning they asked her to pick them up at nine. Livia showed them around the campus all day. Exploring the gym, library, the buildings, the student center, the gift shop, a couple of the statues. It was a good time all around. That night, since it was Saturday they headed over to Ratco.

"So, who all is here?" Tavian asked.

"Um, Terrance and Felicity from Rattus."

"Aw, Felicity is so sweet," Adrian said. "Tender-hearted soul. How is she?"

"It's been a hard adjustment," Livia said. "I've tried to help here and there, but she's still down a lot of the time."

"Aw, hopefully, we can cheer her up," Tan said.

"Then there's Corvin."

Tavian asked. "How is Corvin?"

Livia sighed. "I never know. He's Corvin."

"What's that mean?" Tan asked.

"He's emotionless," Livia said. "Can't read him."

"Really?" Adrian asked. "That sounds like he's having a rough time."

"It does?" Livia asked.

"Yeah," Tavian agreed. "I wonder if it's Bella or the shooting he's not over yet."

"Bella?" Livia asked.

Arik hooted. "Bella Aurelius, Livia."

Livia scoffed. "I know, Arik, but I doubt he's still upset about that."

"Why do you say that?" Adrian asked.

"Yeah," Arik encouraged. "Explain that."

"Just the way he acted when they broke up—"

"How did he act?" Adrian pressed.

Why were they giving her such a hard time over this? Livia huffed. "He gave Bella an ultimatum that if she wanted to fix their relationship she had to give up her job, which is totally unacceptable."

"What?" Tan asked in shock. "He actually gave her that option? He is way too nice—"

Livia growled. "You mean he was a controlling jerk, right?"

Tavian interjected before Adrian or Arik could, thankfully. His voice was calm and kind instead of short and frustrated. "You're responding like you don't know what happened. Right before you came to Caesarea, she spilled Corvin's political secrets to get an unpaid position on Aquila house staff."

"It paid off," Arik said. "She's got a cushy job now. Unheard of for a woman in Caesarea to have a full-time paid position on the staff of the consul."

"Wait. What?" Livia demanded. "What political secrets?"

"Corvin was obligated by family connections to donate to the political campaign of one of his cousins," Adrian explained. "Except, Corvin didn't agree with his platform. Instead of making a fuss over it, he donated a larger monetary amount to the campaign he supported under the name of a business he owns—"

"Corvin owns a business?" Livia asked.

"He registered his own business so Justin Aurelius could hire and pay him to work on technical writing projects for TARP," Tavian explained. "Most of the pamphlets they pass out on mental illness, addiction recovery, and abuse are written by him."

"Wow," was all Livia could manage. She'd known when she'd stayed with Justin and Flavia's family that Bella was being shunned. It was impossible to ignore but no one had told her the reasons. Livia and Bella had become good friends. Livia often took her out bird-watching to get her away from all the drama in Caesarea. Bella had been patient and kind to Livia when Hyrum left for eight weeks. Livia hadn't been easy to live with—paranoid, anxious. Livia would wake the house up with night terrors, refused some days to leave her room. Justin had walked her through all that nonsense. She didn't know what would have happened to her without Justin's help and advice.

"That's not even the worst part," Tan said. "After Bella exposed Corvin for donating to two political campaigns, Lupus house split into factions. There wasn't enough consensus when the votes came around to look after Lupus house interests. So they weren't given the funds from the budget to take care of needy Lupus house families. Lars has been feeding them with emergency funds for nine months. Corvin keeps trying to make amends but it looks like the same thing is going to happen this fall. There isn't enough money left to take care of those families next year without a welfare budget."

Livia gulped. If that were the case then Corvin was way too nice. Livia would have cut Bella off completely. Livia's friendship with Bella was probably the reason Corvin had given her a cold shoulder. Livia's heart sank as she saw the situation differently. It probably looked like she had taken Bella's side. It was a wonder Corvin had offered his friendship at all. Then she'd been a jerk about it. Livia felt guilt clench her heart in its fist. Why was she always so stupid?

"You didn't know?" Tavian asked, seriously.

"No."

"You were friends with Bella, right?" Tan asked.

Livia shrugged. She wasn't at a high point at that time in her life. In fact, she was doing so much better now that she was almost surprised at herself. She'd healed, she'd changed, grown-up, and gotten tougher in ways she hadn't thought about.

"Bella never explained any of that to me. Does that surprise you?" she asked.

Adrian laughed. "No."

Arik asked. "Probably thought you wouldn't remain her friend."

Livia didn't like that she wondered about that very fact. She was extremely unsettled that the most vulnerable people of the community were punished for Bella's decision. Had Bella done anything to fix that?

"Do you think—" Livia had to ask. "If they had gotten back together that the split in the senate would have resolved itself?"

"Probably better that they didn't," Arik said. "I think Lupus house would have considered that a betrayal of them on Corvin's part."

Tavian disagreed. "Yeah, but the Aurelian faction would have thrown their support behind them and they have a lot of influence. It might have worked—"

Adrian snorted. "No, there is no way that wouldn't come back to haunt everyone. She sold him out for an unpaid position. She didn't love him. Better it happened last year instead of in five years. The welfare system needed reform anyway because of this exact situation."

Livia swallowed. Her heart hurt for those in Lupus house that were suffering insecurity because people valued their pride above feeding their fellow house members. She couldn't think of many things more awful.

Tavian interrupted her thoughts, "How have you been doing here, Liv? Do you like school? Things going good?"

Livia sighed. "Not as easy as I expected it to be in some ways. But it's not bad. Some moments are good."

"So, it's okay?" Tan said.

"Yeah," Livia nodded. "I'm comfortable here."

"That's good to hear," Adrian said. "It's nice to hear you're happy."

Livia wasn't sure if she'd describe herself as happy—happy was a tricky state—but she was close to it.

"Thanks," Livia said, pulling into her visitor's spot at Ratco. "We're a little early. Let's hope they aren't too annoyed with us."

Chapter 15

They weren't annoyed at all but excited. Terrance especially, to see anyone from Rattus house. Terrance hugged each Hall member at least three times before he could talk properly. "I don't know how you guys live outside. I miss being with other Rattus folk so badly. It's so good to see you."

"Eh," Adrian said. "We've gotten used to it. Livia knows how it is—"

Livia didn't know if she knew, though, it wasn't getting easier pretending around Whitney. This week was especially difficult. Especially since she'd hurt Whitney when she chose to sleep over hanging out. Livia didn't know how to explain how badly her body needed sleep without revealing how Taurus members worked. Livia was relieved to come to hang out at Ratco tonight. She needed it.

Everyone looked at her. She picked at one of her fingernails. Adrian waited. When Livia didn't say anything he looked surprised. She didn't know what he expected her to do. So, she walked into the kitchen and got a glass of water. Tavian followed her.

"Can I have a glass too?" he asked.

Livia got a second glass and handed it to him. Corvin was in the kitchen, squinting at a recipe, deeply involved in a baking project.

"Do you want help, Corvin?" Livia asked.

"Um, that'd be nice, Liv," he said. "I'm supposed to do this."

116

He turned the recipe book toward her.

"You're making pretzel bites?"

"I thought it would be easy. It's not."

Livia smiled. "You got an apron? We're gonna get pretty messy."

"We don't have any," he said.

Livia shrugged. She'd have to deal. "Okay, then. Let's do it."

Tavian didn't leave. "Liv, you acted weird in there."

She glanced at him. Then looked away.

He frowned. "You miss Caesarea then?"

Livia found a measuring cup. Then stilled. "It's kind of bigger than missing, Tavian," she admitted. "If I just missed it. It'd be easy."

"What does that mean?" he asked.

"It's like…I don't know if I could live outside the way I thought I could. The way I wanted."

"Why not?"

"I thought I could switch back to who I used to be, but…I can't…I need people who understand me."

Tavian's eyes widened. "That's…something I never thought I'd hear you say."

"That I'd need anything," Livia joked.

"Well, that too. But you were pretty committed to doing things solo."

Livia shrugged. "Maybe this is a phase. It might pass."

"Are you hoping it does?" Tavian asked.

Livia sighed. "It'd be simpler if it did."

"Liv," Corvin looked at her. "You know it's normal, right? To need people?"

Livia looked at him, surprised.

"The fact you can feel and acknowledge that need is evidence that you've healed," he said.

Livia froze. "I don't know if I like that. It's harder to need people."

"I know, but it's good. It's healthy," he said.

"But it's hard…" Livia said.

"Yeah, but that means you're growing, you're learning. It's an amazing place to be."

"So, you don't think it's going to go away," Livia said.

"Not in the way you'll want it to," Corvin said. "It'll go away when your needs are satisfied."

Livia sighed. "I hate being human."

Corvin laughed. "Me too, Liv. Sometimes it sucks, right?"

His openness about his feelings surprised her. "You feel that way?"

"Yeah," he nodded.

"A lot?"

Corvin pursed his lips. "Depends."

Livia considered him. "Is it worse out here or in Caesarea?" she asked.

Corvin sighed. "Again, complicated. I think I needed a break from Caesarea. But I miss my family—a lot. It's hard."

Corvin's expression didn't change but Livia looked at Tavian and saw such a genuine sadness on his face. She realized he was echoing Corvin's emotions.

"That's a fierce ache, Cor," Tavian said. "Go visit them."

"We keep talking about going the week of fall break. It coincides with the founding festival so it's perfect. Liv, you wanna come with us?"

"Um, let me think about it...wait, you guys will be gone that entire week. I..." *need you.*

"Come with us," Corvin begged. "I'll worry about you here all alone."

Livia worried about herself too. "I need time to get used to this idea. What's the plan?"

Corvin and she baked together as he gave her all the details. "Felicity is struggling hard, Liv," Corvin said. "She needs it more than I do."

"What else can we do, Corvin?" Livia asked. "We met up for lunch a couple of days last week on campus."

"I don't know if there's more you can do than that, Liv. That's already a big help. She'll figure it out, eventually. She either toughen up and ride it out or cave and learn a big lesson about herself. Either way, she'll be okay if we support her through it."

The more familiar Livia became with Corvin, the more she realized how non-judgemental he was of other people. He didn't care what Felicity decided as long as he knew she was safe and happy.

"She'll be okay?" Livia repeated, looking at him for reassurance.

Corvin stepped closer. "Yeah, Liv. She has a good family and friends that love her in both places. She'll find her best way."

Without thinking Livia moved into his personal space to drink in the reassurance he exuded. "I worry about her."

Corvin smiled, his stance opening to invite her closeness. "You worry about everyone, I've noticed."

Livia sighed. "I can't help it. You think she'll be okay?"

Corvin settled his hand between her shoulder blades. "She'll be fine and so will you."

Livia startled away. "Sorry, I—"

"You're fine," Corvin said, voice warm.

Livia could still feel the sensation of touch on her skin and instead of disliking it, she savored it. She regretted pulling away.

"I'm slacking off," she scolded herself. "The pretzels won't make themselves."

Livia dedicated herself to the baking enterprise, putting space between her and Corvin. She looked up at Tavian. His wide eyes switched between them, as he suppressed a smile.

She rambled about nonsensical things, clearly flustered. Corvin interrupted her when he stroked a flour-covered finger down her nose. Livia looked at him startled.

"What are you doing?" she asked. "Is there flour on my nose?"

Corvin laughed. "When was the last time someone told you that you're adorable?"

Livia was too surprised to respond. What was she supposed to read into this? Was Corvin playing with her? Flirting? He thought she was adorable?

Livia looked at Tavian, who was laughing openly. "Is there flour on my nose, Tav?"

"No," he laughed. "You're fine."

Arik took that opportunity to come in. "Oh, excellent! We're baking?"

He went over to the sink and washed his hands. He handed Livia the rag.

"Wipe off your nose, Liv."

Corvin and Tavian both chortled when she glared at them both. "I am not adorable!"

"Of course, you are," Arik said without missing a beat.

"Not cool," Livia glared at him.

He took out his phone and glanced at it and frowned.

"Something wrong, Arik?" Tavian asked.

He sighed. "No."

"Expecting a call?" Corvin asked.

"Yeah." He placed the phone on the counter in front of him. He looked at Liv. "Are you going to stop glaring at me every time I come near?"

Livia jerked her chin back. "I'm not glaring at you—" That much.

Arik raised a single brow at her. "Right."

Oh no. He was in a mood. She knew if she denied glaring at him there would be a fight. It was time for a different tactic.

"I think you're being lazy," she barked at him. "Standing there looking at your phone when there's work to do in here."

He rolled his eyes. "Yes, Liv, what would you like me to do?"

"Roll this dough out into strips and cut each into one-inch pieces," she said.

"Yes, Ma'am," Arik said and got to work.

"Corvin, will you watch over them while they boil in the baking soda?" Livia asked.

"Got it, Fabulous," he said.

Arik's head shot up at the use of the nickname. Livia tried to remember if he'd ever heard it before. It was something that had started in the TARP office. She was continuously running little errands for them as the intern and they started to tease her by saying things like, "That's our Fabulous Fabius." Until, one day, Corvin shortened it to straight Fabulous and it stuck.

"I'll get the pans all ready to go in the oven," Livia said, trying to avoid Arik's gaze. Was he going to say something?

Soon, they were a productive little assembly line. Thankfully, Arik went

120

back to work and didn't get upset. There was a cooperative bustle in the kitchen that made Livia feel warm and pleased. She slid two pans of pretzels into the oven and released a triumphant sigh. She liked efficiency.

"Alright, we have to let those cook," Livia said. "When does Felicity get here, Corvin?"

He looked back at the clock as he washed his hands. "Ten minutes, if she's on time."

"Does she know the Halls were coming?" Livia asked.

"We thought it'd be fun to keep it a surprise," Corvin said.

"Think Felicity will react like Terrence?" Livia asked.

"More excited," Corvin said.

Livia laughed. "That will be fun. My roommate was struck speechless."

"She was?" Corvin asked, drying his hands off and looking at her now.

"She might have been overwhelmed with three hunky guys in her apartment." Livia grinned.

Corvin laughed. "Compliments to Mrs. Hall."

"She does good work doesn't she," Arik joked.

"I've always liked your mother," Corvin said. "She strikes me as very loving with just the right amount of sternness to keep three boys in line."

"Oh," Tavian said. "But Tan is the wild one. She tests my mom's patience to the limit."

"I am very familiar with the difficulties of reasoning with females," Corvin said. "I'm related to a strong-willed cluster of clever machinators myself."

Livia laughed. He had five younger sisters. "Do they know you describe them as such?"

"You should hear what they call me," he said.

Livia shook her head, amused.

At that moment a knock came at the door. "Felicity's here!" Livia cried.

Terrance opened the door. "So, we have a surprise..."

"What surprise?" Felicity asked.

"Come see," Terrance invited them in.

"Visitors!" Felicity squealed with delight a moment later.

Corvin and Livia cracked up together, gazes locking.

This provoked another intrigued look from Arik. Livia quickly looked away and stopped laughing. Corvin glanced between her and Arik, then frowned.

"Tan!" Felicity greeted. "Are you Adrian or Tavian?" she asked from the other room.

Arik and Tavian exchanged a look and grinned at each other.

"I'm Adrian," Adrian said.

"Adrian!" Felicity squealed.

Arik and Tavian laughed outright then slipped out of the kitchen to the front room. Livia sighed in relief to be out from under Arik's scrutiny.

"Arik!" Felicity squealed.

Arik took the opportunity to taunt Adrian that his name was more memorable. Livia grinned at Corvin as Tavian got the last happy Felicity greeting. "She's happy."

Corvin came alongside her. "See? She'll be fine."

They were alone in the kitchen now. Corvin opened his mouth to say something when Arik's phone vibrated with an incoming call. Livia's eyes widened as the caller's name flashed—Lauren. The name was accompanied by a picture of a young red-haired woman clutched in a passionate embrace with Arik. He'd picked up a new girlfriend. Well, that hurt but also...she was relieved.

Corvin swiped the phone. "I'll be right back."

He disappeared from the kitchen giving Livia a much-appreciated space to breathe. Corvin came back a moment later. "Arik slipped outside to chat with Lauren."

Livia took a deep breath. "That's the call he must have been waiting for."

"You okay?" he asked. "That's a brutal way to find out your ex is dating someone new."

Livia sighed. "It's a little painful but also...I'm relieved?"

Corvin smiled. "Not a bad feeling."

"I mean, he moved on. It's over—"

"Closure?" Corvin asked.

Livia nodded. "I think? I don't know."

Corvin shrugged. "We don't need to analyze it."

Livia sighed with relief. "Okay. Let's just...do something else."

"It's a mess in here," Corvin said, carrying a bowl to the sink and starting to scrub it out.

Livia had the urge to give Corvin a huge hug. She couldn't ask him directly without him assuming she was deeply upset. And she needed something lighthearted right now. She'd have to settle for a playful game of revenge instead. She discreetly scooped up a handful of flour and headed toward him.

He heard her coming and looked over his shoulder briefly. Then did a double-take and turned fully to face her.

"Liv," he drawled low in his throat, head tilting toward her.

Dang, how did he know she was up to no good?

"Corvin," she said back in the same tone.

She hesitated but he grinned and reached out a hand for her. So, she stepped closer. She should have known it was a trap! When she reached him he sidestepped so she was facing the sink. One hand found her hip while the other encircled her wrist and held it over the sink and away from him. He attempted to break her grip on the flour and failed. Due to the advantage of being Taurus, no doubt. Livia laughed and twisted her wrist to break his grip.

Corvin hid his face in her hair and laughed as he lost their battle. The sound of his mirth vibrating in her ear sent happy tingles skittering down her arms. Corvin wrapped both his arms around her and pulled her tight against him to shield himself. Livia closed her eyes and surrendered herself to the embrace for one delicious moment. Then she set herself back to her revenge plot. She cackled and threw the handful of flour directly onto his hair.

Corvin immediately shook his head and got flour everywhere. He nuzzled his head along her shoulders and neck getting her covered in flour too. Livia laughed and turned in his arms so she could push him away. Only to find herself lacking the will to push when her palms came to rest against his ribcage. She looked up into his grinning face and froze. Did understanding what happened between him and Bella change things between them this much? Corvin released her from his hug and placed his hands lightly on her lower back, sending tingles down the length of her spine. Yes, definitely. The knowledge had lowered her reticence dramatically.

Corvin batted his eyelashes playfully. "How ridiculous do I look, Liv?"

When she saw the flour coating his long lashes, she snickered at him.

The spell was broken.

Corvin heaved a sigh and released her to face the sink. He turned on the tap water and splashed his face with water, washing the flower off. He put his hair under the stream and tried to finger the flour out, but he was missing spots.

"Here," Livia reached out before she considered the consequences. "Let me help."

She ran her fingers through Corvin's wet curls, shaking out the sticky flour. She stilled for a moment as the sensation of his hair between her fingers overwhelmed her. She enjoyed it. Too much. Suddenly, all this familiarity intimidated her.

Corvin waited. "Did you get it all?"

"No. I—" Livia moved her fingers through his hair again, washing out the flour spots. She was more careful and timid than she'd been at first.

"You're fine," Corvin insisted. "Thanks for the help."

Corvin closed his eyes. He looked like Ares when he was getting his head scratched.

"You like that?" Livia whispered.

"Feels nice," he said, simply.

Livia got the rest of the flour and removed her hands from his hair, heart racing. She turned off the faucet. Corvin grabbed a dry kitchen cloth and rubbed his neck and head. He turned toward her.

He grinned as he took her in. "You're a mess."

Livia was too shy to look him in the eye. "Not as bad as you were."

Corvin reached out and placed a hand on her lower back to draw her close again.

Livia inhaled sharply and stiffened.

Corvin turned half away to turn the faucet back on and soak the towel. "I'll be gentle, Liv. It was all good fun. No hard feelings."

Livia swallowed as he turned toward her and brushed a corner of the towel against her cheek. Livia flinched instinctively.

"Is that too cold?" Corvin asked, hesitating.

"No, it feels nice," Livia admitted. "I'm just not used to that."

"To things feeling nice?" Corvin asked, concerned.

Livia tried to swallow down her emotion as tears flooded her eyes. Thankfully, she was able to blink them away before any of them fell but Corvin wasn't blind.

"Sorry," Livia whispered.

Corvin lifted the towel again and brushed her cheek gently. "I'm not afraid of tears, Liv, as you know."

Livia laughed, breathless. TARP agents negotiated their way through a lot of tears weekly. He brushed the flour off her other cheek and the cold rag was soothing against her skin. Livia knew her expression softened in response to his touch and she attempted to draw away, afraid she'd reveal her feelings for him.

Corvin tugged her back gently. "Did you think less of me for enjoying your touch?"

"No." Livia scoffed. That was ridiculous.

"I won't think less of you," he said, directly meeting her gaze. "May I?"

Livia closed her eyes hoping that would make it easier. "Okay."

As Corvin wiped the flour off her face with the cold rag Livia's tension eased. She realized that her skin was irritated and itchy from the flour. The cold soothed away the irritation. A sigh of relief slipped out of the back of her throat. Corvin's hand lifted from her back and cradled the back of her head as he tilted it back so he could wipe the flour off her neck and shoulders.

"All done," he said.

Livia opened her eyes, and Corvin smiled. Both his hands feathered over her hair, "Except, for your hair. Shall we rinse it the way we did mine?"

"Can't you just brush it out?" Livia asked.

"I'll try," Corvin's fingers brushed lightly over the strands of her hair as he tried to dust the flour out. "It looks better. But—"

Their gazes met and he stopped mid-explanation. Livia wasn't thinking clearly. She felt too relaxed, too comfortable because she slid her hands up his chest and over his shoulders. She didn't have a plan or an endgame. The gesture just felt right, as natural as exhaling after inhaling.

Corvin's expression softened and his forehead lowered to rest against hers. He inhaled deeply and his hands tangled deep into her hair.

Livia imagined the taste of his lip against hers and inched her chin upward.

"Livia," Arik said, strolling into the kitchen. Livia leaped out of Corvin's arms so fast he had to grasp the counter to keep from falling over. She turned to face Arik, cheeks flaming. His eyes went wide, flying from her to Corvin and back the same way Tavian's had.

Arik grinned and leaned against the doorframe. "So, how long are you keeping it a secret?"

"What a secret?" Livia asked, baffled.

"Your relationship," he snapped. "I've been watching you two the entire time and it's clear as day—"

"Watching who?" Livia asked, confused.

Arik tsked and an impatient look crossed his face. "You and Corvin, Liv."

Livia's face flamed and she cast Corvin an embarrassed look. "We're not dating," she whispered.

"Why not?" he demanded.

Livia glared at Arik. "We're not dating, Arik."

Corvin said, "Arik, there's no secret. Liv and I are not in a relationship, currently."

Arik was not deterred. "Corvin, you should take Livia out."

Corvin coughed. Livia was suspicious it was to hide a laugh and she glared at Corvin. Corvin took one look at Livia and sobered. "You-you hold that opinion?" he asked.

"She's hard on herself but she's amazing girlfriend material. Loyal, supportive—"

"Arik," Livia exploded. "What are you doing?"

126

"I am not talking to you," Arik gave her a snooty look and turned back to Corvin.

"Liv's not interested," Corvin said, firmly.

"She's not?" Arik asked, looking back at Livia. "Have you asked her?"

"Several times," Corvin answered.

"No you haven't," Livia snapped. Then she remembered more than one invitation she'd shot down immediately. She closed her eyes and put her forehead in her palm.

Arik laughed. "He did ask, didn't he?"

"He was only being nice," Livia defended herself.

"Cause that's a crime," Arik drawled.

"Why are you making it your business?" she demanded.

"I want you to be happy, Liv," Arik said. "Also, not a crime."

"Don't be this way," Livia ordered.

"What way?" Arik asked, innocently.

"Meddling," she said.

"Cause you'd never meddle to help someone you cared about," Arik said, a single eyebrow raised.

Livia growled through clenched teeth. "Arik."

"Be persistent, Corvin," Arik said.

"Arik, this is not cool," Corvin said. "You're embarrassing her and that's extremely unkind despite the fact you claim to care for her."

"She doesn't understand her position, Corvin," Arik said. "She thinks I'm a higher class than her. She thinks her status is so far beneath yours that it's impossible to bridge the gap."

"Thanks, Arik," Livia said. "Thanks for that."

"I understand what you're saying," Corvin said. "Now, stop. I won't tolerate this discussion anymore."

Livia was trembling with the effort it took to suppress her tears.

Arik opened his mouth to speak again, a smug look on his face, but Corvin interrupted, harshly. "Don't speak. Leave this kitchen. Now."

Arik looked at Livia and his amusement evaporated. "Liv?"

She inhaled a shaky breath and turned her back to him. There was a long, tense silence, and then she heard Arik shuffle away.

Corvin approached her. Livia tried to breathe away the tears but only managed to sound like she was hyperventilating, as tears slipped down both cheeks.

"This is so stupid," she squeaked.

"Don't worry about it," Corvin said, calmly. "That must have hurt. He was a little too eager to hand you over to the next guy, huh? Right after you were ambushed with the Lauren call."

Livia put a hand over her heart. "I don't know. I don't know."

"What don't you know?" Corvin asked.

"I don't know why I'm crying—" she whispered.

"You're not hurt?" Corvin asked, surprised.

"I feel...so...anxious..."

"You scared?" Corvin asked.

"I don't want you to think...I'm...I'm preying on you—"

Corvin laughed. "No, I don't think that, Liv."

"And it does make me feel...worthless," she whispered.

"Cause he doesn't want you?" Corvin asked in a low voice so no one else could hear.

"I'm not good enough," Livia whimpered. "Nothing I do is ever good enough."

Corvin put his arms around her. "You are amazing just the way you are, Liv."

Livia cried on his shoulder. "I didn't want to do this again."

Corvin chuckled. "I'm here. Just cry all you need."

"It's so stupid. Why do humans have feelings? It's so useless," she muttered.

Corvin rubbed a single hand up and down her back. "Let it all out, Liv."

Livia was grateful that the tears passed quickly and she pulled back. "Thanks, Corvin."

He shook his head. "No problem. Let's get those pretzels out of the oven before they burn, huh?"

She nodded. Corvin found the perfect balance between distracting her from her emotions and offering her support and validation at the same time.

She reminded herself he did this all day for a living, of course, he was good at it.

Chapter 16

They carried a bowl of hot, fresh pretzels into the room. The only way to stay a safe distance away from Arik was to sit down next to Corvin, which was something Livia usually consciously avoided. Arik looked repentant and wouldn't meet her eyes when he muttered, "Sorry, Liv. I overstepped."

Tavian and Adrian both gave him displeased glares. Terrance and Felicity both looked like they were waiting for something else to go wrong. Tan was the only one that still seemed chipper but Livia knew her well enough to see that it was a facade.

Tavian offered her a way out. "Liv, I saw a path outback. Wanna go explore it?"

"Yeah," Livia agreed.

"Want me to come, bro?" Adrian asked.

Tavian shook his head. "Nah, we'll go check it out for ten minutes or so and come back."

Livia sighed with relief as she slipped outside with Tavian. She was overwhelmed with all the drama.

"Arik is an idiot sometimes but he feels awful," Tavian confided. "I had to get out of there."

Livia laughed. "Me too, Tavian."

"So, dating Corvin is a sensitive topic, huh?"

"Well, Arik is dating again—" Livia said, trying to deflect the conversation. "We saw the picture of Lauren come up on his phone when it rang in the kitchen."

Tavian winced. "We debated telling you against Arik's wishes but he wanted to drop that bomb the last day we were here."

Livia sighed. "He's such a coward sometimes."

Tavian sighed. "So, what is up between you and Corvin? I noticed the attraction too."

Livia blushed. "Corvin's not attracted to me."

Tavian laughed. "He put flour on your nose and said you were adorable. He calls you Fabulous—"

"That's a joke," Livia interrupted.

"Well, why don't you consider it?" Tavian asked.

Livia used to think Corvin was a controlling sexist but after Tavian revealed the details behind his relationship with Bella she knew that wasn't true. One of the reasons she'd been so upset about Corvin pulling that move on Bella was that it didn't fit with the values he professed in a professional setting. Now that his personal and professional values mirrored each other in her head her belief in the inherent goodness she's glimpsed in him was restored.

She looked at Tavian. "What do you think about him donating to two different campaigns? Does it make you angry?"

Tavian sighed. "That's a hard question, Liv. Sometimes, Corvin's life isn't fair. His position in Caesarea makes so many of his personal relationships political and that's disturbing to watch, honestly. Like how you asked in the car—if he'd gotten back together with Bella would the welfare reforms in his house be resolved? Who wants to be in a position where the girlfriend you chose determines if 600 people in your house get to eat next year?"

Livia winced. "It would feel like political blackmail if they got back together—"

"Yeah," Tavian agreed. "So, I'm personally glad he didn't do it. I don't think any relationship could remain healthy with that kind of baggage."

"Yet, you ask me why I won't date him?" Livia asked.

"Well, you're in the same position, Livia," Tavian said, bluntly.

Livia missed a step. "What?"

"Anyone you date will want to take advantage of the fact that you have familial relations to Gaius and Hyrum. You're patrician, Liv. That means your opinion influences the political and financial decision of Taurus house."

"I still don't get why you think I'd be any different than Bella—" Livia said.

"Since Corvin has similar influence and power within his family the relationship wouldn't be as unequal," Tavian said. "I mean, being Patrician is one thing but you and Corvin are next-level Patrician. You're Paterfamilial Patrician and that's next to impossible to reconcile with Plebeian politics. Believe me, we've all watched Corvin try. He's had many difficult breakups."

This line of reasoning irritated Livia. Part of her still wanted to be right that she and Arik could have worked things out if he hadn't bailed on her. That door was closed now, though, firmly. Arik was dating someone new and that shifted Livia's internal focus. It was a lost cause and wasted energy to hang on to it any longer.

"But Lupus house is way more powerful than Taurus house," Livia argued.

Tavian sighed. "I know you see that as a bad thing but there's so much potential for good there—"

Livia frowned. "How?"

"His family is secure and strong and yours is chaotic and struggling. It would bring stability to the entire community if Taurus house had the support of the Tullian clan. Gaius and Hyrum can't do everything on their own indefinitely."

Livia knew this and it hurt. It hurt to watch Hyrum struggle. It hurt to accept that Caesarea would break him if things remained the same. It felt gross to date a man to save her brother, though. You could call it selfishness or self-preservation but Livia wasn't willing to do that. It offended her sense of integrity.

"So, it'd be all about politics," Livia glared at Tavian.

"Good relationships, Livia," Tavian said. "Are the foundation of good politics. They're not inversely related."

"Your arguments don't mean we even have to date. We could just be friends!" she insisted.

"You could," Tavian agreed. "That would help Hyrum and Taurus house immensely if you were able to smooth a political understanding with Lupus house. In Caesarea, things aren't about individuals. It's about taking care of the House. He knows so much about what Hyrum and Gaius need to do. Try to learn from him at the very least."

Livia frowned at him.

"This is my best advice," he said. "Don't punish Corvin for Arik's mistakes. Pretend like tonight never happened. Continue as you were before we got here."

That hit Livia hard because she didn't want to be that person. She didn't want to be the person that punished someone who didn't deserve it because she was upset. That was what her mother would do. Livia had to prove to herself that she wasn't going to be like her. She was going to be more rational. She was going to be fair.

"Okay, Tavian," Livia agreed.

They walked in silence a few moments more and then decided to head back to Ratco. Livia mulled over all the arguments Tavian gave her but it was a lot to take in. It wasn't something that she could process on a ten-minute walk or ten days even. She needed space and time and probably a long talk with her brother Hyrum to sort it all out.

When they walked back into the townhouse things seemed less tense. Terrance was chatting with Arik. Felicity was sitting close to Adrian, who was grinning a tad more flirtatiously than usual. Corvin and Tan were slamming down cards as fast as they could, intent on their game of speed.

Tavian and Livia both scooped up a handful of pretzel bites and found a place on the couch.

"Tav," Livia asked. "How's school? You like it?"

"I do," he said. "My Trig class is hard but I'm passing. Then I'm finishing up the rest of my general requirements this year."

"You're gonna be an accountant, right?" Livia asked.

"Yeah," he said.

Livia's brother was studying to do the same and was currently rooming with the twins while they completed the same program.

"Does Lucas see Mom much?" Livia asked. Tavian and Adrian had already reported that he was doing fine and that he wasn't currently dating anyone.

"No, they talk on the phone but he doesn't visit her more than once a month. Tad comes out to see him occasionally."

Livia smiled. "Tad is awesome."

"He is," Tavian grinned. "Tad went on a hike with us and I now know why you're a birder."

Livia laughed. "Right? He knows everything!"

"Seems like it," Tavian agreed, finishing off his last pretzel bite.

Livia's smile fell, as an ache filled her. She turned to look at the wall.

"You miss him," Tavian said.

"A little," Livia admitted.

"A lot," Tavian contradicted.

"I miss Lucas too. I wish he'd come out and visit," Livia confessed.

"I'll try and talk him into coming with us to fall vacation," Tavian said.

Livia couldn't hide her eagerness as she turned to Tavian again. "I'd love that. I was debating on going back but if I could see Lucas again—"

"You were seriously considering not going back for fall break?" Tavian asked, confused.

Livia lowered her eyes. Sometimes it was hard to remember that even if Tavian could sense her emotions he couldn't read her mind. "I wasn't going to go back ever, Tavian," Livia said, quietly.

He studied her a long time before saying anything. "But we had that whole conversation in the kitchen about—"

"I know," Livia pressed her forehead to her knees. "I know."

Sometimes Livia thought that torture would be easier than dealing with this limbo she was in and then she remembered her childhood and told herself she needed to stop being dramatic. She had safety, food, and shelter. She had loyal brothers and good friends. She should be happy with what she had.

"Caesarea is a weird place," Tavian said. He glanced at the rest of the room, as if he worried about what the lifetime Caesareans were going to think of him, then carried on. "There's this culture there that implies because we have characteristics in common that we're all one big family. So, there's this weird messaging that you'll get universal acceptance and it's simply not true. No one in Caesarea has universal acceptance."

"I don't need everyone to like me, Tavian," Livia said. "That's ridiculous."

"Then what do you need, Liv?" Tavian asked.

"I need to have a place where I can be my authentic self and have respect," Livia said. "Caesarea offers me authenticity with no respect. Out here I know how to gain respect but I have to hide who I am."

Tavian's expression turned thoughtful. "What do you get respected for out here, Livia?"

"I work hard. I follow the rules. I help people when I see a problem I can solve. That's enough out here. In Caesarea...well, I keep learning there are new rules even after a year. People don't let you help them because they have people assigned to them that do that? I don't know? I never figured it out. But on a good day it's awkward, on a bad day it's humiliating. Work in Caesarea? I guess people respect it but...they care about things that don't matter more. Like what you wear. Who you're related to. Weird things, Tavian. I don't understand it."

Tavian sighed heavily. "Well, yeah, most people think your family is more important than work in Caesarea. Having a good relationship with your family is...highly valued."

"So, I'm punished because my parents are messed up? Like I had any control over any of that! That was done to me, Tavian. I didn't cause any of the awful things my parents were—mentally unstable, alcoholic, dysfunctional—" Livia said.

"Liv," Tavian spoke, gently. "I'll admit, people are going to judge you because of your parents. You can't stop that. You need to let that go. Instead, focus on the relationships you can control. People notice that you and Hyrum are close. They notice that you're loyal to and supportive of each other. That's been observed and is generally known. It's gonna take time for people to trust that lasts. Understand? Longevity is part of the deal. Keep nurturing that relationship with Hyrum. Support him. Take care of him.

People will start to let go of that history if you and Hyrum show them you treat each other differently."

"I can do that," Livia said. "But...I can't stand not being able to help people Tavian. Like...I...I can't figure out how to make friends if...I'm useless to them."

Tavian laughed.

"It's not funny—"

"Liv, we can be friends without you doing things for me all the time—"

"Like, how?" Livia asked. "What do we do?"

"We just went on a walk—"

"So, you could help me calm down. What's the point of the walk if I didn't need that?"

"Maybe you wanted to show me a bird—" Tavian said.

"You don't like birds—" Livia said.

Tavian frowned. "Maybe I just like walks—"

"Okay, physical exercise..." Livia agreed.

"We both like to exercise. You're taking care of yourself. I'm taking care of myself. That's friendship. You don't have to be useful to me."

Livia stared at him.

"That makes you feel super insecure—" Tavian drawled.

Livia put a hand to her forehead. "I hate you."

Tavian laughed.

"Why are we friends again?" Livia demanded, irritated with his empath powers.

Tavian laughed again. "We talked about this. We both like walks."

"For physical exercise—" Livia joked.

"Yes."

"We both know that's not why we're friends," Livia growled.

"Then why? For real, not pretending?" Tavian said.

Livia answered. "Cause you don't make me feel bad because bad stuff happened to me. And you don't get upset that I'm short-tempered and impatient."

Tavian smiled. "You're my friend because you're considerate. Also, I like

136

that you're honest about when my empathy bothers you. You'll straight up tell me you're inconvenienced by it. A lot of people get uncomfortable and avoid me instead."

Livia sighed. "It is uncomfortable but...sometimes it's nice to not have to explain."

Tavian nodded. "I get that. Lucas doesn't like to talk about the past either. Hyrum doesn't feel the same."

"You've talked to Hyrum about the past?" Livia asked.

"Once or twice," Tavian said. "He's processed his emotions over it a bit more. I think he's talked to a professional about it—"

"Justin made me do that—" Livia confessed.

"Did it help?"

"Enough," Livia said. "It helped enough for what I needed at the time. But it didn't fix everything—"

Tavian shrugged. "It's a process."

"I'm pretty sure Justin would prefer I go back—" Livia said.

"Why not?" Tavian asked.

"Didn't help anymore," Livia shrugged. "Being here has helped me a lot more than anything has in a while."

Tavian smiled. "Well, Liv, there's no way we'd have had this conversation two years ago. You've grown."

Livia sighed. "I know."

"It's good," Tavian said.

"Hard," Livia grunted.

"Sure, but good," he said.

Livia pressed her hands through her hair. "You think I should give it another go, Tav?"

"Counseling?" he asked.

"No." She pushed his leg. "Caesarea."

"Yeah, Liv, I do. But accept you're not going to win everyone over. You just need a team."

"You guys come and go—" Livia said.

"Yeah, we love you but we can't be there the way you need us to be," Tavian agreed. "Stop focusing on being useful. That's codependent and insecure. Focus on being present and kind. Let everything flow organically from there."

"I'm not good at kind—"

"Practice," Tavian scolded her. "You're kind, Liv. You like to show it instead of saying it. Start saying it."

Livia groaned. "I don't have it in me, Tavian."

"Yes you do, Liv," Tavian argued. "Stop whining."

"It feels manipulative—"

"Yeah, cause doing favors for people to make them feel indebted to you is less manipulative—" he said, sarcastically.

Corvin laughed.

Livia looked at him, surprised. Felicity and Adrian were still ignoring them. Terrance and Arik had their faces glued to a phone screen but Tan and Corvin were watching and listening.

"Is...is that what I'm doing?" Livia asked Tavian, honestly.

"That's what it feels like to Caesareans," Tavian answered. "It's just how the culture translates there."

Livia sighed, defeated. "I'll try it your way then."

Livia drove the Halls back to their room late that night. They arranged a time for Livia to drive them to the airport in the morning. It was hard to say goodbye when she dropped them off but they assured her they would call often. Livia noticed that Arik never brought up his girlfriend but Tan assured her that Arik knew that she knew. Livia was frustrated with him but that was nothing new. So, she let it go and hugged them all goodbye.

Chapter 17

L ivia texted Corvin a couple of days later. *If I come by around 5 will you be home?*

Corvin didn't answer instantly and Livia wanted to take the text back. Did she really need to have a discussion with him about everything the Halls had told her? The weight of the consequences of Bella's actions settled on her shoulders. Yeah, it was important to talk about the welfare crisis in Lupus house.

Corvin texted an hour later. *Class until 5:30. Can we do 6?*

Livia's heart pounded. She could make excuses. She could decide to spend the evening watching Romcoms with Whitney. There were a million other things she could do besides having emotionally fraught conversations with Corvin Tullius. But she owed him a sincere apology and she wouldn't let herself off the hook. Not over something like this.

Livia texted. *See you at 6.*

Corvin: I'll pick up something to eat together on the way home.

Livia wanted to protest. That seemed too much like something people in a relationship would do. That freaked her out. Especially, after all the comments Tavian and Arik had made. Before panic made her react harshly Livia took a deep breath and thought through responses that wouldn't cause conflict.

She settled on. *Let me know how much I owe you.*

There. That made it more of a friend thing.

Livia sent prayers up to her dead ancestors again as she walked up to Corvin's door. Terrance joined them for dinner and some of Livia's nerves disappeared because Corvin had bought food for him too. It was totally a friend thing. Also, Terrance smoothed over the conversation when Livia got too nervous to think of a reply.

After dinner, Terrance excused himself to study. He patted Livia's arm on the way out of the room.

"Relax, he doesn't bite," he whispered.

Livia glared at him.

Terrance grinned and disappeared down the hallway.

Corvin sat on the couch in the front room. Livia followed him. She hesitated, then blew out all her breath as she knelt on the ground in front of Corvin. He gave her a questioning look. Instead of remaining on the couch, he followed her lead and slid off the cushions until he sat on the ground too. That almost made her lose all her courage. She'd liked the distance between them. Now, with his eyes level with hers, she felt her throat tighten with the heaviness of her apology.

"What's going on, Liv?" Corvin asked. "Tell me what's on your mind."

She had been awake all night trying to figure out how to have this weird conversation. She didn't know what point to start with first, but she'd decided to start with Bella. She took a deep breath and hoped she didn't offend him forever.

"The Halls told me something I didn't know," Livia said.

Corvin looked surprised. "Oh? What'd they say?"

"They told me what happened with Bella."

A resigned look crossed his face and he nodded.

"I-I didn't know," Livia confessed, awkwardly.

"Really?" he didn't hide his disbelief as he would have before. "She never talked about me?"

Livia shook her head. "It wasn't that. We talked about you. We didn't talk about...how she sold out your secrets to get that political appointment."

"Interesting," he said, but his expression had gone neutral again, he'd gone

140

back into hiding.

Livia pressed on. "I only knew that she was being shunned. So, we'd go out and try to forget for a couple of hours how messed up our lives were."

"Justin didn't tell you?" Corvin asked.

"It was all Justin could do at that point to keep me functional," Livia said. "So, I completely understand why they didn't invite me into their drama."

"Functional?" Corvin asked, confused.

So, he didn't know either. "I went a little crazy after Hyrum left. Didn't sleep well at night. Nightmares. Panic attacks. Didn't want to leave the house. I'd feel unsafe all the time. I'm surprised they even put up with me." Livia looked down at her hands.

"I knew you struggled," Corvin said. "I didn't know it got that bad, I'm sorry."

Livia shook her head. "Don't be. None of it was your fault. My family was...my family is...My mom...she's unstable. She never makes good decisions. And when she does, it feels like good luck. But that's...not what I'm here to talk about. So—" Livia made a motion of putting that aside.

"Okay," Corvin nodded.

Livia had to regroup. "Okay, I guess, I need to ask if what they said was true. Did she betray your political secrets to get a job?"

Corvin sighed. "Her motivations were more nuanced than that, but yes, that's essentially what happened. I gave her a choice to apologize and leave the position to prove that I could trust her. She chose the position over me, which hurt. She expected me to forgive her and to reconcile for a while so it was messy. But she'd showed me she was more infatuated with my position than she was with me. I already know from past failed relationships that's not enough to sustain a healthy relationship."

Livia was surprised at the level of personal detail he shared. It wasn't like him to be that open. Also, what he said made a lot of sense. It reflected the situation with her mother. Maybe that's what happened. Honor was infatuated with Drusus Fabius' position and it wasn't enough to make either of them happy.

"Well, I realized yesterday," Livia gulped. "That it might be my fault she didn't give up the position."

Corvin lifted a single eyebrow. "Explain."

"Because I didn't understand what she'd done, I influenced Bella to keep that job. I thought you were being unfair and...sexist. She was good at that job, Corvin. She hadn't ever had an opportunity like that before. So, I told her over and over that if you cared about her you wouldn't ask her to compromise."

Corvin sighed and wouldn't meet her gaze.

Livia whispered. "Since no one told me, I didn't know that the Lupus house welfare crisis was caused by her actions. I'm sorry if my actions made that more difficult."

Corvin closed his eyes. "I should never have donated that money."

Livia remained silent.

"Justin hoped that if I removed myself from the situation that things would get better and they'd be able to negotiate a deal," Corvin said, folding his hands together.

Livia asked, "Do you feel like it's working?"

"No."

"I am so sorry—"

Corvin shook his head. "Livia, you did nothing wrong. Honestly, I'm relieved you were able to be an impartial friend when no one else was capable. Justin and Flavia have told me more than once that your friendship saved her. It was an excruciating year for everyone involved."

Livia whispered, "I realize how...my actions looked to everyone. I took her side over yours."

Corvin spoke sincerely. "Livia, I didn't resent you for that. You made the best of a hard situation. That said, I'm surprised. I thought you were going to try and talk me into getting back together with her at some point over the last year."

Livia frowned. "No. Bella never asked me to do anything like that. I think we both knew you wouldn't listen to me."

Corvin blinked several times before he asked, "Why'd you both think that?"

142

"Cause, you know? I'm a nobody in Caesarea." Livia laughed.

"That's not true," Corvin said.

"Then…you're blind to the way people treat me there."

Corvin sighed, as if frustrated. "Liv, the power of your influence and position is not diminished by how people treat you. They'd like you to think that, but it's not true. You are my peer. Custom dictates that if you had a concern that someone in my father's circle would give you an impartial audience and hear you out."

"Really?" Livia asked.

"Yes, you are one of the few in Caesarea that has a legitimate claim on that privilege," Corvin said.

"So, does that mean I always have to listen to you?" Livia asked.

"If I made a formal request for an audience you could appoint someone to hear me out if you were uncomfortable with a direct conversation—Gaius, Hyrum, Justin—"

Livia thought about that a moment. "Corvin, I need to apologize for how I treated you when we first got here. I'd like to be your friend. If your offer still stands. I'd understand if you don't want—"

Corvin put his hand on her knee to stop her rambling. "Livia, I'd love to be your friend still."

"Okay. Good. Um—Arik. I-I-"

Corvin smiled, his hand still on her knee. "Too bad he doesn't have a bit more brain to go along with that beauty, huh?"

Livia sighed. "He reminds me of Adrian sometimes. They're clueless."

"Sometimes the inexperience of youth translates as insensitivity," Corvin agreed. "It's a thing."

Livia nodded. She grew self-conscious as Corvin's eyes settled on her and stayed. He removed his hand from her knee then lifted the back of his fingers to her cheek and brushed them briefly over her cheek.

"You know what I can't get off my mind?" he asked, extending his fingers to smooth her hair back.

"What?" Livia whispered, finding it hard to maintain eye contact with him.

"The tears in your eyes when you told me you weren't used to affection feeling good," Corvin removed his hand from her hair and placed it on his own knee.

Livia didn't know why she confessed. "I think, I'm broken."

She covered her mouth with her hand and then hid her eyes in the crook of her opposite arm. She took deep breaths to keep her emotions at bay.

Corvin's hand cupped her arm. Then moved up and down in a soothing motion. She pulled her face up. "I'm sorry."

"No, no," Corvin spoke. "Don't be. Can we talk about it?"

"What's there to talk about?" she asked.

"Were you open with Arik about how you felt?" Corvin asked, removing his hand from her arm.

"Yeah," she answered. "We liked opposite things. So...I tried to make it 50/50 where we kissed the way he wanted and then kissed the way I wanted."

"So, did you like it when you did it your way?" Corvin asked.

"At first, yeah, but then I started resenting him when it was his turn. I got so tired of it."

"That's hard, Liv," Corvin said. "Justin is open about this. Taurus have a hard time feeling pleasure. The same abilities that make them resistant to pain also impede feeling pleasure. He and Flavia spent a lot of time figuring out how to make their relationship good for her too."

"Is...is it good for her?" Livia asked.

Corvin's eyes sparked with amusement at the same time his lips turned up in a grin. "Famously so. They had to work hard for it and don't keep that a secret. They wanted other Taurus women to know they weren't alone."

"Really?" Livia asked, feeling relieved.

"Really," Corvin assured her.

Corvin continued, "My uncle Lucius and Aunt Garnet were the same. They're more discreet about it but things improved for them after they talked to Justin and Flavia. It saved their marriage."

"That's good to hear," Livia said.

"There's nothing wrong with you," Corvin said, gently. "And you are not alone. Both Justin and Flavia and my aunt and uncle would be willing to answer any questions if you run into that problem again."

"What if I hadn't talked to you?" Livia asked.

"What if?" Corvin joked.

Livia smiled. "Thank you for telling me."

"It's the least I can do, Liv," he said.

"I didn't think I was going to try a relationship ever again," she admitted.

Corvin looked at her. "Liv, more guys would be understanding about it than you'd think."

"Really?" Livia asked.

Corvin laughed. "Really, Liv. You should be blunt about it. You'll know right away which guys are interested and which are not."

"What if they're not interested?"

"Then what's the point, anyway? It won't be good for you," he said.

"That's…true," Livia admitted

Corvin asked, "Do you want a family, Liv?"

"Not if I have to give up certain things," she said.

"What things?"

"Independence. Financial Security. I always want to be able to work."

"Those things are not insurmountable challenges," Corvin said.

"You don't think so?" Livia asked. "Caesarea seems…not that way. Very traditional."

"We're Caesarean's," Corvin said. "We're biased toward relationships and family and that won't change. But I think you're not looking at the whole picture of what you have to offer. There will be a man who will be willing to negotiate with you. You have a lot of power. You should not settle before you've even gotten started. Ask for *everything* you want."

Livia had a lot of questions about what he meant. She opened her mouth to ask him and then shut it. She heard Hyrum saying in her head. *Mom's biggest mistake was letting her value be defined by the men around her. Don't do that Livia. No one defines what you're worth except for you.* She worried asking Corvin to explain what he meant would be akin to asking him to define her worth. That wasn't a trap she wanted to fall into. But Corvin had made her feel like she could ask Flavia and Justin these things. It'd be safer to ask them what they thought Corvin meant.

"You have a question?" Corvin asked, face open with invitation.

Livia shook her head.

"Ask," Corvin encouraged.

"No," she shook her head again. "I should go. I have class early tomorrow."

Corvin sighed. "I'm glad you came over. I'd love to talk like this again."

Livia nodded. "See you, Corvin."

Chapter 18

L ivia didn't like using Whitney as a social experiment but she didn't know what else to do. She was going to Caesarea in two days and she had to start somewhere.

She found Whitney in the living room studying. Livia deliberately didn't bring a snack with her like she usually would have. That made her anxious. It'd be much easier if Whitney rejected her food instead of Livia herself.

"Hey," Livia said.

"Hey," Whitney greeted, not looking up from her textbook.

"So, fall break in two days," Livia began.

"Yep."

"I like having you as a roommate," Livia said.

Whitney looked up, confused.

"I'll miss you over fall break," Livia continued.

Whitney smiled. "I'll miss you too, Liv."

"Maybe we can do something together when we get back?" Livia asked.

"I'd like that," she said.

"Sorry, I'm boring lately. I need sleep," Livia said.

Whitney shrugged. "You can make it up to me when you get back from fall break, alright? We're good."

Livia sighed with relief. That did not go too bad. It seemed irrational to spend thirty minutes making a batch of cookies when you could say something and patch things over within thirty seconds. Maybe Tavian had a point? It was going to be an interesting break.

* * *

Everyone piled into Corvin's black SUV, bags packed, lunch bagged, at noon Friday. They planned to arrive in Caesarea around four o'clock that afternoon. They ate and chatted the first two hours of driving. Then took a quick pit stop at a rest stop to go to the bathroom. When they started again Corvin asked to listen to music. Terrance acted like a typical DJ for awhile. Then he dug into his backpack. "Okay, I have a surprise, guys."

"A CD?" Corvin asked. "We're going old school."

Terrance loaded it into the player.

"Wait," Corvin said two measures into the first song. "You didn't."

"Whoohoo!" Felicity cheered. "Turn it up."

"I've never heard this song before but the voice sounds familiar," Livia said.

Felicity and Terrance laughed.

"It's Corvin!" Felicity shouted.

"Guys, I can't do this," Corvin said and reached to turn it off. Livia leaned forward and grabbed his arm to stop him.

"Wait," she said. "You sound..." Livia closed her eyes and listened. Younger. But that wasn't what struck her about his voice. She opened her eyes at the end of the song.

"That Corvin is...happy," Livia said.

The car went silent. Corvin shook her hand off and turned the music off. Livia wanted to ask questions but Corvin put the blinker on and pulled to the side of the highway.

"Corvin?" Terrance asked.

"I need a minute," he said, voice strangled.

He parked and put his head on the wheel and a breathy sob shook his shoulders. Livia flew into action. She pushed open the car door. Livia flew to the driver's side door and jerked it open. Livia froze. She knew what she wanted to do. She wanted to put her arms around him and cradle him the way he'd cradled her. Sometimes, though, her body didn't cooperate with what she wanted to do. So, she had to gather her courage.

She slid her palm across Corvin's back and tingles skittered up her arm but they settled as she tucked her arm around the curve of Corvin's shoulder. There was something grounding about the shape of him huddled in the curve of her arm.

Livia pressed her cheek to the side of his head. "I'm sorry, Corvin."

It had been her fault that they listened to the entire song.

Corvin pulled away from the wheel and turned toward her. His arm wrapped around her middle and his face found shelter against her shoulder. Her other arm curved around him and he melted into Livia's embrace. Livia was relieved at how steady the embrace made her feel. Strength poured into her as Corvin's sobs sent vibrations into her shoulder. She wasn't sure if it felt good but it did feel right. There was no better place to be than here, offering her body as a refuge to the man who'd given her the same gift in some of her darkest moments.

She spoke into Corvin's hair. "It's okay. I'm so sorry. I'm here for you."

Livia held him until he stopped crying. She pulled away. "Get out."

Livia noted the confusion on Corvin's face and realized how abruptly she'd pulled away. Corvin's hand still rested lightly on the curve of her waist.

"I'll drive," Livia insisted. She still didn't sound comforting enough.

Corvin pulled both his hands back over his thighs. "Liv, I'm fine now."

Livia disliked how the lack of his touch made her feel adrift, uncertain of the right way to balance herself. She could ignore all that for now, though, because she had a purpose.

"I'm driving," she insisted. "If it were me, you'd do the same thing, Corvin Tullius."

"I can drive."

Livia shook her head. "I don't care! Get in the back seat. You deserve to rest!"

"Livia—"

"Do. Not. Argue. With. Me." Livia said in her strongest don't-mess-with-me tone.

Corvin undid his seatbelt and got out and slid into the backseat. Livia hopped up into the driver's seat and moved the seat forward. Corvin had extremely long legs. Now she could reach the pedals and he had more room.

Livia took a deep breath. "Okay. Does anyone need anything before we start again?"

Everyone chimed that they were good and Livia shifted the car into drive. Corvin's car was different from hers and it took a couple of miles to adjust to the feel of it. The car was quiet for the next half-hour and they were soon twenty minutes outside Caesarea.

"How's everyone back there, Terrance?" Livia asked.

"They're both asleep," he said, quietly.

"Even Corvin?" Livia asked.

"Yeah, Corvin went out first."

"Is he okay?" Livia whispered.

"I guess I shouldn't have done that," he said.

"What was that? He did a CD?"

"He was the lead singer for a band called the Owls when he was younger. It was a different time of his life. He wasn't as serious. He wasn't always happier but more...carefree, I guess."

"So was it a local thing?" Livia asked.

"Yeah, never went past Caesarea, but for a lot of us, it was the music of our teen years. Really nostalgic."

"So, did he write the songs too?" Livia asked.

"Yeah, with his girlfriend, Cassia."

"Where is she now?"

"She passed away," Terrance said.

"What happened?" Livia asked.

"She was killed. It changed Corvin. He gave up music. Lost a year doing nothing. Then he made a friendship with Justin and they founded TARP together. Corvin finished school and went to work for him. Pulled himself back together really well but when it comes to relationships? Man, he makes bad decisions. Chooses all the wrong girls."

"Okay," Livia said. "That's a lot."

"Yeah," Terrance said. "Don't assume his life is perfect. He's done his fair share of the life sucks thing."

"Got it," Livia said, getting off on the exit for Caesarea. There were miles of flat land out here interrupted only by the occasional hill or greenhouse. Caesarea disguised itself as a rural agricultural college. Most of those greenhouses were skylights for underground offices and buildings. They were coming in from the west side—land associated with Aquila house and the security patrol training facilities. They drove past the outdoor track and training fields, which were busier than Livia expected.

"They're busy—" she muttered.

"They're getting ready for the snatching of the Sabines reenactment," Terrance said.

Livia shook her head. She'd been offended by the whole production last year and still felt the same this year. "Who came up with that idea?"

"It's all good fun, Liv," Terrance said. "No one is forced to do anything they don't want."

Livia huffed. "If you say so..."

Livia dropped everyone off and helped them unload their luggage. They were careful to be quiet so Corvin wasn't disturbed. Livia pulled up to Terrance's house. He was the last one to drop off.

"You okay?" Terrance asked, looking back at Corvin.

Livia nodded. "I'll wake him up and get him to take me home."

"Okay, I'm a phone call away and I have access to a car here so if you need anything? Ring me."

"Got it."

Livia went back to the car, though, and didn't want to wake Corvin up. There was something too intimate about it. She was scared to face his emotions again. Alone this time. She thought about how Corvin would treat her and the answer came immediately. Corvin was the type of guy who drove you home and unloaded your bags and saw you were safe in the arms of your family before he'd leave you. Livia made the decision.

She called Hyrum. "Hey, we're in Caesarea but there's been a complication."

"What's up?"

"I need you to pick me up at Corvin's house."

"Lars' place?" Hyrum asked. "Or Corvin's townhouse?"

"His parents' house. Lars' place."

"Okay," Hyrum said. "See you in fifteen."

"Yeah, thanks, Hyrum."

"Okay, Corvin," Livia whispered to his sleeping form in the backseat. "We're taking you home."

When Livia pulled into the driveway at Corvin's parents' house there were a ton of cars parked on the street and in the wide driveway. There was even a group of people waiting around on the expansive porch around the front door. Livia immediately felt awkward. Maybe this was a bad plan? Too late now.

She pulled in slowly and parked, careful not to hit the empty trash can on the curb. She got out of the car. People who had started toward the car froze.

"Hey, uh," she said, gesturing. "Corvin fell asleep. Backseat."

Livia picked out the familiar faces of Corvin's sisters. Epiphany, Mel, Alia. Epiphany made it to the car first. She opened the door.

"Corvin?" she asked, worried. "Hey, Corvin."

He woke. "Whoa, Piph?"

"You okay?" she asked.

"Where are we?" he groaned.

"Home. You're home," she said, gently.

"Livia drove me home?"

"Yeah," Mel chimed in. "Freaked us out, a little."

"Sorry, she forced me to take a break. I guess I needed it."

"Forced you?" Epiphany said. "That's a feat."

Corvin yawned. "Everyone here?"

"Yeah, come on," Mel said. "We're so excited!"

They dragged Corvin out of the car and to the head of the driveway where he was swarmed with more hugs than Livia got in a year. Alia didn't immediately trail after them. "Nice to see you again, Livia."

"You too, Alia," Livia said. Alia was the most friendly of Corvin's sisters and often stopped to chat with Livia when they crossed paths. She was two years younger than Livia and didn't have the same hazel eyes as the rest of her siblings. Instead, she shared the same steady brown eyes as her mother. "How have things been around here?"

"Pretty stressful, actually," she answered, honestly.

Livia's eyes shifted toward Corvin. "Yeah, I only recently realized how stressful. I'm sorry."

Alia nodded. "Thanks for taking care of Corvin."

Livia waved that off. "He's done more for me. Don't worry about it."

Alia walked off and Livia was left alone. If Hyrum was going to come to get her, then she needed to get her bags. She didn't want to make Corvin or his family take care of her. She opened the back of the SUV. She tried to find her bags but they were behind Corvin's—two huge duffels that were ridiculous in size for a weekend. What had he brought home? She hauled them out easily, almost dwarfed by the size of them.

A deep voice stopped Livia. "Let me," he said.

"I got it," she said, firmly. "Where do you want them?"

"In my hands," the voice jested.

Livia looked the lanky man up and down. He was tall but had more meat on him than Corvin. His hair was silver and his skin tough from exposure to the sun and elements. "They're pretty heavy," Livia told him doubtfully.

The man grinned. "I am married to a Taurus Miss Fabius. I can handle it."

This was Corvin's Uncle Lucius then. He was married to Garnet, who was born in Taurus house. He'd have adopted her powers upon their marriage so could easily handle the bags.

"Alright then," Livia said, handing the bags over.

Livia went back to the SUV and pulled out her suitcase and backpack. She noticed that the backseat had a lot of trash in it. So, when she stowed her stuff at the end of the driveway she rolled the trashcan back toward the car. She started clearing all the trash out.

She had moved to the front seat when she heard Corvin behind her. "Livia, what are you doing?"

"Cleaning up a mess."

"Stop doing that."

"I'm almost done."

"Livia, stop," Corvin ordered.

"There's only three more things," she said, ignoring him. She leaned into the car to grab something on the footboard in the passenger seat. Just as she grabbed the last of the wrappers an arm wrapped around her waist and lifted her up and back.

Livia was so strong that she thought of herself as solid, immovable. Like a rock. This conception of herself wasn't shattered very often. Corvin lifting her down from his truck with one arm pretty much destroyed this illusion. She felt feminine and small and vulnerable. She didn't like it.

"Put me down!" she cried.

"Livia," he sounded annoyed. "You don't need to clean my truck."

He set her feet on the pavement. Livia grabbed his hands and tossed them off her. "You don't need to touch me!"

"Liv, stop fussing. I'm fine."

Livia threw the trash in her hand into the garbage. "I am not fussing!"

"Oh really? What's your definition of fussing then?"

Livia took on the imitation of a dozen simpering females she'd seen interact with him. She pressed a single hand on his chest and spoke in a falsetto. "Oh Corvin, we'll just die if you don't come to this party with us. You are the air we breathe. How could we live without you?"

"That is not funny," he snapped.

But his family erupted in a huge gale of laughter. Livia smirked. "They think it is because it's true!"

Corvin glared.

Livia removed her hand from his chest and swung the garbage can lid closed and then grabbed the handle.

"What are you doing?" Corvin asked, stopping her from pulling the trashcan by putting his hand on the other handle. Livia inhaled through gritted teeth and had to stop herself from running him over with it. This made her almost fall over.

Corvin grabbed her again to steady her, hands splayed on either side of her waist. "Whoa."

Livia gave him a defiant glare, trying to hide her embarrassment. "Let me take the trashcan in."

"Why?" he asked, disbelieving.

"Because I'm Livia Fabius, Corvin," she snapped. "I see a job that needs to be done and I do it."

"Come meet my family," he said.

He still hadn't let go of her. Livia feared she was too upset to break his hold without hurting him. It made her heart beat hard and fast to be held so decisively.

"I need you to stop touching me, Corvin," she begged, voice low.

He looked surprised and immediately released her. Livia's tension lowered.

Livia gestured at the trashcan. "You can't leave this in the middle of the driveway. How are these people going to pull out later?"

"We put the trash can away, you agree to be introduced to my family," he argued.

"Fine!"

Corvin, in a ridiculous move, kept his hand on the trashcan the entire time they pulled it. Two people hauling an empty trash can up the driveway—one of them Taurus. It was a ridiculous sight. His family should be laughing, instead, they buzzed with excited chatter.

They parked the garbage can against the side of the house.

"Happy?" Corvin asked, giving her an amused look.

"Yes, thank you," Livia snapped.

"Are you ready for introductions?" Corvin asked.

Livia inhaled. "Not really. Do I have to do that chin thing?"

"No, that is only for when you're in public. We're at my home now with my family. Things are very informal and relaxed."

Livia took another deep breath trying to calm her nerves. Getting thrown back into Caesarea like this was not part of her plan. She was scared she'd offend Corvin's entire family. Her face went red as she realized she'd already got in a fight with him over a trash can. Talk about a bad first impression.

"I'm sorry, Corvin," Livia squeaked.

"What for?" he asked, leaning in closer.

"The trashcan."

He leaned back and laughed. "Relax, Livia. You're fine."

Livia took an audibly shaky breath. "Let's do this, I guess?"

"Hey," Corvin said. "If you need emotional support you're welcome to slip your hand into mine anytime, alright."

Livia's eyes went wide. "Then everyone would think we were dating!"

Corvin laughed again. "That ship has sailed, Liv. The second you pulled in that driveway they assumed we were a couple."

"Well, how do we fix that?" she hissed.

He shrugged. "They're smart. They'll get it when they don't see you around."

Chapter 19

C orvin led her over to the first group of people. "Liv, this is my cousin Atticus. He's Lucius and Garnet's oldest. His wife Dulcia is Aquila house and these are their two kids."

Atticus clapped a hand on Corvin's shoulder. "You're lucky she didn't run you over with that trash can, Corvin."

Dulcia gave Corvin a scolding look. "You know better than to get in a determined Taurus woman's way."

"She is Taurus, isn't she?" Corvin mused.

"How did you forget?" Livia asked, unsettled.

Corvin's cheeks went pink. "Sorry, Liv."

She stared at him and confessed honestly. "I did almost run you over. It scared me."

"I won't forget again, Livia," Corvin said.

"Nice save," Atticus told Livia. "Mom's not that agile. She would have turned him into Corvin pancake."

Atticus slapped his hands together and laughed. Livia flinched and did not laugh. She looked away and didn't respond to the joke.

Dulcia bumped her husband with her hip. "That's not funny to her, love."

Atticus assured Livia confidently, "He would have been fine. A trashcan is fairly light and so are you. Probably, no more than a scrape or two."

Livia thought it was irresponsible to underplay the risk like that. She imagined Corvin trying to catch himself to keep from falling over and spraining a wrist or an elbow. In the worst scenario, he'd sustain a concussion or fractured bone. People were a lot more fragile than they liked to think about.

Corvin touched her elbow to draw her attention. "Liv, no one got hurt. No use in worrying about what might have happened."

"It's possible you could have ended up with a concussion or—"

"I'm aware," Corvin said. "They are right to call me out for being careless."

Livia let out a sigh of relief. Corvin didn't take it lightly as his cousin. She believed he would be more careful in the future. "Be less careless."

He nodded. "I will, Liv. We okay?"

"We're okay," she agreed.

She was introduced to Garnet and Lucius' second daughter Azurea. Her belly was curved with late pregnancy and her husband held her close against his side.

"I would have expected a baby by now, Azurea," Corvin teased. "I'm looking forward to meeting your girl."

She rolled her eyes. "Trust me, Corvin. I'm more eager than you."

He laughed. "How are you feeling, Az?"

"Fat," she spat.

"Own every pound of it," Corvin encouraged. "You're doing an amazing job."

She sighed and looked at Livia. "You are Livia Fabius."

"I am," Livia agreed very quietly.

"You're at the same school as Corvin we heard."

Livia nodded.

"Do you see each other often?" she asked.

"Only when my roommate leaves on the weekends."

Corvin turned to Livia. "She leaves every weekend?"

"Yes."

His brow furrowed. "I didn't know you were alone that much..."

"I don't mind it," Livia said. "There are parts of being alone that are nice."

Azurea turned to her husband. "Let me introduce you to Jonas, my husband. He's Rattus house and works in the praetor's office."

Livia knew that meant he worked in the Caesarean court system.

"Are you a lawyer?" Livia asked.

"Yes, and I believe you are acquainted with my sister."

"What's her name?" Livia asked though she had an idea. He was Rattus house, married into a patrician family, and had that style.

"Salina Antonius."

One of the maidens of malevolence indeed. Livia nodded. "Yes. I hope her health has improved."

Jonas looked confused. "Her health?"

"Yes," Livia spoke lightly. "We both like to cook. I offered to send her recipes or invite her over to try a dish. But she had severe diet restrictions that fluctuated from week to week. I assumed she was on an elimination diet. I hope her health is better."

Livia hated using her mother's tactics. It made her stomach churn but she didn't know any other way to be both honest and civil.

"She's never gone on any sort of diet ever," Jonas laughed. "That's so awful. I'll have to scold her for being so rude."

Azurea shared an amused look with her husband. "She hopes her health is better! It would serve Salina right if rumors went around that she was chronically ill."

"We shouldn't," Jonas insisted, but he laughed.

"We can't let this pass. We must ruthlessly mock her," Azurea said. She turned to Livia. "She's a beast, Livia. She threw a fit when it turned out I was pregnant before she even got married because I'm younger than her."

"I hope that she has not continued to be rude to you," Livia said, empathetically. "Especially, not after the baby comes."

Azurea looked surprised. "She won't—I should probably be prepared for that shouldn't I?"

Livia shrugged, helplessly. "If sending recipes would make it better, I'm willing—"

Azurea's face lit up. "I'd love that. It'd be good to have some ideas after the baby comes. Please, send them. Corvin can give you my contact information."

Jonas smiled. "I liked meeting you, Livia Fabius. Feel free to approach us when we're out and about."

Livia nodded and gave them a timid smile. Corvin interjected. "I'm sure you'll be so pleased with Livia's recipes. She keeps bringing the treats she makes on the weekends. Everything she touches turns out amazing," he said. "And it's just like her to offer. She's so generous."

Livia looked up at Corvin in genuine surprise. She didn't expect his warm praise. He looked back at her and smiled. She lowered her eyes and ducked her head to hide how much the words meant to her. Livia heard genuine praise very rarely.

Corvin reached out and touched the small of her back very briefly. "This way, Liv. I have more cousins."

Corvin was different among his family. He was a consummate conversationalist. He filled the awkward spaces in their conversations with a warm, affectionate voice that spent chills of comfort down Livia's spine. Without thinking she moved closer to him and let her arm brush against his.

He bragged about her shamelessly. Protective, caring, helpful, talented in the kitchen. Livia would have asked him to stop but she was too intimidated by how outnumbered she was. Also, she was curious. Was this the way he saw her? Was she this amazing person he'd described? Her face turned warm with his endless praise.

Corvin told his family that Livia wasn't much for hugs. Though he suspected she had exactly one reserved in her that night for his mother. Livia was so grateful for this thoughtful bit of protection, she squeezed Corvin's hand briefly in gratitude. He squeezed back before she let go. Livia looked up at him, her heart expanding with warmth for him in a way that surprised her. She couldn't hide the smile that turned up her lips.

Her attention was pulled away as he introduced Livia to his Aunt Garnet and Uncle Lucius. Their greeting was particularly warm. Livia was more curious about them than she cared to admit. Garnet was born Taurus after all. By the end of their exchange, Corvin's aunt promised to invite her over for dinner the next time Livia returned to Caesarea.

"That would be wonderful," Livia said. "You'll have to let me bring something. Maybe my mother's famous honey rolls."

Garnet laughed. "We'd love that. We're so proud of Honor. What a strong, independent woman."

Livia felt tears come to her eyes. It was the first time anyone in Caesarea had said anything kind about her mother. "Thank you," she managed miraculously without crying.

Corvin moved on but Livia hid her face for a moment against the back of his arm to collect her emotions. Corvin paused. He lifted his arm and wrapped it around her, pulling her against him.

"You okay?" he asked, softly above her ear.

Livia nodded, but she was blinking back tears fiercely.

Corvin put up a hand to pause the introduction they were having. He pulled her into a tight hug and held her silently. Livia tried to hold herself apart but that lasted all of three seconds. She melted into his embrace and took strength from it. Corvin's kindness served as a salve for her rogue emotions and Livia pulled away ready for another round of introductions.

Corvin urged her. "Come meet my Aunt Silvia and Uncle Marcus."

"They're with Silvanus," Livia noted.

Silvanus was Corvin's older cousin, who was also one of Justin's officers. Livia was excited to see him again and so was Corvin. The two men swept each other into a fierce hug. Corvin and Silvanus were incredibly close and looked very similar. It wasn't uncommon for people to mistake one for the other when they weren't paying proper attention.

"How's the team?" Corvin asked.

"Missing you," Silvanus said, pulling away.

Silvanus grasped Livia's hand. "How are you, Liv?"

"I'm good, Silvanus. How's work?"

"We miss you too," he said. "No one quite realized how much you did until you left. The new intern is not as organized. Took us a month to figure out how you made things run so smoothly."

Livia grinned. "I was good at my job."

Silvanus laughed. "Too good, Liv. We had to shift things around to get back to how it was when you were there."

"Good to see you, Silvanus," Livia said.

Silvanus released her hand. "It's a surprise to see you two together. You were both rather intent on ignoring each other at the office."

Livia shrugged. "Sometimes you believe wrong things about people."

"Livia thought I was a shameless sexist," Corvin said, amused.

"No!" Silvanus laughed heartily in shock.

Corvin continued, "And I thought she was going to try and argue me into getting back together with Bella. When the entire time she was talking Bella out of it."

"Whoa," Silvanus said. "That's a plot twist."

"We have lots to catch up on," Corvin said.

"We'll talk," Silvanus said, easily. "Say hello to my parents before they call us out for being rude."

Corvin grinned and gestured. "This is my Aunt Silvia, my father's sister. Everyone loves her because they remember her fondly as their primary school librarian."

His Aunt Silvia laughed. "Stop bragging about me, Corvin."

Corvin introduced Silvia's husband. "This is my Uncle Marcus, he's a physician at the clinic. He's revolutionized the way they do medical care there over the last decade."

Livia shook his hand and looked at them both. "You're Silvanus' parents."

They nodded and Silvia caught sight of Livia's ring. Her eyes flew to Corvin, alighting with hope. "Corvin, is this?"

"No," Corvin said, quickly. "That's a gift from her paterfamilias, Gaius."

The hope in her expression dimmed. "Oh, the way you interact, I wondered—"

"Livia and I have only gotten to know each other recently. We're friends now and that took some time," Corvin interrupted.

Silvia's eyes softened. "Well, you keep us updated."

"Same with you," Corvin said and they moved on.

Livia tried not to giggle. Corvin bumped her with his hip. "Go ahead and

162

laugh."

"Maybe I should stop wearing this ring?"

Corvin shrugged. "Maybe switch it to another finger, instead. If it means something to you, keep wearing it."

"It doesn't fit on another finger."

"You can get it resized," he said.

"You can't resize an heirloom, Corvin!" Livia insisted. "It might get ruined."

Everyone took notice of the ring now. "It's from Gaius," Livia repeated. That seemed to increase their fascination with it.

Finally, they met Corvin's parents. Livia had only interacted with Lars and Aurelia briefly, mostly on formal occasions. Though, she knew that Hyrum interacted with Lars frequently over house business when Gaius was visiting family in Istanbul. Livia hugged Aurelia and smiled at her.

Aurelia smiled back at her, black hair streaked with silver. "Thank you for bringing my Corvin home. That was very kind to let him get some rest. He pushes himself so hard."

Livia grinned. "It was a pleasure. He's done so much for me, it was nice to even the score."

"Then I introduced you to my entire family all at once," Corvin said. "That'll erase all my good deeds for a decade at least."

Livia laughed and so did everyone else. "It's slightly overwhelming," she admitted.

"Only slightly?" Corvin teased.

Livia frowned. Why wasn't Hyrum here to rescue her by now? She pulled her phone from her pocket and when she saw the time her eyes flew to the road with fear. It had been 30 mins. Hyrum was punctual and she could understand him being ten minutes late. But fifteen? Without contacting her? That wasn't usual.

"Livia, what's wrong?" Corvin asked.

"Hyrum is supposed to be here by now."

"You asked him to pick you up?" Corvin asked.

"Yes."

Her phone pinged. It was Caecilia. We are on our way. ETA 10 mins.

Livia put a hand over her heart. "They're coming."

"Did something happen?" Corvin asked.

"I don't know. It was Caecilia. Not Hyrum texting. Said they'll be here in 10 mins."

"Hey, we would have taken you home," Corvin said.

She met his eyes. She joked, "Yeah, but then I'd owe you again."

He rolled his eyes. "Remember, I'm in the red for a decade."

Livia laughed. "Stop saying that or I might think you're serious and take advantage."

"I'd like that," Corvin said, warmly.

Livia flushed at the flirtatious look on his face. She shook her head, flustered. "No, you wouldn't."

"I disagree," Corvin said. "It feels good to be needed."

Livia snorted. "You've no shortage of people who need you, Corvin."

Corvin sighed. "But...I do have a shortage of genuine friends."

The change was subtle but Livia recognized sadness on his face. Her defensiveness evaporated. She thought about how the welfare issue in Lupus house probably cost him as many relationships as it had cost Bella.

Livia bumped her hip against his with extreme care. "Hey, me too!" she said with faux enthusiasm.

Corvin laughed and responded in the same tone. "I have a great idea! Let's be friends, Livia."

She rolled her eyes. "We're already friends, Corvin."

"Just checkin'." He winked at her.

It wasn't fair that look sent a whirl of butterflies fluttering in her stomach. She looked away casting about for a distraction and her eye settled on Epiphany.

"How did your book drive turn out?" Livia asked her. Epiphany had spearheaded an effort based out of the Aediles office to increase the selection of books available to the community Library. Livia and Hyrum had compiled a collection of non-fiction animal and agriculture juvenile books and donated it together.

"The librarians and teachers loved the collection of books you donated," Epiphany said.

Livia shrugged that off. "Oh, they were things we would have liked to read when we were kids. I never was into fiction and Hyrum could never find enough stuff about plants."

"Hyrum encouraged me to apply for several library grants. They notified us last week that we were awarded one," Epiphany said. "It will double the size of our science and technology section. The news brought Aunt Silvia to tears."

"Did you write the grant proposal or did Hyrum?" Livia asked. "His professor hired him as a research assistant and all he did for four years was write grant proposals. He earned his department a lot of money," Livia said.

Epiphany's eyes widened, enlightened. "Ah, that perhaps is why he was so specific in his criticism. He told me to send it to him to review before I sent it off and we revised it three times before he approved it. It injured my pride, but I did it."

Livia nodded. "Hyrum is a perfectionist."

Epiphany's face turned sober. "We were surprised he'd take that much time and care over it. But throughout our collaboration, I came to understand that I had very little practical knowledge of what materials normal children needed to learn. Most Lupus house children are capable of reading difficult texts at very young ages so they don't suffer for the lack. About 90% of our educators are Lupus house and since we figured out how to make do without them we didn't realize the need for the Rattus, Aquila, and Taurus house children. Hyrum was personally offended at the inequity and made sure I met each deadline."

A look of frustration crossed Epiphany's face clear as day. Livia had personal experience dealing with Hyrum's stubbornness and offered sympathy. "I hope he was not too infuriating to work with. We all learned really young that if we wanted anything we had to do it ourselves. Hyrum doesn't trust people to be reliable even if they're competent, and I'm sure he saw you as competent."

Epiphany was surprised, but something vulnerable appeared in her eyes.

It was as Livia suspected. Hyrum often came across as disapproving.

"Why do you say that?" Epiphany asked.

Livia spoke reassuringly to her. "Because if you were incompetent he would have diverted your attention to another project and written the grant himself. You must be a very good writer."

Surprise and relief crossed Epiphany's face at the same time. "Thank you for saying that. I didn't doubt my skill as much as I assumed he hated me."

"Hyrum comes across that way," Livia agreed. "Wait a bit; his true colors will show. He'll find some way to say thank you when you least expect it."

At that moment Hyrum came up behind Livia.

"Liv," he greeted, quickly. He stepped to Epiphany. "Ms. Tullius, I think congratulations are in order—"

He was interrupted when Livia laughed out loud.

Hyrum glared at her. "What?"

"You've turned me into a Sibyl."

"What?" His eyes narrowed on her.

"I told her you'd thank her somehow for writing the grant."

Hyrum grunted. "So you know. She worked hard."

He lifted a gift bag and handed it to Epiphany.

Epiphany took the gift tentatively. "What is it?"

"Open it," Hyrum gestured.

Epiphany opened it and found a jar of honey and a recipe book. She read the cover and looked up surprised. "Your mother wrote this?" she asked.

Hyrum nodded.

Aurelia came up beside Epiphany. "May I see?"

Epiphany handed over the book and the honey. Aurelia's eyes rose to take in Hyrum. "This is very thoughtful. This honey is from the Caesarean hives?"

"Yes," Hyrum nodded. "It's fresh. Jarred only this morning."

Lars took the honey from Aurelia's hand. "That will be an adventure. What shall we make with it?"

Aurelia handed the recipe book back to Epiphany. "You'll have to select which recipe we should try."

Epiphany looked up to Hyrum with a smile. "This wasn't necessary but thank you."

Hyrum lowered his head and didn't give any reply. Instead, he looked at Livia. "You ready to go home?"

"I worried," Livia said, quietly.

Caecilia stepped past Livia to greet Aurelia and Lars.

Hyrum sighed and his eyes fell on Caecilia. "I know we're late. Caecilia, well, she…slowed us a bit."

Livia could see by the tightness in Hyrum features that he was frustrated. Her muscles instantly went tense. She looked at Caecilia. She was talking to Lars and Aurelia and exchanging an emotional-looking hug with the matriarch.

"Is everything okay?" Livia asked.

Hyrum didn't get to reply before Caecilia came to Livia. "Liv! I'm so happy—"

Caecilia's eyes filled with tears. Livia was alarmed and stepped forward to face Caecilia directly and grasped her under both elbows. "What's the matter?"

"I'm just so happy you're home," she said, then burst into tears.

Livia awkwardly pulled her in a hug then gave Hyrum the sternest glare she could manage. "What did you do?" she mouthed at him.

Hyrum laughed and so did Corvin and his family.

That surprised Livia because that was out of character for Hyrum. Caecilia pulled back. "I'm sorry we're late. I got sick, again."

"Again?" Livia said, alarmed. Caecilia was never sick that she remembered. "What's wrong with you?"

"Nothing that a few months won't fix," she smiled.

Livia was baffled. "A few *months*? You have pneumonia or something?"

Corvin's family laughed.

"I'm pregnant, Livia."

Livia's eyes widened. "Oh."

That's why Hyrum was laughing! "Wow," Livia said. "Are you sure you're okay? Oh, let's get you home. I need to feed you."

Hyrum and Caecilia both laughed.

"Her answer is to feed you," Hyrum said. "That's Livia."

"I'm afraid not much sounds good right now," Caecilia said.

"Oh, you just need some good cookies," Livia waved a dismissive hand. "You can't say no to Livia cookies."

Caecilia laughed. "I've missed your cookies."

"We'll put your feet up and make you lemon ginger tea while I bake. Hyrum will put on his 'time to relax' playlist and you'll down an entire plate. You'll see."

Caecilia laughed. "Oh, Livia! I knew you'd spoil me."

"We'll if Hyrum hasn't, he's not doing his job right," Livia declared.

Caecilia tossed Hyrum a playful look. "You hear that?"

"Loud and clear," he made a show of grumbling but he was smiling.

Livia looked at Corvin. "I have to go. Caecilia needs cookies. Stat."

Corvin laughed. "See you around, I suppose."

Livia nodded. Of course, he'd say that but she didn't expect to see him much. She seldom saw him in Caesarea unless they were at work and at work he ignored her. Caecilia threaded her arm through Livia's and they started toward the car. Livia looked over her shoulder and gave Corvin one last wave.

Chapter 20

Livia should not be so depressed about the cookies. The tea had gone over well, then Caecilia had taken three bites of a cookie and heaved it into the toilet. It didn't help that there was a parade in two days. Gaius said her attendance was required. She was even supposed to participate in some Taurus house ritual that she had skipped out on last year.

Gaius thought that watching videos of past parades was enough instruction for Livia to figure out what to do. So, Livia spent two hours analyzing and trying to decipher what she was supposed to say. She could only make out only every third word. Eventually, she threw down her pencil. She tried to call Gaius to complain but he didn't pick up.

It was almost midnight now or she would have called Corvin for help. The next morning, she searched for Hyrum to see if he could help her. Instead, she found an exhausted Caecilia sipping ginger tea and eating a bowl of oatmeal one tiny nibble at a time.

"Are you feeling any better today?" Livia asked.

Caecilia looked up. "Yeah," her voice was hoarse. "I'm keeping this oatmeal down...so far."

Livia hated to bother her. "Is Hyrum home?"

"He went to work."

Livia sighed. "Do you know if there's another way to find what I'm supposed to say for this ritual thing? I know I'm supposed to chant something before I light the pile of grain on fire."

Caecilia narrowed her eyes. "Gaius should have a book, I think. It has all the ceremonies in them. Didn't he give a copy to you already?"

"He sent me a video?"

"Oh, right," Caecilia's face fell. "The video. Hyrum had to go to Gaius' office to look at the books cause the video was bad. They're setting up for the parade tomorrow. So, there's no way they'll let you into the office—"

"I'll call Gaius," Livia said.

Gaius still wasn't answering his phone. Livia waited until ten and then called Corvin.

"Hey Liv," he answered.

"Corvin, hey, I hate to bother you—"

There was a low rumble of noise going on in his audio. "No problem. What's going on?"

"I'm supposed to do this…ritual…at the parade—"

"Yes, the one you didn't do last year," he said.

Livia's heart slammed against her chest as she heard disapproval in his tone. "Well, I'm trying to do them this year but Gaius sent me a video and the audio is pretty mangled—"

"There's a book of ceremonies—"

"It's locked in Gaius' office and Caecilia says you can't get in today—"

"Come to my parents' house. There's a copy in our library—"

"When may I do that?" Livia asked.

"Best to come right now. It'll take a while to learn the Latin—"

"It's in LATIN?" That explained hardly being able to make out any of the words.

"Yeah, Liv," Corvin said. "We'll see you in ten minutes, then?"

"Ten minutes," Livia ground out.

Livia couldn't remember the last time a stream of curse words flowed out of her mouth so furiously. The entire car ride over to Lars' house she cursed Gaius, Caesarea, traditions, parades, and every single ancient Roman she could name. She parked on the street because the driveway was full of cars

170

again.

She slammed the door as she got out. "Great, just great, now everyone is going to think we're dating—" she muttered. She'd planned to avoid Corvin's house for the duration of the vacation to avoid rumors. If Livia had her car she might have driven straight out of town. But she couldn't steal Hyrum's car. Maybe she could get lost on purpose during a hike and accidentally camp out overnight?

She felt too guilty to do that knowing that Justin and the TARP officers would be called in to find her. They would worry and spend all that time away from their families during the holiday. Livia was so upset by the time she got to Corvin's door that she had tears in her eyes. She took a couple of deep breaths and wrestled down her emotion before she knocked.

Alia answered the door. "Hey, Liv, come in."

Livia nodded. But she couldn't release the tension in her throat enough to speak. Instead, she walked into the house. She froze as the sheer size of the place overwhelmed her. The ceiling of the foyer soared over her head and contained a huge crystal chandelier. Livia hadn't ever seen anything so fancy outside of a hotel ballroom. She suddenly felt very small and very intimidated.

"The library is this way—" Alia offered.

Livia's voice had deserted her so she followed silently. If the foyer made her anxious, then she was completely unprepared to walk into the library. It was huge and had at least four leather sofas set up in the center of the room for reading. Floor-to-ceiling windows and a huge skylight flooded the entire room with light. Livia's eyes flew to the shelves on every spare wall space of the room. There had to be thousands of books. There were two stories of bookshelves and most of them couldn't be reached unless you climbed the stairs in the corner and accessed a metal walkway.

Livia had to remind herself to breathe because she was so stunned. Real people lived this way? She heard voices and in a distant corner, she saw that Corvin was standing with his father and his uncle Marcus. They were studying a book that was as big as Livia's torso.

Sometimes you lie to yourself about how badly you hoped for something until you're confronted with solid evidence it's impossible. Livia knew she and Corvin were too different to ever be together but she couldn't have imagined that reality would make it this painfully obvious. She was crushed. Utterly. She did not fit into this world and she never would. She wished she'd never stepped across the threshold of his door. Livia trembled with the effort it took to act like everything was normal.

"Did you find it?" Alia asked as she crossed the room.

"We found it," Corvin answered. "Come see, Livia."

Livia did not want to see. She wanted the book to spontaneously combust into flames. Since that wasn't going to happen, she stepped forward.

Corvin came around the table, turning the book as he came. "It's all right here, Liv. It's only three lines of Latin. Not too complicated either."

Livia's eyes wouldn't focus on the words in front of her. Corvin started reciting in Latin and the foreign sound of the language made him feel like a stranger.

The sound of silence finally filled the space between them. Corvin turned away from the book and looked at her. "Liv?"

Her voice was still trapped somewhere inside. So, she didn't respond. Corvin's hand came to rest on her back. "You're shaking? Are you cold? No, you're Taurus…"

Silence fell again. "You…afraid, Liv?" Corvin asked.

"I can't do this!" Livia cried. "I can't!" It meant everything. It meant to be his friend. It meant to be attracted to him. It meant reciting Latin in front of an entire crowd. It meant to be a good patrician. It meant to stay in Caesarea. She couldn't do any of it.

"Hey, hey, hey," Corvin crooned. He pulled her into a hug. "You can do this."

Livia shook her head. "I can't. I-I wish I had my car. I'd drive away and never come back. On the way here I was thinking of getting lost in the woods on purpose but I didn't want all the TARP staff to get bothered—"

Corvin laughed. "Take a deep breath. I'm not going to let you do this alone. We'll break it down into manageable steps."

Livia couldn't relax. She held herself stiffly in Corvin's arms. She scoffed at his reassurances. "Steps? Like it's some kind of recipe? This is so beyond anything I'm capable of—"

"Then, we're in for some personal growth," Corvin said, pulling her in tighter.

Livia usually enjoyed Corvin's touch but today his closeness felt awful. Livia shifted uncomfortably in his arms. "Are you trying to keep me from running away?"

Corvin released her and stepped back. "You're stressed out, huh? So, that is not the slightest bit comforting, is it?"

"No," Livia admitted, bluntly. "Feels terrible."

Corvin grinned at her. "Well, don't run away," he joked.

"I'm not sure I remember how to get out or I would," Livia joked back.

"Why don't we walk around then?" Corvin asked. "I'll show you the way out."

"So, I can run?"

"So, you don't feel as scared," Corvin said.

Livia looked away feeling transparent.

"This addition to the house is fairly new," Corvin said.

Livia's attention whipped back to him. "Addition?"

"Only been here for three years," Corvin said. "I did not grow up with the house this way."

Livia's eyes widened. "Oh."

Lars interjected. "Aurelia and I spent three years arguing about building it but we both agree it was the best thing we did for ourselves."

"Why was it built?" Livia asked.

"Work-life balance," Lars answered. "It takes thirty minutes to get to the forum from here and with all the traffic and congestion that can be extended to over an hour. I'd leave at seven and not get home until seven. When I work from the home office I can start work at 8 and be done at five and spend the lunch hour with the family. When so many of our hours are taken up involved in the community that extra morning and lunch hour are sacred."

Livia looked around her. "So, this is an office?"

Lars shook his head. "No. The office is the next room over."

"Come see," Corvin urged.

Livia followed him through the library and let him show her around the entire addition. It was high class, no doubt, but it wasn't as huge as Livia assumed. There was the library, Lars' office, a storage closet, and some bathrooms.

Covin took her into the foyer and led her to the french doors that were opposite the entrance. "This is the old front door."

He pushed it open and the sound of laughter drifted through the door. He gestured for her to look in. Livia poked her head through the door and was surprised to find a normal house. Expensive marble flooring transitioned to wood, cushy rugs, and worn furniture. Livia could see a living room fireplace on the right and into a small kitchen on the left. The island only had three spaces at the bar and while the appliances were nice there wasn't a lot of cupboard space.

Livia looked at Corvin in surprise. It was a normal house.

"Hey, Liv!" Azurea called. "You came to visit?"

Oh no. She'd been spotted. Her face flushed. "Uh, needed help with the ceremony thing tomorrow."

"Sure," Azurea winked. "It must be nice to see Corvin too."

Livia ducked back into the foyer and gave Corvin a panicked look, but he thought the entire thing was funny. He was grinning. "See ya, Az. We're going to hole up in the library and memorize some Latin."

"Sure," she teased. "That's what I told my parents when I wanted to make out with my boyfriend too."

Livia cringed. Then she became aware that Alia, Lars, and Marcus were watching her. Corvin shut the door and turned to face her.

"Sorry," she whispered.

Corvin's brow furrowed. "What are you apologizing for?"

"They're going to say—"

Corvin waved that away. "I've had worse rumors spread about me, Liv. Besides, you're way too stressed out for kissing to be fun anyway—"

He strode past her leaving her wondering what would happen if she wasn't stressed out. Would he try to kiss her? Livia suddenly remembered their almost kiss in his kitchen before Arik interrupted. Neither one of them had ever brought it up again. That must mean Corvin wasn't interested, right? Even though his reaction right now made it seem he might want to kiss her when she was relaxed.

Livia was sure the confusion was written across her face when she turned to follow Corvin.

Lars interrupted her. "Marcus and I wanted to review some papers in the library if that wouldn't make you uncomfortable..."

Oh, that was a relief! It took the ambiguity out of the situation. "That's great! I mean, fine. I'm fine," Livia said, trying to rein in her initial enthusiasm. "With that."

Marcus chuckled. "You really aren't dating."

"No, we're not," Livia said.

Alia spoke up. "None of us would be against it if you were, you know?"

Livia's eyes widened. "Oh," she choked out.

Lars grinned. "We'd be rather pleased, actually."

Livia didn't know how to respond to Lars' show of support. She was so surprised that she laughed. She wondered if Corvin knew his family was matchmaking behind his back—literally. She looked up and Corvin was leaning halfway out the library entrance.

"Fabulous, we have work to do," he barked.

She exchanged a look with the trio and they all burst out in a round of laughter together. The unexpected moment of camaraderie left Livia with a warm buzz in her chest. She exchanged a conspiratorial smile with Corvin's family.

"I do have Latin to learn," she told them.

Lars winked playfully at her. "Women are renowned for multitasking."

Another burst of shocked laughter startled out of Livia. "I gotta go. You lot are nothing but trouble—"

Their laughter echoed in the hallway as she marched toward Corvin with a red face.

"What'd they say?" he asked quietly.

Livia pressed her lips together and shook her head.

Corvin's eyes widened. "What'd they say?" he pressed.

Livia couldn't look him in the eye. "I can't say—"

He laughed. "Are they teasing you? I can tell them to stop…"

"It's okay," Livia said, softly. "I don't mind."

"You let me know, Livia," Corvin insisted. "If they cross a line and we'll fix it together, alright?"

She nodded. She lifted her eyes to his and the sunlight streaming in behind him highlighted the warm-colored specks of amber in his eyes. Livia's breath caught and she couldn't look away.

"Come on, Fabulous," Corvin said, walking into the library. "We got Latin to learn."

Livia followed him to the large book. She sighed. "Where do we start?"

"With the first three words. How's that sound?"

"Deceptively easy," Livia muttered.

Corvin laughed. "Livia, you can do this. I'm going to prove it to you."

Two hours later Corvin had invited his entire family into the library. Livia hid in a corner until Corvin dragged her out. So, they were holding hands in front of his family. She shot him an irritated look but he ignored it.

"Okay, Liv, they've agreed to the test run," Corvin said. "Show them what you know."

"I don't think this is necessary," she said, removing her hand from his.

"Oh, it is totally necessary," he insisted. "It's going to be uncomfortable reciting in front of all those people tomorrow. So, the last step is to make sure you can recite the lines while uncomfortable."

"Is that supposed to make me want to do this?" Livia asked.

Corvin laughed. "Of course you don't want to do this, Liv. I can't fix that. My goal is that you'll be prepared to do it."

Livia stared down Corvin's family and they stared right back at her. Even the children were oddly well-behaved like they understood their mission. She sighed and resigned herself to her fate. It was harder to remember the lines with people watching, feeling the pressure to not mess up. It took her about four tries until she managed it.

Livia put her hands over her face. "This isn't going to work."

"Livia, Livia, Livia," Corvin grabbed her hands so he could look her in the eyes. "You're going to do fine. This is why we're practicing this way. Okay?"

Tears welled up in her eyes. "I can't do this, Corvin."

"Liv, hun, I know it's hard but there's no one else to do it," he said, gently.

"What happens if I mess up in front of everyone?" Livia cried.

"Then you take a deep breath and start over again," Corvin said.

"They will hate me forever," Livia whispered, horrified. "They'll never let me forget it."

"Liv, you won't be the first person to mess up at one of these things. It happens. No one holds it against people."

Livia laughed bitterly. "That's only because they're considered Caesarean. No one thinks I belong here in the first place."

"I think you belong here," Corvin insisted, fiercely.

"No, you don't," Livia snapped. "Admit it. You disapproved of all the rules I broke and the people I hung out with—"

Corvin looked confused. "The people you hung out with? TARP? I never disapproved of that—"

"Arik. You thought he was beneath me—"

Hesitation crossed Corvin's face.

"See!" Livia accused.

"I didn't understand you," Corvin said. "But that never meant I thought you should leave. You belong here as much as I do."

"You say that." Livia pointed a finger at his chest. "But you ignored me for an entire year. So, if that's the best I can expect from the most decent person I know, I can only imagine how others will treat me."

"Livia, that's in the past," Corvin insisted. "I'm not going to ignore you if you make a mistake."

"Will you go back to ignoring me if I decide not to do this?" She challenged.

Corvin sighed. "Livia, let's be reasonable about this—"

"How am I being unreasonable, Corvin?" Livia demanded. "What rational being places themselves in front of a hostile crowd knowing they'll appear weak and incompetent? Tell me of any other creature in the animal kingdom that would do that. Humans are INSANE!"

Some of Corvin's family laughed.

"She's technically not wrong—" Melanie muttered. "Humans are the only animal that stupid."

Corvin shot his sister a glare.

"Livia," Corvin looked back at her. "First, they're hostile because they believe you look down on Caesarean traditions."

"That's ridiculous—"

"Oh, then what would you conclude if someone new came to live at your house and then proceeded to ignore all the rules and traditions you'd established?"

Livia shouted. "No one taught me the rules!"

"Did Gaius ask you to perform the ritual last year?" Corvin asked.

"Gaius didn't even find what I was supposed to say in that book," Livia gestured, wildly. "He said I should get up there and mumble incoherently and eventually a prompter would tell me what to say! So, you can call me disrespectful for hiding in the audience with Arik but faking my way through a ritual some people might still consider sacred was way worse, Corvin!"

"Did Gaius actually say that?" Corvin asked.

"Yes! That's what Hyrum did. Didn't you watch him last year?"

"Yet, Hyrum has their respect and you do not," Corvin said. "What does that tell you?"

Livia glared at Corvin.

"It's natural to be frightened, Livia, but humans would not have survived millennia of challenges and catastrophes if we couldn't act despite our fear," Corvin said, firmly.

Livia shook her head. "I just don't believe it will do any good, Corvin. And what's the point of getting up there if it makes things worse? I already can't deal with living here—"

"I need you to trust me—"

"I don't," she quipped. "Remember?"

Corvin shook his head. "Livia, trust me. Doing this—even if you make huge mistakes—will do so much good."

"Why?" she asked. "Why does it matter so much?"

"Let's go back to my earlier analogy. Imagine a stranger came to live in your house and they disrespected all your rules and traditions."

"Okay—" Livia agreed. "I got that part—"

"What would you want them to do to make it up to you?"

"Leave," Livia said, immediately.

"Or—" Corvin prompted.

Livia thought but she couldn't come up with an answer. "I don't know."

"Start following the rules and traditions," Corvin said.

"Oh," Livia said. Then the understanding sunk deeper. "Oh, I see."

"That's why, Livia," Corvin said. "That's how you fix it."

"What if it doesn't work?" Livia asked.

"That's a possibility. You can't control how people will respond to your efforts or how long it will take until they decide to trust you again—" Corvin stopped in the middle of his thought.

Emotions crossed over his face and at first, she thought he was upset about how she'd joked about not trusting him. Then she considered the wider circumstances. Caesarea was still upset at him for donating money to different campaigns.

"But if you keep doing the same things nothing will change. You have to show up, take risks, and hope it's enough to create change—" he said, voice hoarse.

Corvin's show of vulnerability gained her trust more than any argument could. Their situations were different but they were both currently in a form of exile—his political, hers social. His advice was being offered from a place of empathy.

Plus, he was right that repeating the same mistake she'd made last year was only going to make things worse. This was one of those crossroads moments. Livia could decide to ditch the parade out of fear like last year, or she could face her fear and discover if she could earn the respect she craved in Caesarea. If the entire thing backfired, she didn't have much to lose. Nothing, except her new friendship with Corvin.

"If I do this...and I mess up in front of everyone...you'll still be my friend, right?" Livia asked. "You won't hate me?"

"No, Livia, of course not," Corvin said.

"Promise?" she pleaded.

"I promise," Corvin vowed.

"I just need one person to like me besides Hyrum," Livia confessed, voice shaking. "I just need one person to stand by me no matter what—"

Corvin lifted his hands and gestured around the room. "What else do I need to do to prove that I support you, Livia?"

Livia laughed. "I know...I mean, thank you. I needed your help and you didn't turn me away."

"You should ask for help more often," Corvin said. "I wish I knew sooner how awful Gaius treated you."

Livia frowned. "He's not awful."

Corvin looked confused. "You don't think so? Cause I think he's not very helpful or supportive—"

"Well, that's...irritating... inconvenient even," Livia admitted. "But you have to do a lot worse to be awful."

Corvin gave her a look.

"What?"

"We're going to have to disagree here," Corvin said. "He treats you awful. The only reason you don't think so is that you don't fully understand how much consideration you deserve."

"Consideration?" Livia laughed like that was a joke.

Then she realized Corvin was not amused and maybe even genuinely angry by the look on his face. She froze. "Are you angry at me?"

"No. I'm angry at Gaius."

"You're angry at Gaius?" Livia was genuinely bewildered.

"Who sends a young woman up in front of thousands of people without teaching her what she's supposed to say? That's reprehensible, Livia. Not a single competent parent in Caesarea would stand for their child to be humiliated that way."

Livia looked away, pained. "I still can't believe Hyrum did it."

"Does he know what to say this year?" Corvin asked.

"I—Caecilia seemed to think he did. She said he found the information in the same book you looked at—"

"I'll call her," Corvin said.

Corvin pulled out his phone and made the call immediately. He confirmed Hyrum did have the right information. Then tried to see if Livia had everything she needed to wear. Finally, he arranged for Livia to come to the house again the next morning. So Caecilia only had to worry about Hyrum and not spend hours doing Livia's hair while her morning sickness was so intense.

Livia was irritated that he was making arrangements without asking her. Then he ended his call and asked, "Will we see you here tomorrow morning?"

Livia's irritation eased a tad. At least he was asking her instead of telling her. Also, his concern for Caecilia seemed genuine. Was Livia going to refuse and pile a load of work in her sister-in-law's lap?

"Fine," she said, sharply. "What time?"

Corvin turned to his family and locked eyes with his mother. He'd made plans without consulting her either Livia realized. She wished she hadn't agreed so hastily. Livia shot Aurelia a panicked look. "Only if that's not a problem—"

She spoke warmly, "It's not a problem. Please, come at six."

"Are you certain?" Livia asked. "We could manage...somehow...I think?"

Corvin's family laughed. Livia's cheeks heated. Everyone in the room knew there was no way she'd manage and she hated looking so incompetent.

"The hairstyle and makeup required are quite specific," Aurelia said. "We'd prefer that you were correctly presented this year so more important issues can be the focus of the ceremonies."

"I'd prefer that too," Livia agreed. "I'll be here at six."

"So, we're doing this," Corvin confirmed.

"We are," Livia confirmed. She didn't like it but Livia didn't want another big scandal. "Thank you, Corvin."

Chapter 21

The next morning Livia got up early, took a shower, and loaded her dress—an authentic roman stola—into her car. She drove over to the Tullian home.

Alia opened the door before she knocked. "Quiet, Prudence and Verity are still sleeping."

They passed through the formal atrium and through into the original house. There was a small fire burning in the front room. The kitchen counter was a mess but it smelled like fresh bread. They walked past an open eating area with a dining room table. Then they turned down a hallway and opened the first door. There was a long set of steps. They tip-toed downstairs and locked themselves into Alia's room. "How are you, Liv? You looked stressed."

Livia rubbed her eyes. "Didn't sleep much."

Alia nodded. "Nervous?"

"Yeah, I'm hoping I don't mess everything up."

"You'll be fine," Alia reassured her. "Also, I will still like you even if you make a mistake."

Livia looked at her surprised. "Thank you."

Alia grabbed a hairdryer. "Okay, Dry your hair, real fast. I'm going to ask Epiphany to come help."

Ten minutes later Livia had her hair dry and opened the door to find Alia.

She was in the bathroom helping Epiphany hairspray her hair.

Alia gestured her over. "Your turn."

Livia came and sat on a stool while both Alia and Epiphany took a curling iron to her hair at the same time.

Livia heard Melanie's voice outside the bathroom. "Verity! Prudence! Time to wake up. Mom wants you upstairs!"

Alia and Epiphany were silent as they worked. Livia watched in amazement as they pinned and curled her hair into the same elaborate style that Epiphany wore. In twenty minutes her hair was perfect.

"You are so fast," Livia said.

"We have practice," Epiphany said. "Let's do your makeup. It doesn't need to be fancy but you don't want to look shiny in the pictures."

"Thank you," Livia said. "There's no way I could have done this on my own."

"How's Caecilia this morning?" Alia asked.

"She seemed okay," Livia said. "She was drinking tea and keeping it down pretty well—"

"That's good news," Epiphany said, and she dabbed foundation on Livia's cheeks. "Mom and Dad have been worried about her. She's under too much stress."

"Is she?" Livia asked.

"Yeah, Gaius isn't doing his job and so Hyrum and Caecilia have to do emergency management all the time. It's bad."

"It's not good for the baby to be under that much pressure constantly," Alia said, "My mom lost her last baby that way."

Livia gasped. "Oh, no."

"It was four years ago," Epiphany said. "Twelve weeks along."

"That's why they built the addition—" Livia said.

"Mom has been a lot healthier with dad around more," Alia said. "It's been good for everyone but especially Corvin."

"Is he still asleep?" Livia asked.

"I don't think he's here yet," Epiphany said. "If he is, he'll be upstairs helping mom with the girls."

"He's not here?" Livia asked puzzled.

"He sleeps at his townhouse," Epiphany said. "But he's here a lot of the time still. Sometimes when mom needs a break we pack up and head over there to hang out."

"Is…your mom…unwell?" Livia asked.

Epiphany hesitated. "She's had health challenges since she miscarried. She's resolved all her physical issues currently but hasn't had the chance to catch up emotionally…if that makes sense?"

Livia nodded.

Epiphany stepped back and smiled. "Your makeup is done."

"Alright," Alia said. "Go get dressed. We'll be upstairs. Come up."

Livia got dressed and went up to the kitchen. Corvin was coaxing his little sisters Prudence and Verity to eat breakfast. Their hair was done in adorable pigtails but they were still in their PJs. They were squirrely, giggling, and trying to balance their cereal spoons on the tip of their noses.

"Girls," Corvin said, sternly. "You got three seconds to use those or I will eat your cereal all up."

This caused them to jump to the business of eating again.

"Livia, did you eat?" Aurelia asked as she bustled around the kitchen. She was stacking boxes of rolls on the counter.

Livia had not eaten. "I'm fine."

Epiphany turned on her. "Eat. You'll need the energy to focus."

Corvin reached over to the back of the counter and grabbed some bananas. He held them up. "Want one? We also got cereal, toast, waffles, bagels, and cream cheese."

"Bagel, please," she asked, accepting a banana and peeling it.

"Verity," Corvin glared at his little sister.

She took her spoon off her nose and smiled innocently at him.

"We don't have time, hun, eat. We'll play this afternoon."

"You won't be too busy?"

"No."

"Swear it!" she said, dramatically.

"I swear." Corvin leaned across the counter and crossed pinkies with her.

Verity took a big bite with her spoon, newly motivated. Corvin went to the pantry and came back out with a bag of bagels. Epiphany brought Livia a tub of cream cheese. Corvin made the girls clean up their bowls and ordered them downstairs to change.

Corvin looked at Livia. "How are you this morning, Liv?"

"I'm well."

He smiled. "You look beautiful."

Livia looked away as butterflies erupted in her stomach. "Alia and Epiphany did the hair and makeup."

Corvin tried to catch her eye again but Lars and Aurelia walked into the kitchen.

"Livia, may I speak with you?" she asked.

"Yes, ma'am," she answered.

Aurelia smiled. "Do you have your palla?"

The palla was a long but narrow rectangular fabric that was worn like a shawl. Livia went over to the couch and picked it up from where she'd laid it. "It's here."

"Let me show you how to wear it," Aurelia said.

"Don't I wear it over my shoulders?" Livia asked.

They were interrupted when Lars spoke. "Corvin, Epiphany follow me to my office. Verity, Prudence," Lars addressed his younger daughters with firmness. "Go downstairs and change into your tunics and sandals. If I hear that you've caused any trouble for your mother I'll be assigning extra chores, understand?"

Both girls nodded solemnly.

Lars smiled. "When you've gotten ready come join us in my office. So your mother can help Melanie and Alia finish getting ready."

The two youngest scampered off and Epiphany and Corvin followed Lars out of the room.

Aurelia called Livia's attention again. She explained the palla was placed over the left shoulder, pulled under the right arm, and draped over the left forearm.

Livia frowned as they arranged the garment over her correctly. "Seems strange."

"Yes, but it allows your right arm to be free for the ceremony," Aurelia said. "Also, I do not know if Corvin or Gaius explained that before you perform the ritual you must pull the palla up to cover your head?"

Livia shook her head. "No."

Aurelia gave Livia a reassuring smile. "Let me show you how and we'll practice."

Aurelia showed Livia the way to pull the palla over her head. Then requested her to recite the Latin she'd memorized the previous day. After she finished, Aurelia insisted Livia practice several more times. Satisfied, she placed her hands on Livia's shoulders and looked into her eyes. "I'm so proud of you, Livia. You will do fine."

Livia nodded, surprised at the supportive words. In her experience, this kind of kindness was rare. At that moment, she recognized the characteristic goodness that Livia admired in Corvin. He had inherited some of it from his mother.

"Thank you," Livia said, touched.

Aurelia left to help Alia do Melanie's hair and told Livia to make herself at home. Livia sat alone on the couch in front of the fireplace, wondering why she needed to stay longer. She should tell Corvin she was leaving but she didn't know if she was allowed to interrupt his meeting with Lars. So, Livia sat awkwardly in the silence and looked around. Picture frames full of cameo family photos instead of formal poses intrigued Livia. She walked across the room to study several on the mantel. Corvin openly laughed in one photo, which made Livia smile. Then a sense of sadness filled her as she realized she had never personally seen him look that happy. The laughter she heard was always laced with a wry cynicism. That was something they both had in common, though. Livia wasn't an optimist.

She wondered suddenly did people feel sad that her happiness was always diluted with pessimism? It made her pause to reflect on it. She'd come a long way over the past two years but maybe she had more work to do with herself.

"What are you thinking?" a voice asked.

Livia gasped and almost dropped the picture frame she held in her hands. Corvin stood so near that Livia was surprised she hadn't heard him approach.

"I was going to come to tell you that I was leaving," Livia said.

"Why?" Corvin asked.

Livia blinked. "Why would I stay?"

"Come in the car with us. It will be simpler to go together. The parking and traffic will be insane," Corvin said. "I don't want you to get lost in the crowds and not make it to the parade."

Livia frowned. "You mean you want to make sure I don't run away."

Corvin grinned. "Do you still feel like accidentally getting lost?"

Livia sighed. "I'm resigned to my fate now."

He reached out and took the picture frame from her hands. "Which one is this? Ah, I remember. I was so young." He shook his head and placed it back on the mantle. "Why did it make you sad?"

"Did I look sad?" Livia asked.

"Yes."

"I wondered why you never look that carefree anymore," Livia said.

"Life happens, doesn't it?" Corvin mused.

"Well, I don't think I've ever looked that carefree," Livia said. "So, I'm not trying to judge."

"I didn't take it that way," Corvin said. "Life has happened to you too."

"I also wondered...if it's ever possible to go the other way. Could I let go of...my cares...be happier someday?"

"Are you unhappy, Liv?" Corvin asked.

"Less unhappy than last year," she answered, honestly. "Are you happy Corvin?"

"Sometimes," he answered. "I think that's okay, Liv. We don't have to be happy all the time as long as we're headed in the right direction."

Livia nodded. Her heart lightened a bit. "I think I have that. I think I'm headed in the right direction, Corvin. Are you?"

Corvin frowned. "Honestly, Liv? I feel a little lost. Not sure what my next step should be. But my relationships with my family members are better than they have been for years. So, that makes me hopeful that things will work themselves out one way or another."

"Seems like things are never good all at once, doesn't it?" Livia asked.

Corvin nodded. "Sometimes it does feel that way."

"There was this lady who I stayed with when I was young," Livia said. "Gave me the most comforting advice I've ever gotten. She said, 'Things always change. If you're unhappy, it will change. If you're happy, it will change.' She said if the change was hard to deal with right now then that would change too because people get good at things that are hard to do and so they become easier."

"That was comforting?" Corvin asked.

"Yeah," Livia said. Then she laughed. "Arik reacted that way too."

"What way?" Corvin asked.

"Didn't understand why it was comforting—"

"You're resilient, Livia. I might not think it's comforting but it sure makes me admire your strength and grit."

Livia looked at him in surprise. "Oh," she laughed, awkwardly. "Didn't expect that."

Corvin suppressed a smile. "Arik needed to use his words more. There are lots of things to admire about you, Liv."

Livia blushed and look away. "I-I admire a lot about you too, Corvin."

"Like?" he drawled.

"Like you need my compliments?" Livia muttered.

"Well, I was under the assumption that you hated me for most of the semester so...what exactly changed your mind?"

"I admire how compassionate and kind you are," she said.

Corvin made a face. "People take advantage of that."

"That means something is wrong with them, not with you," Livia said.

It was Corvin's turn to look surprised.

"Anyway, even when I hated you I admired your work ethic."

"Did you? That is not usually what I get admired for..." Corvin mused.

"Apparently," Livia said, a tad sarcastically. "I can't even admire you the right way—"

Corvin laughed, again with that undertone of cynicism. "I don't mean you're doing it wrong. I mean, no one ever gives me credit for that. I like that someone noticed."

"I had this conversation with Tavian. No one gets respect for working hard in this town," Livia said.

Corvin looked thoughtful. "Maybe you're right? Funny, I kind of resent it too. But no one has ever validated that for me before. Interesting. It's really that different outside Caesarea?"

"Absolutely."

"Hmm," Corvin's eyes drifted away from her and he appeared lost in thought.

"What do people usually admire about you?" Livia asked.

Corvin's eyes shot back to her. A look of mischief crossed his place. He changed his stance so that he leaned against the mantle and closer toward Livia. "Certainly, you can guess?"

Livia rolled her eyes and stepped away from him. "No, thank you."

He laughed and there was a less sardonic quality to it. Livia liked that. Corvin played offended. "You didn't fall for my trap!"

"Someone so accomplished doesn't need their ego inflated."

"Oh, ho!" Corvin teased her. "You're back to insulting me. Our pax has ceased."

"Be prepared," Livia said, wryly.

Corvin did a double-take. "Should I be worried?"

"Very," Livia assured him.

"I can't tell if you're joking or not—"

"That's to my advantage then."

Corvin hesitated and then laughed again without the bitterness. His entire face lit up and Livia's heart lightened. She liked seeing him happy. She couldn't stop a smile from spreading across her face and her facade went up in smoke.

"You're funny," Corvin said as if it were a surprise. "I didn't know that about you."

"I'm insulted," Livia drawled.

"You're so quiet and shy I've never noticed."

"You think I'm shy?" Livia asked.

"You are absolutely shy—" he said. "At least, around me. I've seen you loosen up around Cam and Tavian."

She didn't have a crush on Cam or Tavian. She shrugged it off, hoping he didn't make the connection.

Corvin sighed. "Maybe one day, huh?"

"One day, what?" Livia asked.

"One day you'll feel that at ease with me."

"Maybe one day," Livia agreed.

That wasn't the response Corvin wanted. She could tell. She should feel guilty about that but she didn't.

He changed the subject. "I came in here to let you know that Hortensius will be here in five minutes."

"Hortensius?" Livia asked.

Corvin smiled, pleased. "He and Epiphany will be signing matched papers. You are invited to observe. We'll leave for the parade directly after."

Livia followed Corvin to the library where Epiphany stood bouncing on her toes next to her father. He spoke to her reassuringly with a file folder in his hand.

Aurelia, Mel, and Alia came in only a few moments after Corvin and Livia. Prudence and Verity were in a corner reading books. The doorbell rang and Lars went to answer it. The whole thing wasn't very fancy. Hortensius entered with his parents and two siblings. They greeted Aurelia and Lars then the papers were laid out.

"Please, review the papers are correct, Hortensius," Lars invited. While Hortensius looked over the papers Lars called to Verity and Prudence to leave their books and come over. Corvin's family bunched up together to observe. Livia felt very conspicuous as the only person in the room standing alone.

"Livia is here?" Hortensius asked Epiphany.

"She came to take care of some business for the parade," she answered.

"Oh. Liv," Hortensius gestured her closer. "Come closer. Don't stand over there."

Livia stepped closer.

"Nice to see you. It's been a while," he said, easily.

She nodded. "It has. Congratulations."

Hortensius grinned and looked at Epiphany. "I'm lucky, aren't I?"

"You don't get luckier," Livia agreed, sincerely.

Epiphany shot her a surprised look, but a pleased pink flushed her cheeks.

Hortensius spoke, "Lars everything is in order with the papers. I'd like to sign them."

Lars nodded. "We'll go first then."

Epiphany signed her name. Then Lars after her. Hortensius took up the pen and signed the paper and his father signed after him. Hortensius tried to kiss Epiphany and she ducked away.

"I—I'm sorry. We're in front of all my sisters," she seemed extremely embarrassed at her instinctive reaction.

Hortensius smiled. "Perhaps, a respectable peck on the cheek then?"

Epiphany nodded and offered her cheek.

Hortensius placed a polite kiss there and then put his arm around her. "I'm excited to start this new adventure with you."

Epiphany nodded. "Me too."

She seemed tense but relieved too. Livia wondered if she liked him or if it was one of those arranged political matches that Lupus house was notorious for arranging.

Then Epiphany peeked up at him shyly while he spoke a few words to Corvin and her infatuation revealed itself. Epiphany liked him. Livia grinned. She wished them well.

Chapter 22

P arking was already overflowing onto the training fields. Security patrol officers wore bright vests. They directed drivers into areas cordoned off with stakes and ropes. Signs marked the rows so people could remember what area they had parked in. The whole thing was rather ad hoc. The forum didn't usually see this much traffic all at once, but on those rare days it did, it was clear to everyone that their community had outgrown its public spaces.

Corvin asked Melanie to carry five-year-old Verity on her hip so she didn't get lost. Corvin carried his seven-year-old sister, Prudence, piggyback. Alia and Livia pressed in close as they pressed through the crowds together in a little herd. Livia pressed in against Corvin's side more intimidated by the crowds than she'd ever admit to anyone. She was glad she was with Corvin and his sisters. She felt like she had a place in the mass of humanity—a shelter.

The crowds got thicker as they approached the entrance to the subforum. When you approached it from this direction the three entrances looked like a singular glass mansion. The central entrance was the largest glass structure, built in the basic shape of a rectangle; the most interesting part of the architecture was the soaring barrel-vaulted ceiling.

The central entrance was flanked by two smaller rectangular glass buildings. In reality, the flanks were set much further back. However, the land was so level that the illusion of them being a unified building remained. Citizens had to transverse the buildings to access the elevators at the back, which descended into the subforum.

The large central building descended into the headquarters of the Security Patrol. The smaller building on the left descended directly into the Curia. You had to have a special pass to enter that way. It was reserved for senators and other government officials. The entrance on the right descended into the Department of the Treasury located in the Temple of Saturn. Parade participants entered through the treasury or Saturnalian entrance.

Livia had never entered the forum through the Saturnalian entrance before. She had always gone through the Security Patrol headquarters. When she approached the building she didn't know what to expect.

Four Security Patrol guards flanked the outside doors and verified they were parade participants. Once inside, more guards greeted them. They recorded the number of their party and assigned them to an elevator line.

The Saturnalian entrance only had two elevators as opposed to the headquarters' bank of six. The guards assigned Livia's group to line B. Verity sighed heavily in Melanie's arms and rested her head on Livia's shoulder. Melanie shifted the girl's weight in her arms and it was obvious she was struggling with the girl's weight.

"You okay?" Corvin asked his sister. "It's hard to hold a five-year-old this long."

Melanie looked around the crowds. "I know, but I'm worried about setting her down."

"Pru can walk a bit if needed," Corvin said, bending his knees. "Pru, I gotta let you down."

As soon as Prudence's feet touched the ground she attached herself to her sister Alia, who entertained her with groan-worthy puns that made Prudence belly laugh. Livia shook her head, holding back a smile. Melanie passed Verity into Corvin's arms.

He smiled at Verity. "Want to sit on my shoulders, Ver?"

She shook her head and wrapped her arms around his neck. "Stay here."

He gave her back a gentle pat. "Alright, hun, thanks for being patient. I know the wait is long. I'm proud of you for being so good."

The wait was so long that people requested to use the stairs. The Security Patrol guards refused their requests. They had orders to keep the stairs clear for emergencies.

Once they reached the floor of the treasury antechamber they split into the staging areas set aside for each house. The Lupus house staging area was first and was roped off from the others with blue cords. Lars, Aurelia, and Epiphany waved when they caught sight of Corvin and his sisters. Verity scrambled to be let down and Livia lowered her down to the ground. She ran over to Lars and asked to be picked up. He smiled and pulled her into his arms with a warning that it was only for a minute.

Leaving his sisters with his parents, Corvin walked with Livia to find the staging area for Taurus house. They found the area marked out with red ropes. Gaius and his wife Lauretta were waiting for Livia. Lauretta's hair was flawlessly curled and a delicate golden tiara rested in her hair. The wheat stalk design was interspersed with diamonds. A bullhead pendant hung on a chain around her neck with bright rubies shining in the eye sockets. The ostentatious jewelry surprised Livia and she tried to remember if Aurelia had worn similar pieces. All Livia could remember the materfamilias of Lupus house wearing was an orange-colored stone carved with a she-wolf and teardrop earrings to match. Beautiful pieces but simple and practical. Nothing as ornate as Lauretta currently wore. Was Lauretta trying to make a statement of some kind?

Livia confronted Gaius. "I tried to call."

"We'll talk later this week," he said, dismissively.

Did he think he could ignore her until later in the week? After everything was over? Livia's anger flared and she glared at him. He smirked. The situation was amusing to him. Livia walked past him and determined to ignore his presence for the rest of the day. Corvin was right about him. Livia remembered how she felt tucked up against Corvin's side with his sisters squished in around them, like a herd of ducklings taking shelter in each other. She longed for that suddenly as she approached the group standing behind Gaius and Lauretta.

A handful of Pleblian Taurus house teens gathered together in a bunch. Livia only recognized Clara Porcius—daughter of the only Plebeian Tribune from Taurus house. Hyrum had invited their family over for dinner more than once to ask their advice on senate matters. They were polite but distant. Clara made it clear she would be civil but wasn't interested in being Livia's friend.

Bella Aurelius stood with them, looking a tad out of place. Bella was technically a plebian from Aquila house. Same as her father, Justin, but ever since Justin became Livia's patron Bella was often included in Taurus house events. Especially since her mother, Flavia was Taurus house.

Clara stood in the center of the group and greeted Livia cooly with reserved brown eyes. "So, you decided to show up this year."

Livia's cheeks went hot. "I did."

Clara muttered something indecipherable that made the teens around her laugh. Livia was used to being the butt of jokes, but it had been months since she had to confront such rudeness directly. Some of her emotional armor had fallen away and she had to look away to hide her hurt and mentally gather her defenses. Livia turned back to them, her old armor pulled tightly around her. She could compete with Corvin for showing the most emotionless face.

Bella frowned at her, eyes still trailing Corvin as he moved through the crowd toward Lupus house. "You came with Corvin?"

Livia nodded. "They helped me get ready this morning. Caecilia has morning sickness."

"You were at Corvin's house this morning?" Bella asked in disbelief.

"Yes." Livia was confused. Shouldn't it be a bigger deal Caecilia was pregnant?

Clara Porcius was also visibly surprised by this. "Are you dating Corvin?"

"No," Livia snapped. "I asked him for help."

This changed the entire demeanor of the Taurus group. They gave each other hopeful glances. Clara's face conveyed sheer relief and then she smiled.

Bella narrowed her eyes. "They don't just invite anyone over before events. It's a family policy."

Livia shrugged, pretending indifference. "Is it?"

Bella's expression hardened and her stare turned into a glare. Was this how Bella was going to welcome Livia back to Caesarea? Livia stared back, refusing to look away first.

Clara looked between Livia and Bella. Unexpectedly, Clara came to Livia's defense. "So, they made an exception. Don't let it ruffle your feathers, Bella."

Bella turned her displeasure on Clara. "Stay out of this. It's none of your business."

Bella was out of line and Livia had lost all her patience. She stepped forward and put herself between the two girls. "Watch yourself, Bella. She didn't do anything to deserve that kind of tone."

Clara blinked and pulled her chin back with surprise. "Stay chill, Livia. I'll mind my own business. Unlike some people here."

She sent a glare in Bella's direction. Then she turned and stood in her position, waiting for the parade music to start.

"So," Bella said, turning to speak only to Livia. "You and Corvin..."

"Are friends," Livia emphasized.

Bella grinned. "Good, because I've been looking forward to talking to him this week about our future together."

Clara audibly snorted.

"So, stay *friends* with him," Bella said with faux sweetness.

Livia exchanged a look with Clara. *Is she serious? For real?*

Clara shrugged. "Not my business."

"Has Corvin mentioned me?" Bella asked Livia.

Livia wasn't sure how to answer this question. "We had one conversation about you," she admitted.

Bella's face lit with hope. "Does he want to get back together with me?"

"Bella," Livia shook her head. "Let him go."

"What did he say?" Bella asked.

Livia shook her head again, surprised at how quickly her anger turned to pity. "Bella, he won't get back together with you."

She snarled at Livia. "I never should have listened to your advice. I should have known you wanted him for yourself all along!"

Apparently, Bella's friendship only lasted as long as Livia had a nonexistent relationship with Corvin. The betrayal cut deep because Bella's friendship was one of the things that Livia relied on in Caesarea. Now, that was no longer true.

"I shouldn't be surprised that you've turned on me. You have a history of stabbing people in the back," Livia growled.

Bella stepped back. "He told you—"

"You should have told me!" Livia cried.

Bella was going to argue back until Hyrum strode over and stared her down. "We're not going to have any drama today," he said, firmly. Then he turned his head towards Livia to include her in his displeasure. "Understood?"

"Yessir," Bella said, cowed.

"Yes," Livia answered.

Livia could tell the other Taurus were pleased that Hyrum had intervened. Clara subtly arranged for all five of them to stand between Livia and Bella in the parade line. Livia was grateful to her. She took a deep breath and calmed herself.

One of the Taurus boys said, lightly. "Let's not embarrass ourselves, alright? All we got to do is keep our mouths shut and walk."

Hyrum guided Caecilia next to him. Then they took their place in line behind Gaius. Thankfully, the parade started and they were too distracted to say anymore. They walked through the treasury hallway and entered the dark stone chambers of the temple of Saturn. They exited the building, pouring out the front entrance and down the steep stairs. The parade route led them straight across the short end of the forum toward the Curia. After passing the Curia they marched past the Basilica of Aemilianus where trials were held. The three levels of porches along the front of the building were packed with people. The flat roof of the Curia had people sitting up on top. They walked down the length of the forum. Past the temple of Castor and Pollux the stairs of which were lined with cheering people. They reached the podium and seating prepared for the parade marchers at the opposite short side of the forum.

This is where Livia's family split off from the others. She followed Gaius and Hyrum to the stands to sit with the patricians. She marched up onto the raised dais and sat on the platform beneath the two couples. Corvin had explained married and single patricians sat on different platforms.

That left Livia to sit alone on the lower platform. To her right and left the chairs of the other houses were full. Livia's heart raced as she sat alone, painfully visible to everyone in Caesarea. There was no one to distract the gaze from her, no one to share the anxiety of scrutiny with. Livia tried to tell herself that she was fine but she felt abandoned. She'd never been one to seek attention, staying quiet in the background had been a survival technique. Now, she was being forced to sit on display in front of this crowd when all her instincts were yelling at her to hide.

The Aediles office had built the platforms around the statue of a she-wolf feeding two young boys. It served as the symbolic setting for the theme of the parade. Lars started with a speech on providing nourishment to those who were hungry. Considering the situation with Lupus house the message was extremely political but Livia approved anyway. The young Rattus house Paterfamilias Lorin spoke on being hospitable. He was concerned about the numbers of Caesareans who were choosing to make lives outside Caesarea and the need for them to continue being welcomed in the community. Tavian had once told her that Lupus and Rattus house had the highest numbers of members who tried to make their way outside Caesarea.

Hortensius' uncle Benedict, paterfamilias of Aquila house, spoke on growth and potential. He spoke longer than the other two and Livia shifted in her seat with impatience. He was rather boring.

Then it was Gaius' turn. He stood and walked slowly to the rostrum. He was silent for such a long time that Livia worried he wouldn't speak. Then his voice lashed out, dark and sardonic.

"It is a pity my cousins are so prepared this year. I wish we would progress beyond this farcical display where we pretend we're going to improve ourselves each year—"

Livia gasped. She turned back to look at Hyrum. He was horrified. Caecilia had the back of her hand pressed to her lips as if she might hurl at any moment. But it was the lone tear that streaked down Lauretta's cheek that brought Livia to her feet.

"I've prepared no remarks obviously because you deserve none. Hypocrites, all of you—"

She had no memory of walking down the steps but she was suddenly beside Gaius.

"Stop," she commanded him.

He looked at her. "Go back to your seat."

He spoke as if he expected her to obey. He was paterfamilias after all.

"No," she said loudly, clearly, defiantly.

"You're not to contradict me in public," he said.

"It's funny that you neglect to teach me rules of conduct until it specifically benefits you!" Livia accused.

He didn't even look at her. "Livia, we will deal with this in private."

"You lost that privilege when you pitied me in public," she seethed.

He turned to her, face red with fury. "You have no right to tell me what to do."

"I have every right," Livia declared. "You've made your wife cry and Caecilia physically ill. I understand you hate it here and you're angry about being paterfamilias but you will show consideration and respect to the women of this house!"

Gaius' jaw dropped. He looked behind him. Caecilia had a trembling hand clasped over her mouth and her face was an odd shade of white. Lauretta wouldn't look at Gaius.

"This is their home!" Livia cried. "Don't insult it in front of all their family and friends."

Gaius turned a cold look on her. "You think you're any better than me? Acting this way? In front of everybody? It's shameful!" He gestured at her.

"What is truly shameful is that you've let hatred poison you so thoroughly that you'll behave this inconsiderately toward your own family!"

"Livia," Gaius growled.

"Unless you have something appropriate to say we should get on with it," she said.

She turned her back on him and walked to where she would complete the ritual. She stood, chin up looking defiantly out to the crowd. She heard Hyrum descend the stairs behind her. He didn't acknowledge Gaius, a slight that everyone surely noticed. He stood silently next to Livia in support.

"Proceed with the ritual," Gaius said. Then turned and returned to his seat.

Hyrum went first. He recited his Latin and then poured a bottle of wine into a shallow bowl. He lit it on fire with a torch handed to him by an attendant. Then he soaked the grain in front of Livia with the remaining wine so it would burn.

Livia swallowed and took a deep breath. *I can act despite my fear.* She pulled her palla up to cover her head the way Aurelia taught her. Her voice and hand shook but she managed the Latin without a single mistake. She lit the grain with a torch handed to her by the attendant and it was over. She'd fulfilled her duty. Her throat was tight and her stomach churned but it was over. She turned and returned to her seat.

Hyrum hesitated near the podium. Then he made some sort of decision. He approached the podium.

"My sister is headstrong," he said, calmly. "She had to be to survive the upbringing we had. I am grateful daily that even with all we went through, she did not suffer worse. The places we lived were so unsafe…" Hyrum paused to control his emotions. "I was constantly afraid for her. So, I taught her as best I could to defend herself. That meant training her not to trust anyone's authority but her own. She'll never be a conventional woman and I accept the responsibility for that. It was not my mother. It was not my father. It was me, a sixteen-year-old child, trying to avoid having his baby sister become another statistic—missing or dead on the street.

"Having said that, I am concerned that this small family disagreement will distract from the importance of the words spoken by my predecessors. Even Gaius, for all his brashness, had a valid point. What are we doing this all for if we do not change? And there are many ways that we can change for the better. Let us set aside frivolous issues and address the lack of necessities that many in our community face. Let us work together to address inequitable access to food, education, and safe housing. Let us provide honorable work and legitimate economic opportunities. These are the issues that should concern us as a community. Dissecting Livia's mistakes will not feed a hungry family, it will not employ a father or a mother, and it will not provide adequate heat in the dead of winter. Thank you for your time."

Hyrum returned to his seat and the back of Livia's neck burned. Hyrum was making excuses for her. Livia was still furious but now she also felt guilty. She hadn't wanted there to be a fuss about her this year and now she'd failed. Even if she had gotten up and done the ritual correctly, it didn't matter. It wasn't good enough. Just like always.

Livia was grateful when it was time to return to the parade route and proceed out of the Forum. She descended the platform stairs and met up with the others marching with Taurus house.

Clara met her with satisfied glee. "You embarrassed him! That's justice right there. Gaius deserved it. All those times he embarrassed Hyrum and my father because he couldn't get his act together."

But the boy that encouraged everyone not to embarrass themselves had his shoulders pulled up to his ears. "You did great with the ritual, Livia. Hyrum did too. I can't believe that Gaius threw a fit about that up there, in front of everyone. Obviously, he hates you as much as he does us, but Aquila house is going to be livid. He dishonored Lauretta with how he behaved and they'll want revenge."

"Forget Aquila," another Taurus girl interjected. "It distracted from Lars' amazing speech. I wouldn't blame the Tullians if they were pissed. Now everyone is going to be talking about Livia and Gaius fighting instead of how to solve the welfare standoff in the senate."

Livia's stomach dropped to her toes. The girl was right. Corvin's mom had said as much last night when she agreed to help her. She wanted everything to go smoothly so Lars' speech would be the focus of the ceremony. Not only had Livia failed the very people that helped her but she prevented desperate people from getting the aid they needed to feed their families. They might not leave the parade without two Taurus house females vomiting because

Livia was so disgusted with herself she wanted to hurl.

All discussion ceased when Gaius and Lauretta passed by them to take their place at the head of their procession. Gaius refused to look at Livia. Lauretta shot her a disapproving glare. Caecilia followed close behind. She clung to Hyrum's arm. She wasn't trembling anymore but she still looked pale. She gave Livia a wan smile. "You did great!"

Livia snorted. "Right."

"You said the Latin perfectly and completed the ritual," she said.

Livia looked away from her. She noticed Caecilia didn't say anything about her interaction with Gaius. Because even if Livia had done the right thing she'd screwed it up. She felt defeated. Why did she even keep trying? She should never have come back for fall break. She never should have let Corvin talk her into appearing in public.

"You alright, Livia?" Clara asked, stepping close to her.

"I'll survive," she whispered.

Bella studied her but didn't offer any words of comfort.

They marched past the Temple of Venus and the Basilica Sempronia, which held the house offices. They marched back into the temple of Saturn and stood in elevator lines to go back up top. Livia was relieved to feel the fresh air on her face. Refreshments were served in the quad that housed the primary and secondary schools.

Livia watched the crowds for a moment looking for anyone she recognized. Clara slipped away into the crowds without saying goodbye. Livia got the distinct feeling the girl wanted to avoid her. Then Lauretta came to stand next to Livia's side. Suddenly, Clara's abrupt flight made sense.

"Shameful," she hissed in Livia's ear. "I've never been so humiliated in my life."

"Would you have preferred I let him go on?" Livia shot back, defiant.

"I regret being associated with any of you!" Lauretta snapped. She swished the folds of her stola with a dramatic flourish and stomped away, the click of her stiletto-heeled sandals emphasizing each step.

Livia inhaled as her defiance melted into hurt and shame. She'd been trying to protect Lauretta from more embarrassment but she'd only made

202

things worse. She watched Lauretta speak angrily to a group of her family from Aquila house. They kept shooting glares at Livia and made consoling overtures to Lauretta, who looked like she might burst into tears at any moment.

Livia's throat tightened with frustration. Corvin had been wrong about everything. All that work and effort could never make up for the fact that she was an outsider in Caesarea. They'd never accept her. The realization should have made her sad but it settled on her shoulders with an exhausted resignation. There was no point in wasting emotions denying reality.

Two Rattus house girls passed by shooting her sympathetic looks. Livia recognized them. They were patricians but were rarely seen associating with the malevolence of maidens. Stubbornness streaked through Livia. Was she going to give up because Lauretta threw a few mean words in her direction? Livia was tougher than that.

"Good afternoon," Livia said, she lifted her chin to invite them over to talk the way Corvin had taught her. "What are your names?"

They both froze and stared at her in shock. Their eyes scanned over the crowds around them.

Then the taller of the two girls lowered her chin. "Vale."

The second girl followed suit quickly, chin tucked. "Vale."

They both scurried off. Livia hated this city. Here was proof that even when you knew the rules of polite conversation it didn't make any difference. Livia never should have let Tavian talk her into giving Caesarea a second chance.

Alia ran over to Livia and dragged her away from Lauretta's scowling relatives with a protective look on her face. Some of Livia's turmoil melted away, touched at the show of concern.

Alia turned and grabbed both her hands when they were out of earshot. "Are you alright?" she asked. "Gaius behaved abominably! I'm so glad you stood up to him even if it was rude."

"I'm alright," Livia lied.

"Slow down, Alia," Mel snapped, as she came up. "We're supposed to stay together, remember?"

Hyrum approached them. "Liv? I need to leave."

"Is Caecilia alright?" Livia asked, concerned.

Hyrum sighed. "She'll be alright, I think. She just needs to rest. We're leaving so we can pick Lucas up from the airport. We won't be home for three hours or so. Maybe four if we stop to let Caecilia eat something."

"Should I come with you?" Livia asked. She hoped he would say yes. It would be the perfect excuse to escape Corvin's family. Alia was nice but Mel hadn't looked happy to see her.

Hyrum hesitated. "We'd planned on just us going. It's been a while since we've had alone time but—"

"No," Livia gulped. Caecilia needed Hyrum more than she did right now. She'd have to face the Tullians alone. She lied, "I'll be fine. Corvin's family will see I get home. Enjoy your time with Caecilia."

Hyrum frowned. "Are you sure? You're okay?"

Livia nodded, unable to speak.

Hyrum studied her. "Okay."

Hyrum hesitated a moment but turned and walked back to Caecilia. He put his arm around her and started toward the parking lot. For an instant, Livia felt abandoned. Then Alia linked her elbow with Livia's and smiled at her. "Let's go! There's food to eat!"

Alia and Mel pulled Livia along through the crowds, snagging some refreshments on the way. Livia couldn't eat though. They found Corvin chatting with Justin and Flavia. Unfortunately, Bella was with them. Livia wanted to avoid them but Alia and Mel marched right up to them. Livia took a bracing breath and steeled herself for the worst.

Corvin turned at their approach. His expression was distant and cold. She was reminded forcefully of dozens of dismissive interactions in TARP offices. Livia's heart thudded painfully in her chest. Corvin was angry with her and she didn't blame him.

"It's nice to see you, Livia," Justin grinned at her.

"How have things been Justin?" Livia asked, trying to pretend this was an ordinary conversation. Even as her eyes were drawn to Bella easing closer to Corvin's side. A twitching muscle in Corvin's cheek was the only tell that he was uncomfortable.

"About the same as when you left," Justin answered. Livia's eyes flicked back to his face. Justin's gaze had also landed on Bella. His lips pressed into a distinct frown.

Livia marched to Flavia. "I missed you," she said.

Flavia smiled and opened her arms for a hug, which Livia had gambled on. Livia put her arms around her and hugged her briefly.

"How's school?" Flavia asked.

"Good," Livia said.

"Corvin says you've spent a lot of time together," she said, neutrally. Livia was wise to that though. She knew a trap when she saw one.

"Yeah, and his cousin Terrance, too. Along with Felicity from Rattus house. We've had good times."

"But you're rooming on your own?" she asked.

"I'm not alone," Livia insisted. "I have a roommate. Her name is Whitney."

Livia then proceeded to tell her all about Whitney to distract Flavia from the topic of her and Corvin. She angled herself to include the rest of the group in her ramblings. Bella had eased even closer to Corvin. He could no longer hide that Bella's nearness made him uncomfortable. Livia took pity on Corvin.

Livia asked the first question that came to her mind. "Bella, what are your plans currently…professionally, I mean?"

Then Livia realized what she'd done. She'd asked Bella to talk about the job she'd betrayed Corvin to get. Bella leveled a glare in Livia's direction. She tried to backtrack. "I mean, do you plan to leave Caesarea to go to school?"

"I've had enough school to last a lifetime," she said, frostily.

Livia didn't miss the look of disappointment that crossed Flavia's face. Livia recognized that Caesarea Academy had that effect on a lot of Aquila kids. It burned them out so bad they'd do anything to never go back to academics.

"College would be loads easier than Caesarea Academy," Livia encouraged, trying for Flavia's sake to reason with her, though she normally wouldn't.

205

"Not interested," she said.

"I wish you'd consider it," Justin said.

"It's not your life dad," Bella nearly snarled.

Livia's eyes widened at the amount of rebellion in her tone. Justin inhaled and schooled his features. The tension between him and Bella was obvious, which meant it must be extremely bad between them. Justin was pro at staying reasonable about things. He was used to negotiating with hardened criminals and reasoning with insane people.

Though, if Livia had pulled the same stunt with Hyrum—refusing to go to college—they'd be about the same. Maybe it was time to switch topics. "Gone on any hikes lately?" Livia asked instead.

The furrow between Bella's eyes eased the slightest bit. "Went up Whitepine trail."

"See any cool wildlife?" Livia asked.

"A beaver, actually—"

"Really?" Livia was genuinely delighted. "Did you know they're a keystone species?"

One thing that Livia appreciated about Bella was that she was transparent. She didn't pretend to be politely interested. She was interested or not. That meant that even socially ignorant Livia could read her. The tension in Bella's face softened further and her eyes settled on Livia. So Livia kept talking. "That means that because beavers build dams and create pools of water that other animals can survive and thrive. If beavers were taken out of the environment all those other animals would die too."

Bella's eyes widened. "Really?"

Livia nodded. "They also have awesome fur. It's designed to tolerate a whole lot of water. That's why they were almost hunted to extinction in Europe and North America, which was environmentally devastating to a lot of forests. They never recovered because the beaver is so essential to the ecosystem."

Bella's face lit up. "So, I saw something amazing!"

"Yeah," Livia nodded. "I'm jealous. I wish I was with you."

Bella looked confused, then sad. "I wish you were there too. Then you could have told me all about the beaver while I was watching it build a dam."

"You got to watch it build? Do you remember the trail? Maybe we can go back?"

"Not this time of year," Justin cut in firmly.

Bella nodded. "Yeah, the trail is closed for the winter. It's dangerous."

"Spring then," Livia said, firmly.

Bella hesitated, almost as if she didn't believe Livia's offer was serious. "Maybe. Do you think it will still be there?"

Livia shrugged. "That's half the fun of going out. The mystery…"

Bella smiled the tiniest bit. Livia couldn't tell if it was a smirk or not. "We'll see how we feel about the hike in the Spring. Who knows what could happen?"

Livia looked at Justin. He smiled at Livia, gratitude clear on his face. Livia was sure the subtle dig went over his head. Silence fell across the group. Livia looked at Corvin. His face was no longer blank and the angles of his features were sharp with anger. It made Livia's stomach lurch. She didn't know what had upset him. Had he'd picked up on Bella's possessive attitude or was he angry Livia made plans to hang out with her in front of him? Maybe Livia's friendship with Bella bothered him more than he'd admitted. Livia looked between them trying to swallow the tightness in her throat. She was afraid neither one of them would be her friends after everything that went down today.

They were all startled when Silvanus walked up and put a hand on Corvin's back. "How's it going, brother?"

Corvin's angry expression melted away into relief. "Silvanus."

"Can I get a ride home with you? My shift is over." Silvanus had been on duty as a guard and was dressed in his uniform.

"Yeah, I'd love the help with the girls," Corvin said.

"Where are they?" Silvanus asked.

"Right now they're with mom and dad. They'll send them over when they've had enough of the crowds," Corvin answered.

Livia looked over and noticed that Alia and Mel had silently slipped over to their parents. Yeah, she was the only one not smart enough to avoid this minefield.

Silvanus blew out his breath. "Tell me about it. The lines got so bad this year and not everyone that came got to go down."

Corvin frowned. "Really?"

Silvanus nodded. "I think we need to revisit bringing the parade up top like most of the other festivals."

"It's one of the last ones," Justin interjected. "It's because of the symbolism of the Romulus and Remus statue."

"Move the statue," Livia said. Her lingering insecurity made her sound more impatient than she intended and everyone looked at her.

Flavia tried to calm her. "It'd be exposed to the elements, love."

"Build a pavilion then," Livia snapped.

Silvanus laughed. "Make her talk to the senate, Corvin, she'll have them convinced."

Corvin leveled an amused look at her. "She just might."

Livia gave him an impatient shake of her head. "Doubtful."

Corvin's parents approached and dumped the little ones on Corvin at that precise moment. Silvanus picked up little Verity. "Let's go find your other sisters, huh?"

"Piphany staying," Verity told him seriously.

Corvin and Livia looked at Lars and Aurelia.

"Something to do with Hortensius?" Corvin asked.

"He's ending his patrol shift now and we'll head over to his family's house to announce the match," Lars answered.

Corvin smiled. "We'll see you later, then."

Corvin crouched down and instructed Prudence to ride piggyback. She pressed her cheek happily to the back of his shoulder. "I want to go home," she said.

"That's where we're headed, Pru," Corvin said as he straightened up.

"So, they signed the papers?" Silvanus asked, excitedly.

"Right before the parade in the library," Corvin said, smiling.

"Excellent," Silvanus said. "Was she scared?"

"Nervous," Corvin answered. "But happy too."

They gathered Mel and Alia and headed home. Livia was glad Silvanus was with them this time because if the crush was bad before it was worse now.

"Stay close, Alia, Mel, Liv," Corvin barked. "We don't want you trampled."

"Where's Epiphany?" Mel yelled.

"She's staying with Mom and Dad," Corvin said. "They were visiting Hortensius' family on the way home."

They fought their way to the car and squished in together. It took forty minutes of traffic to get back to the Tullius house. Corvin, who was usually calm in every situation, started muttering furiously at other drivers and the car remained tense and silent the entire trip.

When they arrived home everyone scattered. They seemed to forget about Livia, who sat on the first soft place she could find and put her face into her hands and leaned forward, forearms on her knees. In a few minutes, she'd get up and drive home.

Livia didn't know how much time had passed until Silvanus came over to sit with her. "Hey, you alright?"

"I know I need to drive home," she said.

"Don't even think about it for an hour," he said. "The roads are so bad out there."

"Oh," Livia said. "Right."

"You seem upset. Can you tell me about it?" he asked.

"I just...I never do anything the right way..." Livia's voice cracked.

"You upset about what happened during the parade?"

"I put in all that work so there wouldn't be a big issue then I just...got so angry. It's one thing to be incompetent. It's a whole other thing to maliciously sabotage an entire parade—"

"You honestly think it was 'malicious sabotage'?" Silvanus asked.

"You should have seen the smirk on his face when I greeted him before the parade and mentioned that I'd called him—"

"You called him to help you and he didn't respond?" Silvanus asked.

"At least, eight times," Livia said. "He never answered. I had to call Corvin at the very last minute—"

Silvanus' eyes widened. "Wow, did you mention that to Corvin?"

"No." Livia shook her head. "Then Bella was being all snobby to me."

"Oh?" Silvanus asked. "What did she say?"

"She said there are rules against people coming over before events," Livia explained. "She was mad at me for it. Said she was planning on getting back together with Corvin now that he's home."

Silvanus blew all his breath out and shook his head in disgust. "I'm glad you said something. He should know that."

"Really?" Livia asked.

"Yeah," Silvanus said. "Who knows how she'll ambush him? He needs to be ready. Especially this time of year."

"What's this time of year?" Livia asked.

"He lost someone close to him."

"Cassia?" Livia asked.

Silvanus looked surprised. "He told you about her?"

"No, Terrance mentioned it after...he broke down sobbing in the car."

Silvanus' eyes widened further. "When?"

"On the way here. That's why I was driving. I forced him to rest in the back afterward."

"We were all grateful to hear you took care of him like that," Silvanus said. He looked up as if searching for Corvin. "He pushes himself too hard. We don't know exactly why it's so bad this year. Maybe because of the shooting. Maybe it's that Bella hurt him but none of us can seem to comfort him."

"Do you think he'll get back together with Bella?" Livia asked.

"No," Silvanus said. "He shouldn't have gotten together with her in the first place. He did it for all the wrong reasons. Bella, she's no better. She's acting like she has to prove something and it's destroying her and a lot of her relationships. I wish we could talk sense into her before she self-destructs."

Livia saw something in Silvanus' eyes. "You...care about her."

He sighed. "As long as she's interested in Corvin she won't give me the time of day."

"So, Bella's going through...a thing," Livia said.

"Yeah," Silvanus said. "It's starting to get to Justin and Flavia. They've tried everything they can think of and then some."

"It's that stupid school," Livia said.

Silvanus looked surprised. "Say what?"

"I've seen it in the other Aquila kids too. Caesarea Academy crushes them. Bella is smart and likes to learn but the second you mention a book she turns up her nose."

Silvanus blinked. "I've never had that type of interaction with her. What does she like to learn about?"

"Animals, nature, science, the environment. All of that stuff fascinates her."

Silvanus looked intrigued and thoughtful. Corvin came up from downstairs changed into regular clothes. "So glad to get out of that toga. Those things are awful. Liv, you did so well! I'm so proud of you!"

Livia didn't think she deserved his praise. She was waiting for the 'but...' part of the statement to follow any moment now.

The doorbell rang at that moment. "That's the crew," Corvin said.

He walked to the front door and opened it. "Come in!"

A chorus of giggling preceded a line of tiny kids entering the house.

"What's going on?" Livia asked.

"Everyone will come over, stay until dinner, and then leave. It's a family tradition," Silvanus said. "Usually, this is when significant others and big announcements are introduced to the family. It's hard to get us all together otherwise. I'm sure Epiphany and Hortensius will make their announcement later."

Corvin led the kids to the backyard to play. Their parents followed after and settled on the nice patio that was visible through the windows. Silvanus and Livia trailed after them. Livia laughed as Corvin got pulled into playing the horse for the kids.

"Why don't you go change, Liv?" Silvanus suggested. "Take a few moments?"

Alia offered up her room for Livia's privacy. She changed out of her stola. She sat down on a chair and carefully pulled the pins from her hair one by one. A few stray tears fell onto her cheeks and she brushed them away.

"Here one moment, gone the next," she whispered the maxim Flavia often chanted to her children. Livia didn't have a brush to tame her wild hair so she had to finger-comb her tangles into submission and then braided her hair to hide them.

She took her time. She let the stillness and the quiet steady her battered emotions. She might be able to take a chance on leaving now. The worst of the traffic would have worked itself out by now. Livia gathered her things and carried them upstairs, planning to leave.

Chapter 23

The low drone of voices reached Livia as she climbed the stairs, warning her that the house was full of people. As she walked through the kitchen and into the front room she saw groups of people gathered in various parts of the house chatting eagerly, laughing. Everyone was happy and calm.

Aurelia noticed her and came straight over. "Livia, darling, is there anything I can do for you?"

"I should go home," she said.

Aurelia gave her a look full of compassion. "I understand you're upset about what happened at the parade but Lars and I don't hold it against you. You're welcome to stay in our home for as long as you like."

Relief flooded Livia. As well as apprehension. She had a feeling that Aurelia spoke only for herself and her husband deliberately. Corvin probably had his own set of feelings on the matter.

Livia nodded. "Thank you. And I'm so sorry."

Aurelia smiled. "You conducted yourself well today and those that say otherwise are trying to twist the situation to their favor. You remember that. Don't allow anything they say to convince you that you are anything less than wonderful."

What a kind thing to say and Livia had a feeling that Aurelia meant it. She almost cried again. Corvin had an amazing mother.

Aurelia smiled at her and patted her arm. "Don't forget to say goodbye to Corvin and the girls before you go."

Livia nodded. "Where is Corvin?"

"Outside with the children. They are playing something fierce. Hurry, go out and be with them."

Livia went to find Corvin and the girls. Her stomach flipped with nervous anticipation. When Corvin caught sight of her would his eyes flash with anger? Would he refuse to speak to her? Would he be disappointed in her?

Livia watched Corvin through the window. He was laying flat on his belly while he grinned up at Prudence. Verity stood in front of him, face in a pout. She stomped her tiny foot dramatically and he laughed at her. It was probably safe enough to go out and say goodbye. Livia opened the door.

The roar of a dozen tiny children trying to prod Corvin into being their horse overwhelmed her at first. Corvin put his cheek flat against the grass and looked exhausted. "I'm too tired," he whined. "No more."

Livia laughed.

His head popped up to look at her. "Oh look! Livia's not exhausted."

Livia froze as a pack of children rushed at her. "Be our horse," they pleaded.

Livia turned panicked eyes to Corvin. He looked amused at her predicament. Livia wasn't sure if this was his idea of punishment.

"I can't," she said, intending to go home.

Then Verity grabbed Livia's hand and looked directly up at her with the same gold-flecked, green eyes that Corvin had. "Please, Miss Livia?" Verity begged. "Please play with us?"

"I really can't," Livia tried to explain.

Verity's hopeful expression turned genuinely sad.

Livia couldn't bear it. She caved. "Because I'm a pony, not a horse."

Tiny little faces lit up with joy and excitement and a cheer went up.

"Oh no," Epiphany said, amused. "You don't know what you've done."

She was back with Hortensius. They sat next to each other, lightly holding hands. He laughed at Epiphany's remark.

Livia was a pony for a half-hour and then gave airplane rides for another hour. Placing the children on her feet and lifting them into the air while she held their little hands. Livia had never been in a position before where having strength and endurance meant she was the most fun. She loved it and didn't ever want it to end.

Eventually, Corvin made them stop. "It's time to come in. It's announcement time."

Livia panicked. "I'm so sorry. I stayed too long."

"No," Corvin said. "It's fine."

Livia studied him. He didn't seem offended at her mere presence but he wasn't warm either. He looked exhausted and a little frustrated. Was that because of her?

"I should go," she insisted.

Corvin shook his head. "Stay for Epiphany's announcement. She'll like you to stay."

"Okay," Livia agreed, hesitantly.

Everyone knew where to sit, except Livia. They sat in a huge circle divided into family groups. Aurelia called Livia over when she noticed her confusion. "Come sit next to my Alia."

"I'm so sorry. I've stayed too long," Livia blurted.

"Nonsense." Aurelia waved a hand.

Lars grinned. "We're just glad you entertained the small ones so long. They wear the rest of us out. Thank you."

"Oh," Livia said in surprise. "I got caught up in the fun. I wasn't going to stay this long—"

"I told her to stay for Epiphany's announcement," Corvin said.

"We'd be pleased," Lars said. "We're so excited. Come sit here next to Alia as Aurelia asked."

Livia squeezed in next to Alia. There was room but it was tight. Epiphany was glowing with excitement. She could hardly sit still.

"Now, our family will go first," Lars said, smiling at his daughter. "We'd like to announce that Epiphany has made a match with Hortensius of Aquila house."

Hortensius smiled at the murmur that filled the room. He was one of Justin's agents and known for being one of the most adept healers in all of

Caesarea. Livia was sure the family all considered him a great catch. Livia was happy for Epiphany and him.

"How long until the betrothal?" Silvia asked.

"Six months," Epiphany said.

A chorus of oohs filled the room.

Was that significant somehow Livia wondered. If a match wasn't an engagement as she assumed, what was the difference between a match and a betrothal?

"Are you upset, Livia?" Epiphany asked.

"What?" Livia flinched. "No, I like Hortensius. I think you have very good taste. Congratulations."

"Why are you frowning?" she asked.

"I'm...confused."

"About what?" she asked.

"I thought...a match was a betrothal but you talk about them like they're different?"

"It's probably confusing if no one ever explained it to you," Epiphany said, with a tone of inquiry.

"Well, Hyrum was barely even engaged, and with Gaius, it was the same. And everyone knows that my parents didn't get married the convenient way either—"

There was a burst of slight laughter then awkward silence since they didn't know if they should have laughed or not. Honestly, Livia didn't know either. Epiphany looked at her father. "They stopped requiring matches during world war two?"

"That's correct. It used to be how all marriages were done," he said.

"So, how is a match different from a betrothal?" Livia asked.

"It's just an approved boyfriend," Melanie said. "Like your parents agree and his parents agree. Then they sign a paper saying you'll date this long and do these certain things to prepare for your engagement."

"Sign a paper? Like a contract?"

"Exactly," Lars said.

"So, what does your contract say?" Livia asked. "Am I allowed to ask that?

Or are they private?"

Lars looked at Epiphany. She looked at him. He nodded at her. "It is at your discretion."

Epiphany looked at Hortensius. He nodded. "We have nothing to hide."

Epiphany explained, "Ours was very basic. We agreed to be exclusive with each other for six months at which time we would either decide to sign a betrothal contract or split up. That all gifts above a certain monetary amount exchanged between us would be returned if a betrothal contract was not signed. Then…" Epiphany hesitated. "We agreed that if we had an illegitimate child and Hortensius refused a betrothal contract that full custody would revert to me and the child would be considered Lupus house."

"Really?" Livia asked. "Does everyone agree to that?"

Epiphany shook her head. "Everyone makes different arrangements. Some men stipulate the woman agrees not to get an abortion in the case of an unwanted baby. In most of those contracts, the men negotiate to take full custody of the child and pay for all medical expenses in exchange. Some contracts only stipulate what will be the house of the child in those circumstances."

"So," Livia inhaled a big breath. " As I understand it, you sign a match contract, a betrothal contract, and a marriage contract?"

"Oh," one of the younger children said. "That's why they call them three-scrolled women."

There was a silent pause, then a burst of laughter.

"Astute observation," Corvin said, wryly.

"That's a thing?" Livia asked.

"Yes," Epiphany said. "It's a phrase to describe a woman who is traditional, upper class, and a rule-follower."

"I see," Livia said. "What if you are a two-scrolled woman?"

"Then you only signed a betrothal and marriage contract," Lars said. "It's quite common now, as that's how it is done in the world at large these days."

"Sans the lawyers," Livia joked.

"Point taken," Lars dipped his head.

"Really is an expensive endeavor," Livia said. "What if you're poor?"

"The house provides free representation for all marriage contracts," Lars said.

"All houses?" Livia asked.

"Lupus and Rattus house," Lars said.

"So, a rich Lupus man can pull a fast one over on a naive working-class Aquila girl?" Livia asked.

Lars looked uncomfortable. "Aquila house doesn't provide free representation but they have a list of things they won't agree to. So, you can't get away with just anything."

Livia's eyes narrowed. "That is not good enough. Why doesn't the senate set up free representation for every Civ instead of tolerating unequal access to legal advice?"

Lars coughed. "You'd have to ask them. I've done the best I could by the woman in my house. And many Aquila house fathers hire lawyers or pull connections with their Patrons to hire Lawyers at affordable fees. Aquila women are not as defenseless as you suppose."

Lars tossed Aurelia a look and she suppressed a smile, eyes dancing. Livia decided it was time to change the subject before she offended someone.

"If you're Caecilia, are you a one-scrolled woman, then?" Livia asked.

"Ah, ah," Lars made a contradictory noise. "I made Hyrum and Gaius wait sixty days for her. She has two scrolls and a fair contract. Lauretta, however, only has a marriage contract. Something I vigorously objected to, as technically illegal. Though the other patres familias outvoted me and merely called it unprecedented."

Livia was horrified. "Did a competent lawyer advise her before signing their contract?"

"I do not know," Lars said. "That information was never revealed to me."

Livia didn't know what to think. Did she bring it up with Gaius? She didn't want to be seen as insufferably nosy but it'd be better to know now if she was going to have to fend for herself if she ever decided to marry. "I'll have to ask him," she muttered.

"It'd be wise to let him know how you'd like your arrangements to go," Lars said.

Livia nodded. "You're right. Better to know now how helpful he'll be."

"I have a question," one of Corvin's cousins raised a hand.

Lars looked at him. "Yes?"

"Is Livia dating Corvin?"

"No," Corvin said, swiftly. "We're not."

"Why not?" he quipped.

The family laughed. Livia's face flammed.

Corvin said, with an irritated glare. "Why aren't you dating?"

"Can I date Livia?" he asked, hopefully.

Everyone laughed.

"No," Livia said. "It is officially time for me to leave. I'm excited for you, Epiphany. Thank you for your help, Corvin. Alia, I'll miss you if we don't see each other again before I leave."

Alia smiled. "Miss you too, Livia."

Livia looked at Mel. "Try to boss Corvin into relaxing some."

Mel laughed. "Will do."

"He'll love that," Livia joked. "Right, Verity? Prudence?"

"Yeah!" Both girls agreed.

Corvin interjected. "Livia, I get this sense that you're plotting against me."

"Corvin, I'm never *not* plotting against you," Livia teased.

"Careful there, Liv. You make it sound like I'm on your mind constantly," he said, smoothly.

Well, Livia walked straight into that one and she was more guilty of the accusation than she was comfortable with. She made an expression that made his entire family burst into laughter. She was quickly so flustered that she could not come up with a witty reply. Her cheeks heated.

Livia drew herself up into command mode. "You take good care of yourself, Corvin Tullius," she barked. His family's laughter stopped. Livia adopted a playful tone. "Or I'll sic Justin on you."

She turned on her heel and left the house on another wave of delighted laughter. Corvin's the loudest among them. He knew as well as she did that Justin would be delighted his name was being bandied about as a threat to encourage self-care. She remembered hearing Justin ordering Corvin to go home and spend time with his family more than once after a particularly fraught shift. He'd remarked once that she and Corvin were the same—they both needed to be badgered into resting.

When Livia walked into Hyrum's empty house the reality of her situation descended forcefully. If the Tullian clan hadn't taken her in, she would have been in an empty house, alone all day. Livia didn't like to imagine how low her emotional state would have sunk if that had been the case.

She sighed and settled into her room to rest. She thought over her interactions with Corvin. Livia was almost certain he was mad at her over the incident with Gaius. Her memory settled on the sharp way he denied they were dating. He definitely wouldn't want anything to do with her when they got back to school. Livia should expect to be ignored again. She closed her eyes and tried to tell herself it didn't matter.

But it did.

Chapter 24

Hyrum and Caecilia returned home with Lucas in tow a few moments later. Lucas crushed Livia in a long hug until she started pinching him to get him to let go. It'd been a stressful day and the affection was irritating.

"That doesn't hurt," he drawled, unmoved.

"Lucas!" Livia cried.

He laughed and let go. "I missed you."

Livia huffed at him. "Apparently, it was a mistake to miss you."

Lucas laughed again. "Sorry, Liv."

Livia stomped around the kitchen for a minute or two to release the irritation. Hyrum and Lucas watched her calmly but Caecilia was unused to Livia and looked concerned.

After the dishes were secured in the dishwasher Livia was ready to talk again. She turned toward them. "How was the drive?"

"You have a bad day?" Lucas asked.

Livia rolled her eyes. "Don't even get me started—"

"She got in a fight with Gaius in front of everyone—" Caecilia said.

"As in all of Caesarea, everyone," Hyrum said.

Lucas pulled out his phone. "The hordes must be going feral then."

Livia assumed he'd pulled up Tabula as he started to scroll and read. "Ah, Corvin has come out in support of you and that seems to have chilled

221

everyone out—" Lucas mused.

"Corvin wrote something about me?" Livia asked.

Lucas showed her. Corvin had written a note about how important it was to correct a paterfamilias to protect the emotional and physical health of family members. He even praised Livia for her bravery and strength of character.

She was surprised at his praise. She hadn't expected that reaction at all. An unexpected blush

spread across her cheeks.

Lucas grinned at her. "You dating him?"

"No." Livia corrected. "We're *friends*."

Lucas laughed. "Right. So, we're finally in that situation."

"What situation?" Livia asked.

"You've liked him since we met him, Liv. It was only a matter of time till you caught his eye and he fell for you—"

"What?" Livia sputtered. "First—"

Hyrum's laugh interrupted Livia's planned tirade. "She's liked him that long?"

"Totally," Lucas answered.

Oh no, this was bad. Livia did not want to be on the opposite side of an argument with both of her brothers. She was in an untenable position.

"This is none of your business—" she snapped at Hyrum.

Lucas and Hyrum laughed at her, unfazed by her tone.

"What signs has he shown that he likes her?" Lucas turned to Hyrum.

Livia interrupted. "Lucas, be serious, there's no way he'd like me!"

Caecilia answered, "He arranged for Livia to come over to his house this morning so they could help her get ready for the parade. He also helped her memorize the Latin for the ceremony."

Livia gave her a look of betrayal.

"Ooo," Lucas teased. "Sounds serious."

"We're friends!" Livia shouted.

"Come on, Lucas," Hyrum said. "Lay off. She's already had a rough couple of days."

"Why don't you think he'd like you?" Caecilia asked, confused. "It'd be an extremely advantageous match."

Livia sighed. She was going to get another lecture similar to the one Tavian gave her.

"What do you mean?" Hyrum asked.

Caecilia outlined the same argument that Tavian had. Livia watched Hyrum closely to see his reaction. Would he disapprove?

He frowned. "I mean, that's all interesting...but none of that matters if Liv doesn't like him."

Everyone looked at her.

"Did you stop liking him, Liv?" Lucas asked.

Livia gulped. "I've tried to—"

Hyrum grinned. "But haven't succeeded?"

Livia grumbled at them. "It's ridiculous..."

Lucas grinned, looking at his phone. "You look cute together—"

"Cute? Together? What are you looking at?" Livia asked, panicked.

Lucas turned his phone around and there was a photo of them herding the Tullius sisters toward the temple of Saturn. She was tucked in tight against Corvin's side and was looking at him for direction. Alia and Mel were on their opposite side.

"There were crowds—" she tried to explain.

Hyrum grinned. "Ignore all the political stuff. If you like him, go for it, Liv."

"Y-you don't disapprove?"

"Why would I?" Hyrum was confused.

Caecilia spoke up. "I think you'd get along well. You have similarish personalities...hardworking, protective, soft-hearted but unwilling to show it—"

"So, you don't think...it'd make me like mom?" Livia asked.

Hyrum snorted. "Livia, mom had me when she was *seventeen*. Your life is already completely different."

Livia nodded. "Okay."

"I think you'd be smart to give him a chance since you like him," Hyrum said. "You can't avoid relationships all your life because you're scared. You got to take a few chances."

Livia looked at Lucas.

"I'm already a fan," he said. "Tavian highly recommends him."

Livia glared. "Figures, the Halls are gossiping about me."

Lucas started scrolling on his phone again. "People are mad at you but agree with what you did is the gist of it. This place is crazy! How can they insult and praise you at the same time?"

"You can't ever win," Livia agreed. "Never."

"Ignore them," Lucas said. "Just apologize to Gaius and then avoid fighting with him like that in the future. No big deal."

Lucas moved on to teasing Hyrum and Caecilia about whether they wanted to have a boy or girl first. The conversation morphed into a discussion about all sorts of baby plans. It was fun to see Hyrum and Caecilia exchange warm looks and get excited after all the stress that morning.

It got late and Lucas stood up and declared that he needed to sleep. Livia stood up to retreat to her room.

Hyrum called to her, "Wait, Liv, I have a question."

Livia gulped. Well, this was when he was going to give her the lecture about the parade. She'd hear all about how she'd disappointed him and how she should have acted better. She'd gone through enough years with Hyrum to know that he'd never be as harsh with her as their mother. Still, Livia's heart thudded in her chest as she awaited his lecture.

"I'm wondering if…" Hyrum hesitated. "I know it seems like Lucas has had an easier time accepting all this than you but I'm worried that he's expressed so little…reaction. But he's interested in participating in the reenactment in two days. He even mentioned he had started training again. Would you consider joining him in it?"

Livia groaned. This was the last thing she was expecting. She could get back on Hyrum's good side by agreeing but she didn't want to. "I oppose on principal—"

The reenactment was a game that recreated the snatching of the sabine women. A girl and a selected male "guardian" stood on one side of the field to represent the Sabines. The other half of the field represented the Romans who were going to swoop in and snatch them. The guys acting as Romans had to defeat the girl's guardian to haul her over to the Roman side of the line. When they got over to the other side the guy got to kiss the girl and the game was over.

"I know, I know," Hyrum said. "But this is the only time Lucas has expressed an interest in participating in the community. Gaius gifted him a full suit of Roman armor that used to belong to his brother."

Livia's heart fell. It was hard to remember the extended family. There weren't many left after the civil war that had torn Taurus house apart. A small number of their remaining relatives secreted themselves away in Istanbul, Turkey. Mistrustful and resentful, they refused to leave their new home.

Gaius visited often to keep up with relatives there. It wasn't a secret that he preferred it there to Caesarea, which was hard on his wife Lauretta. She went with him wherever he traveled the first year they were married but more often these days she opted to stay in Caesarea with her family.

Hyrum and Lucas were the future of Taurus house in Caesarea. Livia would take on the house of her husband and unless there were special circumstances all her children would also. If Lucas didn't find a way to acclimate to Caesarea, then it would have permanent repercussions for the house. Livia felt obligated to smooth over Lucas' transition into the community.

"Fine. I'll do it."

Miraculously, she escaped a lecture on her behavior at the parade and retreated to her room in relative peace. Her rest was disrupted when her phone vibrated with a text from Gaius.

Meet me in the Taurus house office tomorrow morning. 8:00 am. Be on time.

She hadn't escaped a scolding after all. Hyrum was letting Gaius handle it.

* * *

Livia was ten minutes late, but it wasn't her fault. She hadn't been able to find a place to park. Then the lines to take the elevators were long. She didn't understand why the crowds were still so thick now that the parade was over. Why were people up this early in the morning during a holiday?

She stood before Gaius apologetic. "The traffic was really bad...then the elevators...I tried—"

"Stop, Livia," Gaius snapped, impatiently.

Livia stopped talking and waited for him to say something. He only stared at her for a long uncomfortable moment. Then went to sit down at his desk.

"Can we pretend I punished you and agree never to engage in such unpleasantness in public again?"

Livia's eyes widened. "P-pretend you punished me?"

"I don't have any energy to deal with it. So, let's agree that I will not insult Caesarea in public out of respect for Caecilia and Lauretta and you will not directly contradict me unless we are in private."

"Alright," Livia agreed.

"Good," Gaius said. He picked up a folder on the corner of his desk and set it in front of him.

"Now, I have papers to review. Unless you have anything else?"

Livia stared at him in shock. "Y-you aren't angry at me?"

Gaius laughed, a hard, bitter sound. "I'm too busy doing damage control with Lauretta to spare emotions for anything else."

Livia's eyes widened. "Is she still angry?"

"*Furious*," Gaius said.

"There's nothing...we can do...is there?" she asked.

Gaius gave her an impatient smile. "No."

Livia gulped. "I am sorry to bother you but I don't know when I'll see you again..."

"What is it?" he asked.

"How did you arrange your marriage to Lauretta?" she asked.

Gaius looked surprised. He closed the folder and then sat back and gave her a suspicious look.

"Her mother had a connection to my mother. They arranged for us to meet together several times. We determined to marry and wrote up the contract and signed it."

"Lars objected?" Livia asked.

"Yes, of course, he did," Gaius looked, annoyed. "Lars is a traditionalist."

"How were the papers written up?" Livia asked.

"I told Lauretta to give me her requirements. I wrote back what I agreed to and what I didn't. She had thirty days to review the papers. She asked for a handful of things that I agreed to and then we signed them at the ceremony."

"So, she spoke to a lawyer?"

"Her uncle is a lawyer who often writes up these contracts," Gaius said.

Livia blinked. "Did you have a lawyer?"

"No."

Livia's eyes widened. "You weren't worried she'd...trick you?"

Gaius sighed and closed his eyes. "No, I didn't."

"Why not?"

Gaius shrugged. "What prompted you to ask?"

Livia explained, "I was just...with Epiphany when she announced her match with Hortensius. They explained how it all worked usually."

"Right, where you don't get tricked into agreeing to lose half your property and your entire fortune when your wife divorces you."

"Is...that what you ended up agreeing to?" Livia asked.

"Unfortunately. The only solution is to give it all away."

"To who?" Livia asked.

"You," Gaius said.

"What?" Livia sputtered.

"Hyrum and Lucas too, of course," Gaius said. "I've been advised by Lars already. Funny, he

asked if you'd spoken to me."

"You asked Lars for help?" Livia asked.

"I didn't have a choice if I wanted to save Taurus house," Gaius said.

"So...you are getting a divorce, then?"

"We'll see. I'm minimizing the damage if I do. I wouldn't care really if we'd had a child first. I would have considered it worth it. But to lose all my money and property and have no child? Well, that's just unendurable."

Livia stared at him. She had no idea how to respond. First, the complete lack of emotion over losing Lauretta as a person. The relationship only mattered to him if they had a child? She hated to admit she could see why Lauretta was divorcing him if that was the sum of his regard for her. Still, It didn't make sense. If he wanted a child so badly, why did he spend so much time away from Lauretta?

"Any more questions, Livia?" Gaius asked.

She hesitated. "I only wondered if I could arrange my marriage differently than the way you and Hyrum did it?"

"How do you want to do it, Livia?" he asked.

"If I want to sign three contracts, who will be responsible for the cost of a lawyer?" Livia asked.

"I will pay for it with house funds," Gaius said. "You do not need to worry about that."

Livia's eyes narrowed. "Can I choose a lawyer?"

"If you wish." Gaius grinned as if he'd discovered something. "Who is it that has caught your eye, Livia?"

She shook her head. "I'm not interested in being married right now."

"In case you didn't notice," he said. "It's a rather extended process. If you match for a year and set a year-long betrothal you'll not be married for two years. That doesn't count the back and forth it requires to arrange the match in the first place. That can drag on six months. It's not a quick way to get married."

"Six months?" Livia asked.

Gaius shrugged. "You might as well tell me."

But Livia shook her head. "I'm not certain about anyone right now. I was only curious."

"Anything else?" Gaius asked.

Livia figured she'd pressed his patience far enough and excused herself. She stood in the hall and tried to evaluate the concerns that were plaguing her. If Livia decided to work with Gaius to arrange a match how could she stand to remain in Caesarea? If she left Caesarea how would she navigate any significant relationship without revealing her powers? Livia's mother had kept Tad in the dark for years but Livia couldn't imagine herself doing that. She didn't know how her mother had maintained the deception for so long.

Their multiple moves took on a new dimension in her mind. Would Livia live her life running from city to city to avoid anyone finding out? How had Tad convinced mom to marry him? Maybe Livia could leave for a long time—long enough for Gaius' divorce to die down—then come back. Did leaving have to be permanent? Would people look at her more favorably when she was older?

Then there was this divorce to consider. How much had Livia's actions yesterday affected Lauretta's decision? She'd been extremely displeased with Livia. Did Livia bear some portion of responsibility for the situation? If she did, how did she fix it?

Livia had to drive over to Hyrum's work to find him. He was in one of the greenhouses planting vegetables in the raised beds. She told him everything Gaius had said and asked him what they should do. Hyrum refused to get involved.

"If she wants to divorce him, she probably has her reasons. I'm not going to interfere. Do you know how much better our life would have been if Mom had divorced dad the first time she wanted to?" Hyrum asked.

"What about all the money and property he was talking about?" Livia asked.

"Not my problem," Hyrum said. "We all have food and shelter and an honest way to make a living. Not going to worry about it, Liv."

"But isn't he making a rash decision? Doesn't he realize giving that stuff away to us is going to nuke his relationship? I don't want to be involved but if he gives everything to us then we're involved. We should at least try and stop him!" Livia cried.

Hyrum sighed. "Fine. I'll call him."

Hyrum stopped digging with his hand shovel and pulled out a cell phone. "Gaius," he said. "Liv's over here upset. Maybe you should take some time before you—"

Hyrum was silent. His expression fell. "Gaius, no. We should discuss this first—"

"See," Livia hissed.

But Gaius hung up on Hyrum when he tried to protest again.

"What did he say?" Livia demanded.

Hyrum shook his head. "It's already done. There's nothing we can do to change it."

"What did he do?" Livia asked.

"We'll find out all the details soon enough, Liv. I think I'm going home. I better prepare Caecilia for the shock."

Whatever Gaius had told him, Hyrum didn't look happy. What had Lars told Gaius to do? The only thing Livia could do was follow Hyrum home and listen to what he told Caecilia.

Lucas was on his way out the door to go spar at the fields. "Wait," Hyrum told him. "We're all here…we should talk."

Caecilia came down the stairs a moment later. "You're home early? Is everything alright?"

"Lauretta and Gaius are probably getting divorced tomorrow or the next day," Hyrum said.

"What?" Caecilia asked.

Hyrum shook his head. "That's not the part to get upset about, love."

"Then what is?" she demanded.

"To cheat her out of a divorce settlement he put all that land that Aquila and Taurus house have been fighting over for the last twenty years into a public trust and made the three of us the executors over it."

Caecilia sat down on the stairs. "No," she whispered. "What will all those Aquila families do? They'll have no place to live."

"Wait," Lucas asked. "What's going on?"

Hyrum turned to him. "He turned about 500 families out of their homes. Now that it's turned over to public lands it's no longer permitted for residential use. Aquila house stole the land from Taurus house landlords. Uncle Quin tried to litigate it back into Taurus house control and was successful to a degree but spent almost a million dollars in legal fees."

"What?" Livia sputtered. "H-how is that even possible?"

"So, if it went to Lauretta in the divorce settlement she could have sold it to someone in Aquila house and finally ended the dispute?" Lucas asked.

Caecilia said, "Could have. Now? Now, we have to develop it. There are strings attached to public lands."

"I don't know what we'll do," Hyrum said, wearily. "We'll have to see where the chips fall tomorrow. Maybe she'll decide to stay with him when she discovers her divorce settlement has been significantly reduced."

"I'm sure the Senate will have to give them time to move out..." Caecilia said. "But wow, turning all that land to public space? Caesarea needs that too. The forum isn't big enough anymore..."

"What we need is public housing—" Hyrum said.

"Maybe if you did it in phases, some of the poorer families could move in right when the housing was ready?" Caecilia said.

Hyrum muttered, "They're all poor, Caecilia. Everyone knows those houses should have been condemned a decade ago. It's a political and logistical nightmare so everyone has refused to touch it. Gaius just threw us to the wolves."

"The eagles in this case," Livia joked.

Nobody laughed.

Lucas watched them all with wary eyes. "Sounds like we're clearing out a slum."

"Essentially," Hyrum said. "It's going to make a lot of people angry."

That sounded awful to Livia. Weren't things in Caesarea bad enough for her already? She had come here to find reasons to stay. Now, she only had a longer list of reasons to leave.

Chapter 25

Livia looked out on the field of people dressed in Roman armor and wondered why she'd agreed to this. The weather couldn't be better for mid-October—clear sky with temps in the high 50's. Everyone seemed to be in high spirits except for her. She consoled herself with the fact that she got to be outdoors instead of crammed underground. The reenactment took place on the wide-open fields of the security patrol training grounds. She stood outside the men's locker room and waited for Lucas to come out with his armor on. She played the part of Sabine maiden and wore her stola again.

Epiphany and Corvin crossed in front of her. Livia's heart lurched into her throat. She'd wondered after reading the post that Lucas had showed her if Corvin didn't hold the parade incident against her. However, Livia was too much of a coward to call out to him and put his regard for her to the test in front of all these people. What if he tucked his chin down and bid her a 'vale'? Her heart couldn't take it. Then Epiphany looked over her shoulder and caught sight of Livia. She smiled and tugged on Corvin's arm. They stopped and walked over to her.

Livia took the opportunity to observe Corvin's appearance. He wore polished *lorica segmentata* armor over a white tunic, which had a blue stripe around the bottom. His helmet had hinges at the temples where two long segments were attached to cover his cheeks. A fringed belt protected his front lower half but his legs were bare except for leather sandals. He carried the TARP parade shield—sky blue with a prancing deer on the bottom. A fancy garland was painted around the shield boss and the words *"subvenire, sanare"* were written across the top. It was the TARP motto: to rescue, to heal.

"Liv?" Corvin asked. "We didn't know you were doing this."

Corvin and Epiphany didn't bother with the ridiculous nodding ritual. What did that mean? Was it an insult to skip the greeting? Livia should have asked that question before now. Why did Livia never think of these things until it was too late?

Livia shook her head. "I didn't either."

Epiphany and Corvin exchanged alarmed looks. Oh no. What had she gotten herself into?

"Who has been appointed your guardian?" Corvin asked.

"Lucas. My brother. Tell me, is there any way I can get out of kissing someone at the end?" she asked.

Epiphany looked panicked. "Usually, the girl asks her guardian to arrange who's going to snatch her beforehand so she gets a kiss from who she wants. The rules are that a guy is disqualified from awards for excessive kissing."

"What's the definition of excessive kissing?" Livia asked.

"We all know it means french kissing," Corvin said.

"There's that at least," Livia said. "Can I fight?"

Epiphany answered. "Some of the Aquila girls do. They go over the fight rules at the beginning so you'll have to follow those."

Lucas exited from the dressing room. Livia tried to ignore the pit of dread in her stomach. She forced a smile for her brother. "Hey, look at you!"

Lucas looked good in his armor, and it was obvious he'd been working out. His arms were defined with muscle and his shoulders were broader than the last time she saw him. He hadn't been able to talk about anything but the reenactment since yesterday.

"Hey," Lucas said, grinning. "You ready to do this?"

"As ready as I'm going to be," Livia said.

Corvin extended his hand. "It's been two years, hasn't it, Lucas?"

Lucas accepted his hand and shook it. "Corvin, nice to see you here."

"Liv has mentioned missing you. I'm glad you're here," Corvin said.

Lucas nodded. "Livia was nice to agree to this last minute."

Corvin grinned and glanced at Livia. "Too bad I can't join the other side. I'd steal a kiss."

Livia gasped. *Friends? Right?* She didn't want to think about this going into a fight. She glared at him. "Not without a fight you wouldn't."

Corvin laughed. "Don't fight too hard. It's a game."

"A game where I get kissed against my will," Livia muttered.

Corvin's brows furrowed in concern. "I can do some last-minute arranging. Do you want me to put in the word with anyone?"

"Seriously?" Livia asked. "I'm supposed to admit to you that I want to kiss somebody—"

"That's not a crime," Corvin said, eyes twinkling. "I'm willing to put a word in with someone."

Lucas frowned. "Liv, I thought you were okay with this."

Livia backtracked. Lucas needed her to be on board with this. She didn't want to ruin his fun. "Oh, I am totally okay with this! We are doing this!"

"If you are okay with this then tell Corvin who you want to kiss," Lucas challenged.

"Tavian Hall is here?" she squeaked, face bright red.

"They flew in the same day you got here," Lucas said.

Livia looked at Corvin. "Tavian Hall."

Corvin nodded. "I'll be back in a minute."

"Is there a way she can avoid getting kissed?" Lucas asked Epiphany.

"She'd have to defeat all the fighters," she said.

"How would that work?" Lucas asked.

"Well, the rounds last 8 mins each," Epiphany said. "Once you catch a girl you take her to Rome base and sit out. Most guys go three rounds to have some fun fighting before they catch their girl. You can also get pulled out if you get a 'kill' hit. The judges watch on the sidelines and pull you out."

"So, how many rounds are there?" Lucas asked.

"As many rounds as it takes to catch all the girls," Epiphany said.

Lucas gave Livia a grin. "Wanna try for last man standing, Liv?"

Relief poured over Livia. "Really?"

"Yeah," he said. "And if you decide after round four or something that you've had enough we can call Tav over. It'll be fun."

Livia nodded. "That sounds good to me."

"You sure?" Lucas studied her eyes.

"Yeah." Livia looked at Epiphany. "Okay, where do I get a weapon?"

"You have to win it," Epiphany said. "Guys get automatic weapons. Girls have to win them from someone else."

"You have got to be joking me," Livia said.

"Nope."

"This game is rigged," Livia said.

"Um, that's kind of the point?" Epiphany said.

Corvin returned right before the horn for round one blew. He came to Livia. "Alright, I told Tavian that you wanted to get snatched by him."

"What'd he say?" Livia asked.

"He was agreeable to the idea."

Livia didn't even want to ask for the details. It was way too awkward. Instead, she glared at Corvin. "Do you realize that I have to win my weapon?"

Corvin smirked. "I did know that."

"Do you have any advice for me on how to do that?" Livia asked.

"Well, don't get the guys with the red bandanas around their arms until after the third round. That means they've got a girl waiting on them and there's an unspoken agreement to lay off until round four."

"Okay, so the guys without a red bandana are free game?"

"Yeah, but each guy wears a stripe on the bottom of his tunic according to house colors. Red is Taurus. Blue or Silver is Lupus, Green is Serpens, yellow or gold is Aquila. Go for Green or Blue. Aquila will probably be too fast for you."

An announcer called for everyone to take their places on the field. Once the crowds had settled they went over the rules. There were only two sparring weapons allowed—foam practice swords and pugil sticks. Strikes to the face and head were forbidden. Strikes to the limbs were not considered kill hits but any tap to the trunk of the body with a weapon or hand to hand combat would tag you out of the game.

Then the horn sounded.

A shouting mass of men ran across the field pell-mell and jumped right into the fighting. There was a lot of yelling, but there wasn't a whole lot of hard fighting. Laughter filled the air as playful taunts were exchanged over mock battles. Most of the girls were ignored at this point. They stood and laughed and gossiped as they watched.

Livia, however, was trying to select a target. She was looking for someone with a standard patrol infantry shield—red with a single lightning bolt down the center and two crossed spears. They were the gear for basic, first-year recruits and most likely to have the least training. She spotted one carried by a green-striped tunic youth.

The guy hadn't expected her to approach because she was a girl. It was obvious that he was hesitant to hit her. It was too easy. When he swung down with the pugil stick Livia grasped the center pole in her palm and yanked. She broke his grip easily and claimed the weapon as her own. It was sweet to be Taurus.

"Hey!" the kid cried and tried to attack, but Livia had the pugil stick now. She spun it around, took a fighting stance, and tapped his chest within three seconds. A whistle blew. A ref called, "Green-stripe out!"

Livia laughed and made her way back to where Corvin and Lucas were sparring. The horn blew to end the round and the Romans retreated.

"Got your weapon, I see," said Lucas.

"Yep, the kid was scared to take a full swing at me. Too bad for him," Livia said. She put her stick down to tie up the folds of her stola so she could move more freely.

"Wow," Epiphany said. "First round? Really?"

"They're going down," Livia said, lifting her pugil stick to the sky. "Bring it on Romans!"

Corvin said, "You're gonna have fans by the end of this."

Livia rolled her eyes. "Highly doubtful."

He shook his head. "Don't doubt me, Fabulous. You'll see."

Livia scanned the crowds that surrounded the field. The Aediles office had erected temporary seating around the field. So spectators sat on multiple levels. Two white tents sat opposite each other in the middle of the field. The first was a media tent where a mass of photographers and camera operators camped to film the event. The second was a medic tent, Livia spotted several healers in TARP blue. Others wore bright orange shirts signifying their association with FORMICA, the other specialized unit of the Caesarean border patrol. The two units had an ongoing rivalry, which often expressed itself in humorous ribbing whenever the two interacted. Livia was sure the med tent was an interesting place to be right now. She felt bad for the standard clinic healers in white who had to be in the crossfires.

The Cornicen blew the horn to start the second round and Livia turned her attention back to the battle. The second round passed much as the first had. Except, Livia hovered near Lucas. He had the advantage of wielding a shield, an ancient circular one that differed from the rectangular shields around them with Caesarean insignia on them. Livia noticed a few more Aquila women had snagged weapons, but there were only a handful. The light sparring continued and no one got snatched away. Livia was grateful for the chance to warm up and remember how to fight again. It had been a long time since she'd sparred with anyone seriously.

Then the horn for the third round sounded. The atmosphere of the entire field changed. Some serious fights went down in front of the crowd. Guys hauled girls over their shoulders or pulled them up into their arms to carry. They all screamed with laughter, smiles on their faces.

Hortensius came in for a fight with Corvin. It made sense that he was slated to capture Epiphany. Both men grinned at each other wielding shields of sky blue and short foam swords.

Livia was distracted from their fight when a trio of Lupus house guys approached her and Lucas. They were in an arrow formation—a pugil stick wielder flanked by two swordsmen. Livia almost snorted. Of course, Lupus house would be the tacticians.

"Lucas—" she muttered. "What do we do?"

Lucas' eyes were darting back and forth looking for a weakness. "He's holding his shield on the wrong side—" he muttered.

"He's what?" Livia whispered.

"Limits their mobility. That's where we need to strike. On my count hit the center of the right swordman's shield."

"Wait," Livia hissed. "How hard?"

"Enough, to knock him over but not enough to hurt him," Lucas said.

"I haven't practiced enough to do that!" Livia hissed, ready to revolt. Livia had no idea what type of damage she could cause with the pugil stick since she'd never sparred with one before. Even a practice weapon could be lethal if you used enough force and Livia wasn't going to experiment on a random kid.

"You can kiss him then," Lucas glared at her.

"Fine. Count," she growled.

"—three!" Lucas cried.

Livia disobeyed Lucas' orders. He needed a man down. She'd get him down. *Her way.* She hurled the pugil stick like a spear. Her mark blocked easily with his shield but the point was to distract him. Livia dove towards his feet, ignoring the dust that puffed into her mouth. She snatched his ankle and pulled it out from under him. He fell to his back instantly but Livia had enough experience with hand-to-hand combat that she knew how to keep herself from injuring him. She took a hit from his sword on her forearm then snaked her wrist around the dull weapon and stole it from him. She tapped his chest with the flat side twice and he froze. He was out.

Lucas had taken the second guy out somehow and was sparring with the third. Lucas' shield clashed with his opponents. Lucas shoved, not at full strength but hard enough that his foe caught air. The Lupus kid yelped. He managed to keep his stance when he connected with the ground again but he was so spooked that he ran away.

Livia spat the dirt out of her mouth. Livia glanced toward Corvin and Hortensius. From what she could tell Corvin was pretty proficient with the sword. Corvin let his guard down in a way that made it obvious he did it on purpose, and Hortensius made a solid hit. The ref called Corvin out. He tossed a grin at Epiphany and walked off the field.

Hortensius scooped Epiphany up into his arms. She laughed as he spun her around in a circle. She wrapped her arms around Hortensius' neck.

Epiphany encouraged him. "You don't get a kiss until you cross to Rome's side, hero. Hurry up!"

Hortensius laughed and proceeded to carry her across the field. Maybe, this isn't so bad Livia told herself. The boys get to show off their fighting skills. The girls got to have a fairy tale moment of being carried off and kissed by a strong man in armor. There was a certain romantic appeal there she recognized.

There was a fifteen-minute break after the third round ended. Livia went to the water table and swished around a mouthful and spat it into the grass. Most of the grit was out of her mouth now. She had a few bites of a banana and some Gatorade. Lucas downed an entire bottle of Gatorade.

He glared at her. "You didn't listen, Liv."

"I did too. You wanted the guy down. I did my job," she insisted.

He shook his head. "Liv, no more going rogue. We're a team. You want to pull something like that, tell me first."

Liv nodded. "Okay, but you have to listen when I don't want to do something—"

Lucas gave her a nod back. "Deal."

"Whoa," Livia said, looking around. "They like this three-round thing."

"Yeah, well it's been about 30 mins of fighting," he said. "You're in that stola thing you tied up but I'm in heavy armor. It's starting to suck."

The horn sounded.

Livia shouted, "For Taurus!" and ran forward twirling her pugil stick. She'd hung the sword she'd captured on the tie that circled her waist. It rested against the small of her back until she needed it. Lucas followed quickly on her heels. The fourth round of fighting was a lot tougher. There were more Aquila opponents and they were extremely hard to fight. Livia had to do all kinds of acrobatic moves to avoid getting hit.

In the beginning rounds, she didn't fight directly next to Lucas, but as the fighting got tougher she tucked in closer to him. They held together fairly well until Lucas got tossed on his back. Livia stepped over him and took the hit on her pugil stick that would have 'killed' him. She nailed his opponent out. She hauled Lucas up to his feet, even though he was still out of breath. He'd gotten the wind knocked out of him.

"Stay with me, Lucas," she said. "Watch my back."

She pulled him around so they were standing back to back. Lucas leaned against her while he caught his breath. Livia took on an approaching Aquila kid while Lucas recovered on her back. By the time the ref called a kill hit she was panting with exertion.

Lucas swung them around and he took the lead while Livia caught her breath. The horn sounded for the end of the round. Livia and Lucas were both exhausted.

"Wow, Liv," Lucas said. "This is rough."

"Come on, let's get some water," she said.

They both guzzled down the liquid and then returned. Livia surprisingly was having a good time. It was refreshing to face a challenge that tested her strength and skill to this extent. Also, it had been a long time since she'd felt so connected with her brother. She liked feeling like she was on the same team as him. Livia and Lucas marched back out together. The field was mostly empty on their side now.

The horn for the next round blew. The last dozen or so girls had been captured. Only Livia and Lucas were left. Most of the Romans didn't attempt to come to the fight. They milled around on the other side, resting. Those that were still up for a fight came jogging over.

"Hey! Um, you're outnumbered!" a guy called. "About 50 to two."

Livia cursed.

Lucas laughed. "We're snowed."

"You can take them Fabulous!" a voice yelled on their right.

Livia looked. It was Alexander from TARP. He wore a TARP t-shirt to show his support for his department. He was surrounded by a handful of other TARP agents too—Cam, Silvanus, Luccia, and Pallas.

They punched their fists into the air and started a chant—"Fab-u-lous!" Soon, huge swaths of the audience were joining them. Chanting her name and punching their fist into the air in a show of solidarity.

"Look at that," Lucas muttered, amused.

Livia had to blink back tears as a wave of acceptance washed over her. She was part of them even if some people didn't like it. She still belonged here on the field next to her brother. She kissed the top of her fist and punched it into the air in response to the audience and everyone cheered.

Chapter 26

T he sounding of the horn brought a strange hush over the crowd. Lucas and Livia settled into their stances and prepared for the fight to come. Then a group moved in from the left—Rattus tunics with basic shields.

"We've got it!"

Livia recognized Adrian Hall's voice. She smiled. This was the perfect time to let Tavian take her in and give her an awkward kiss to end the game. Livia and Lucas had a good run and everyone on the field was worn out now.

The other guys held back as Adrian, Tavian, and Arik all approached. Lucas took point against Adrian and Tavian, holding them both off. They were all laughing at being able to spar with each other. That left Livia to face Arik.

He had a pugil stick too. His blue eyes looked concerned. "Hey, Liv, come on in, kay?"

Hold up, didn't he know that Tavian was supposed to do this job? Livia shook her head. "No, Arik."

Arik spoke with a patronizing calm. "Liv, you're outnumbered. Think this through."

Livia glared at him. "You think you're going to sweet talk me into cheating?"

"Cheating?" Arik asked, confused.

"You're dating Lauren," she said.

The ref standing behind Arik pulled a disbelieving face. The soldiers standing by to watch started muttering to each other and shaking their heads.

Realization crossed Arik's face. His eyes darted to the people listening in on their conversations and his face went bright red. "Liv, this is...an exception."

Livia snapped. "No exceptions are necessary, Arik!"

This response was met with mutters of agreement and respect. "He shouldn't take her in." "She deserves better than that." But there was also frustration. "Then how is this going to end?" "Why didn't they have a plan?"

Livia launched into an offense. Arik was experienced with the pugil stick and held Livia off without trouble. She was worn out enough that she'd accepted she wasn't going to make it to the last man standing. But she wasn't going to let Arik be the one to kiss her.

The ref whistle blew as Lucas and Adrian took each other out. Livia made the mistake of looking over, hoping to catch a glimpse of Tavian. That was all the distraction it took for Arik to spin the pugil stick out of Livia's hands and toss her over his shoulder.

Livia was so stunned for a second she didn't react. Then Arik started back to the Roman side and she realized what was happening. Arik probably didn't know that she wanted Tavian to be the one to take her in. Or simply ignored her request entirely. She refused to kiss Arik.

Enraged, Livia grabbed his belt and dragged herself down his back. For an instant, it felt like she was going to fall face-first into the ground. Livia could hear the crowd give a collective gasp, but Arik caught the back of her knees before she fell. She was lucky. It was an extremely dangerous move.

"Livia," Arik growled. There was a strain in his voice. The move had cost him.

But Livia was exactly where she wanted. Her arms could reach low enough to trip Arik up. A second later they both went crashing to the ground. Livia rolled away and ran back to her side of the field.

"You're kidding me," one guy said as she ran past. "No *way*. She got right back up after that?"

Arik was right on her heels. She dropped flat on the ground, hands over her head. Arik had to leap over her to avoid tripping. He swung back around and Livia leaped to her feet to engage him in hand to hand tactics.

"Liv, seriously," Arik said. "Let's end this."

They danced around neither one of them willing to *actually* hit the other person. Livia was thinking that she didn't want to accidentally hurt him. Even if he was a jerk. Someone called out the time. Two minutes left in the round. If she could last that long, this could end peacefully.

"Liv, what are you going to do if you knock me out? Think about it," Arik said. "You know me. I'll take care of you."

Livia snorted. "Right. Do you miss me Arik? Is that why you're here?"

"I'm here to help!" Arik tried to come in close.

"Right, you're so much help," Livia snarled, pivoting out of his reach.

"You're being unreasonable," Arik cried, frustrated.

Unfortunately, frustration made Arik reckless; he closed in and reached for her. Livia spun out of the way and then delivered a roundhouse kick to his chest. Arik went flying and crashed straight into Tavian. They both fell to the ground. Livia was horrified. Arik wasn't the only one letting his emotion make him reckless. Under normal circumstances, Livia never would have pulled that move on anyone but Hyrum or Lucas.

"Arik! Tavian!" She ran to them, hands shaking. "Are you okay? Are you okay? I'm so sorry! I'm so sorry!"

"Livia," Tavian hissed. "Pay attention!"

Livia wheeled around just in time to avoid being grabbed by a huge Aquila guy. The round ended. Livia ran back to Arik. He was gasping and holding his side. "Oh no," Livia's eyes filled with tears. "Arik."

"Nice kick, Liv," Arik laughed. He was putting on a brave face. "Really got me."

Livia was filled with guilt. "I'm so sorry."

"That's the game, Liv. I'll be alright," he groaned in pain.

"He'll be okay," the medic with him said. "But he cracked a few ribs."

Livia ran her hands into her hair that had come completely out of her bun. She didn't know where her hair tie even was. She turned to Tavian. "I'm out, Liv."

"What?"

"I'm out. They counted Arik slamming into me as a kill hit."

"Are you okay?" Livia asked. Tavian was cradling his hand into his belly.

"Broke a couple of fingers."

Another wave of guilt washed over her. "I'm so sorry."

"Three minutes with a healer and I'll be good as new. Livia, you need to focus. You have another round to fight and there are 27 guys. Some of them are not nice people. Avoid the FORMICA crowd. They consider you associated with TARP and taking you in will be a score for them in their rivalry. The Aurelian Aquila guys will be good to you. The Lupus guys too."

"How do I tell if a guy is Aurelian?"

"They wear gold bands, not yellow. They won the distinction because of their clan's military service."

"I'm screwed."

Tavian didn't comfort her. "Go drink lots of water."

There was a fifteen-minute break. They made her drink Gatorade and fussed over her. Livia thought the whole thing was overkill. Until she got back out on the field and a wave of dizziness passed over her. She felt like she was going to puke. Somehow she had to take down 27 guys. She didn't know how to go about that as she watched a line of them approach slowly. If she'd felt a little bit better, she might have laughed. They looked like they were trying to catch a skittish deer.

Livia noticed straight off that the Aurelian and Lupus house guys had banded together and were on her right. Everyone else on the left were all tough-looking Aquila guys. The majority of them carried orange FORMICA shields on their arms. The ones Tavian warned her about. Livia thought about going straight to the right and surrendering. Except, what would that say about Livia? That she folded when things got dicey?

Determination filled her. Livia was a fighter. She pushed through, she dug down, and she fought until she couldn't give anymore. Livia twirled her pugil stick in her hand and waited for the horn to sound. She didn't hesitate. She charged straight into the left flank. She used every dirty trick Hyrum ever taught her. She had five guys down but she had awful bruises to show for it and she lost her weapon. Livia tried to back out to catch her breath and got pulled up onto a guy's shoulders.

There was laughter as he carried her toward the other side of the field. Livia froze with pain. She hurt everywhere. She tried to shake it off and come up with a plan but her body ached bone-deep. The guy was spinning her around in celebration, displaying her like some kind of trophy. Infuriated, Livia ripped his helmet from his head and hurled it at his feet. The guy tripped up and she grabbed his foam sword while he was unbalanced. When he straightened up she had it against his throat.

"Put me down," she hissed.

A whistle blew. "Put her down. That's a kill," The ref called.

The guy swore and flipped her off his back. Livia slammed to the ground. She cried out in pain.

The ref got in the guy's face and screamed at him. "What do you think you're doing? You're out! You don't treat her like that. You could hurt her!"

A medic called a timeout and ran over. "You okay?"

Livia pulled herself to her feet. The pain from before had gone numb. She could walk but there was a heat in her hip. "I'm okay."

"I need you to think about that question again," the medic said, his voice taking on a commanding quality. "Tell me you're injured and you're out. You don't have to fight anymore and this will be done."

Livia shook her head.

"Please?" he said, looking her in the eye. "Nobody wants to see you lose this one or worse, seriously hurt."

Livia shook her head again. That wasn't the rules of the game. She wasn't going out on a technicality. That would be cheating, but she needed to change tactics. Her hip wasn't going to hold up. She wasn't going to be able to fight all these guys off. She needed to end this thing intact and that meant

246

surrendering.

They waited for Livia to set herself up again. She didn't know what to do. She leaned into her hip. There wasn't a sharp pain but there was discomfort and heat. Part of being Taurus meant being able to endure a lot of pain, however, that made it hard to tell how badly you were hurt. Taurus men usually went into rages and passed out. Taurus women only reacted when someone touched them and the pain crashed in all at once.

Justin called it grounding. He and Flavia often worked out together in the mornings. At the end of every session, he touched her shoulder or her hand and asked if she'd hurt herself at all. Flavia had needed Justin to train her how to exercise within her limits to avoid random injuries.

This knowledge had been one of the most useful things about discovering she was Taurus. It freed Livia from a lot of childhood anxiety around being touched. Right now, though, she didn't know how she'd endure a kiss. She didn't want to repeat the pain that had crashed over her when she was on that Aquila guy's shoulders. When she had felt all the bruises and injuries she'd collected over the last hour all at once. Plus, that was before she'd been hurled to the ground like a sack of potatoes. Livia shifted her weight back off her hip. She sighed in frustration. There was no way to tell how badly she'd hurt it.

They should have blown the horn by now. There was some kind of delay on the other side. An announcer came over the speaker.

"Lupus house has forfeited their house points to transfer a player from side Sabine to side Rome."

The horn blew and Livia braced herself for the line to advance. Instead, they split down the middle and parted for a figure clothed only in a white tunic and crimson cloak. Livia wondered briefly if she'd hit her head so hard she was hallucinating. She rested a hand on her forehead, trying to remember if her head had slammed into the ground when that Aquila guy had flipped her off his back. The most disorienting thing was that she couldn't tell. It was aggravating to not know such a crucial thing about herself. She almost wanted…the only way to solve this mystery was to touch someone.

The white tunic guy was still approach—Corvin. It was Corvin. His house had forfeited points to send him out to her. Livia's eyes blurred with tears. He was in front of her now.

"Livia, no more fighting," he commanded, stern.

"I think I'm hurt?"

"We know," he said.

"I don't know how bad it is…" she dropped her hands to her sides, exhausted. "I can't tell."

"We know that too, Fabulous," Corvin said. "No one else could have stood back up that fast after being thrown to the ground like that."

"I'm scared," she confessed. "I'm so scared."

Corvin started untying the knot of the cloak at his throat. He spoke calmly, without emotion, but his eyes were soft. "There's no reason to be afraid. I'm not here to hurt you. I want to help. Will you let me do that?"

Livia nodded.

Corvin's cloak came loose and he removed it. Then he flung it around her and pulled it closed in front of her. "Can you walk?"

The thick heavy wool sat on her skin comfortably. She hadn't realized she was cold, but she'd been exposed to the 50-degree weather for over an hour now. It was nice to have a shield from the breeze.

"I can," Livia said. "But I'm not sure…I should."

Corvin tugged on the cloak urging her forward. "Let's see how it goes."

He pulled again. Livia stepped forward. Livia's knees were wobbly but she walked without trouble. She pulled back against the pull of the cloak. "Corvin."

Corvin stopped. "Yes, Liv?"

"I wanna know how bad it is—"

His brow furrowed. "And that would require…"

"Put your hands on my shoulders," Livia ordered.

"You sure?" he asked, doubtful.

Livia nodded.

Corvin still hesitated.

"Please," Livia begged.

Corvin took a deep breath. His expression cleared of any hesitation and he seemed to be steeling himself. "Okay."

He cupped her upper arms with his hands. The first onslaught of pain was intense and Livia's knees almost buckled under it. Probably, would have if Corvin hadn't held her up. Then the strength came back to Livia's legs and the pain leveled out as she grew familiar with her ache. She groaned but something was satisfying about it too. Knowing the shape and weight of her pain made her feel steady and secure.

"Are you alright, Livia?" Corvin asked.

"Yeah," she panted. She closed her eyes and acquainted herself with her pain. Her hip throbbed fiercely but the pain was dull, not sharp and piercing. She put her hand against Corvin's chest and pushed him back so they could keep walking. The pain in her hip didn't get any worse or better. Another wave of relief poured over her.

"I think I'm okay," she said.

"You're okay?" Corvin asked, still walking backward.

"Yeah," Livia nodded. "I'm okay to walk. It's okay, Corvin."

She smiled up at him. He didn't smile back. His eyes were wide with surprise.

"A-are you sure?" he asked. "There's no pain?"

"Oh, there's pain," Livia laughed. "But it's the satisfying kind. I *earned* all these bruises Corvin," Livia said, proudly.

Corvin laughed in a startled way like it was torn from him unwillingly. He shook his head. "I'm glad then. I expected the worst."

"Me too." She grinned.

Corvin's expression turned playful. "We're on Rome's side now, Fabulous."

"Does that mean you kiss me?" she asked, uncertainly.

"I'll leave that decision entirely up to you," he said.

Livia grabbed a handful of his tunic and pulled him to a stop. "Then, yes."

Corvin smiled. His hands left her shoulders and resettled on her cheeks. He leaned down and brushed his lips against hers slowly. His kiss was like being struck with lightning. Her lips throbbed with the beat of her pulse. She registered for one glorious second the exquisite softness of his lips.

Then her legs refused to hold her weight. Corvin caught her with an arm around her waist before she fell to the ground.

"Fabulous?" he asked.

Livia was able to grasp the fabric on his shoulder. She attempted to pull herself upright but her body rebelled. Her fingers went limp, her arm went slack, falling to hang limply at her side.

"G'night, Corvin," Livia slurred. Then her head lolled back and everything went black.

Chapter 27

When Livia opened her eyes she was in a hospital. A stream of curses flooded from her mouth. She hated hospitals. No, loathed. No, abhorred. There weren't words strong enough to express exactly how much she hated hospitals. She'd gotten some kind of infection when she was little and needed an IV. She had tried to refuse and ended up breaking the nose of the nurse who held her down. Doctors were awful at figuring out what was wrong with her. Once, it had taken three weeks for them to figure out she'd broken her arm. By then they had to rebreak her arm and reset the bone.

Choked laughter made her aware she wasn't alone in the room. She turned. Hortensius was trying to hold back his amusement and failing. Dr. Marcus Tullius watched her with an expressionless face but his eyes were lit with a soft amusement.

"If it's any comfort," Dr. Tullius drawled. "We're not thrilled you're in here either. We'd much prefer you had avoided any injury."

Livia snorted. "Right, I'm sure you'll be happy with your bank account after I've been here the sixth time and you still can't figure out what is wrong with me."

251

"Is that how things usually go for you?" he asked.

Livia turned away from him and glared resentfully at the wall. "Just make sure I don't have any broken bones," she muttered.

"Funny you say that," he said. "Hortensius insists that you're only bruised but I want to recommend an x-ray to make sure. Will you consent to my precautionary recommendation? "

Livia turned her head back around to study Dr. Tullius. "Consent?"

She didn't remember ever having this type of conversation with a doctor before. Usually, he talked with her mom and mom texted Hyrum. Mom always ended up doing what Hyrum said even if Livia disagreed. It used to make her furious, but mom wasn't here and neither was Hyrum.

Marcus Tullius nodded. "Yes, you're over the age of eighteen and in charge of your own medical decisions. If you'd like to counsel with your family we can arrange for you to communicate with them—"

Livia shook her head. "No. I don't want them involved. Yes, I'd like an x-ray of anything you think is broken."

He nodded, pleased. "Hortensius, please take Livia to get her x-rays. Then set her up with an IV after you've returned. We'll take things from that point."

Livia eyed Hortensius.

He teased her. "Liv, you've never looked at me so mistrustfully before."

She huffed. "The last person who gave me an IV ended up with a broken nose—"

He laughed. "How recently was this?"

Livia thought. "I was six? Seven?"

He grinned at her. "Hopefully, you're a more cooperative patient today?"

Livia agreed, genuinely worried. "I hope so too."

"Hey, it's all grand to be Taurus until you get injured. We know how it is around here, okay? We'll be good to you."

Livia swallowed against the tightness in her throat and nodded.

"Liv," Hortensius asked. "Are you in any pain? Dr. Tullius didn't think you'd need any interventions but I can get some meds for you if you're hurting."

"Meds don't really ever work," Livia's voice wobbled.

"We have a couple of specific combinations that work for Taurus house. We've experimented a lot since Dr. Tullius took over and we now have effective methods. Are you in pain?"

"It's just hot. And I feel sick—" she whispered.

"Alright, we're gonna start off without drugs first. Taurus respond well to ice. It'll take about three minutes to get a bucket in here."

Livia didn't expect the size of the bucket they brought in. It was huge and the nurse who brought it in helped Hortensius shovel it into plastic bags and tie them off. They laid a thin linen blanket over her body then settled the ice down the entirety of her left side.

The chill against her skin sent a wave of comfort spiraling through her. Livia's eyes filled with tears and she was embarrassed that she couldn't repress them. They spilled down her cheeks and into her hair.

"Aw, Liv," Hortensius said, gently. "It'll be alright. I'm gonna call up some meds. Okay? It's gonna take longer but the ice should hold you over—"

"I'm okay," she choked, through her emotion.

"Nah," he said. "It's the protocol to medicate Taurus if icing produces emotional distress. Means you've been in pain too long."

"What—what are you giving me?" she asked.

"We'll start with a muscle relaxer. That usually helps and then we'll add a mood stabilizer to keep you calm."

"A mood stabilizer?" Livia asked. "Are you giving me morphine?"

"No, they're anxiety meds. Dr. Tullius will need to sign off on which one he wants to give you. This is the bad part about you not growing up in Caesarea. Most Taurus women know by this age which ones they respond well too—"

"What happens if I don't respond well?" Livia asked.

"You'll cry. Hysterically. Usually, we'll administer a sleeping med if you can't calm down after an hour. We prefer that to restraining Taurus. They hurt themselves and break our equipment if they flip into a rage."

"I thought only men did that—"

"No, women do too under the right circumstances but we're going to treat you too well for that to happen, alright?" Hortensius said. "We know what we're doing here. We aren't going to hurt you and we aren't going to allow you to hurt us."

Livia hoped he was right. Dr. Tullius ended up coming in with the nurse to deliver the meds.

"Icing produced tears?" he asked.

"Yep," Hortensius said.

"How's the ice feel, Livia?" Dr. Tullius asked.

"It feels good," she said. Then two more tears ran down her cheeks.

"That's good." His kind hazel eyes peered directly into hers. "I'm going to get you better as fast as I can, promise. Hang in there."

Dr. Tullius turned to Hortensius. "I'm going to hold off on administering an anxiety med until after the x-ray, Hortensius. If she has a fracture somewhere we'll administer it immediately. I'll have the nurses waiting in here for when you come back. If she only has contusions we'll stick with the muscle relaxers. I've called down and Clara will be waiting at the rad desk."

Hortensius grunted. "Good."

"Livia," Dr. Tullius looked at her. "Do you want me to invite your brothers to be in here when you get back? They're both in the waiting room."

Livia shook her head frantically. Dr. Tullius looked concerned by her refusal. "You're always allowed to ask for them to come in."

Livia shook her head. "Hyrum will try to tell me what to do. I don't want him involved. I want to decide what happens to me."

Dr. Tullius nodded. "I understand. I will tell them they are not permitted until our treatment course is completed."

Hortensius spoke up. "Liv, Justin is training some new recruits in the ER today. We could page him to come down. Would you like to see him?"

Livia hesitated. She wanted to be strong enough to say no but she wasn't. Her emotions betrayed her. "Yes," she nodded. "Yes."

Dr. Tullius looked at the nurse. "Will you please make sure Justin gets contacted in the ER department?"

"Yessir," she said.

The Clara Dr. Tullius mentioned was none other than Clara Porcius. Her black hair was smoothed back in a high ponytail and she wore a set of scrubs. She greeted Livia with a wry grin.

"Well, if it isn't the Bellatrix of Taurus house," she drawled quietly.

Livia laughed. "What are you doing here?"

"I'm doing an internship here for school credit."

Livia nodded. She'd done a similar internship under TARP. "How's it going?"

"Pretty great," she said.

"You like it?"

"Yeah."

"I liked my TARP internship too," Livia said.

"Word is you were better than most experienced people they hire," Clara said.

"They're the only people that like me here," Livia looked away.

"You okay if I go let the techs know we're here?" Hortensius asked.

Clara smiled at him. "Yeah, we're good. I'll keep her comfortable."

"Great," Hortensius said and stepped away.

Clara returned her attention back to Livia. "What happened with the fight today? You didn't have someone picked out to kiss you?"

"Tavian was supposed to kiss me."

Clara's nose scrunched up. "Your ex messed that up."

"He's an idiot," Livia agreed.

"Is it true he was dating someone else?"

Livia nodded.

"Lame," Clara said. "When you get back from school we should hang out."

"You'd hang out with me?" Livia asked.

"Yeah," Clara said.

"You wouldn't hang out with me last year," Livia said.

Clara sighed and nodded. "Yeah, I should have given you a chance. I see that now, but...you know...people change their minds."

"Sure, we'll hang," Livia agreed.

Clara smiled. "Good."

There was silence. Then Clara asked, "Is it true Gaius and Lauretta will divorce?"

Livia closed her eyes. The divorce had been made official the previous evening. "Yes, and he arranged to cheat her out of the property she would have gotten in the settlement."

Clara snorted. "It's what she deserves. Lauretta's disloyal to Taurus house and more concerned with her family's interests. She sabotaged the relationship between Gaius and the Taurus plebs from the very beginning."

Livia opened her eyes. "I-I didn't know."

Clara said, "I assumed you had the same attitude as her at first. But when you told Gaius off I realized you were just as frustrated as the rest of us."

Livia hadn't realized that her reception by the plebian factions in the house were influenced by the actions Lauretta had taken. It was relieving to know that not everything was her fault. There was also a tiny bit of hope that things might get better with Lauretta gone.

Hortensius returned. "Alright, they should call us back any ti—"

A woman came out and called Livia's name.

"Time for your x-rays," Hortensius said. "Let's get this done."

The x-rays went smoothly and whatever drug she'd been given had kicked in. Livia's body felt light and limp. Her thoughts drifted through her head, hazy and soft. Hortensius bid Clara farewell.

"Call me next time you're in town, Liv," Clara called.

Livia gave her a lazy wave that looked so lame that both Hortensius and Clara laughed.

Justin sat in a chair along the wall outside her room. He stood when Hortensius wheeled her near.

"How are you feeling, Liv?" Justin asked.

"Floaty," a spacey quality had transformed her voice.

Hortensius and Justin chuckled as they maneuvered her back into her room.

Hortensius grinned at her. "I'm going to pull your ice now the drugs have kicked in."

He started removing the bags of ice they had packed around her. Justin approached the opposite side of her bed. "They treating you well, Livia?"

"I think so," she answered.

"Well, you're allowed to complain, alright?" Justin said, patting the back of her hand.

"Justin, did I—" Livia stopped, unsure if asking the question would make her sound crazy. But everything was starting to feel fuzzy.

"Did you what, Liv?" Justin encouraged.

"Did I kiss Corvin?"

He laughed. "Yes, you did, Liv."

"I remember thinking I'd hit my head when he started walking out. He did walk out, right?"

"Yes, he did come to get you off the field," Justin said.

"I don't remember how I got here," Livia said.

"You weren't conscious. You fainted," Justin said.

"Is he mad at me?"

Justin's brow furrowed. "Are we talking about Corvin still?"

"Yes, is Corvin mad at me?"

"I don't think so. He's out in the waiting room with your brothers."

"He is?" Livia asked.

"Yeah, he won't go home until he knows you're okay."

Livia let out a deep sigh and closed her eyes. "He's a good friend."

"You falling asleep, Livia?" Justin asked.

"Maybe," she whispered.

"You tired?" Hortensius asked.

"Umhmm," she nodded.

Hortensius said, "Well, I'm going to get you started on an IV. Stay just the way you are and it'll be easy and quick."

Livia's eyes opened when she felt a pinch on the back of her hand. She looked at Hortensius.

He smiled. "You're done. We're gonna run some fluids into you. Nothing funny. We just need you really hydrated before we start healing."

Livia didn't know how long they waited for Dr. Tullius because she drifted in and out of a light sleep.

When he returned he was grinning. "I have good news. Hortensius was right. No broken bones. Healing should go easy and you'll be home tonight."

"Excellent," Hortensius stood. "Let's do this then."

He made Livia turn on her side. Justin got the honor of holding a bowl in front of Livia's face. Livia knew the healing started when a tingling started deep in her hip. The sensation made her stomach lurch and she pulled the bowl closer to her face. Sweat broke out on her forehead but she didn't gag. Not until Hortensius healed her bruised ribs, then the odd tingling sensation made her heave the contents of her stomach into the bowl.

"You're doing great, Liv. There's a nasty bruise on your shoulder and then we should be done."

Livia ended up heaving into the bowl a second time. Healing was not especially pleasant. The cold sweat had migrated to the back of her neck and her palms.

Hortensius had to leave to help another patient but Justin stayed with Livia as she waited for the wooziness to pass. She was grateful for the familiar sound of his voice and his steady presence. After fifteen minutes, Justin urged Livia to sit up and rinse her mouth out with some water.

"I think...I should warn you about the gossip," Justin said.

"The gossip?" Livia asked.

Justin inhaled and pulled a chair over from the wall. He settled into it when he'd positioned it directly opposite her. "Everyone assumes you're dating Corvin."

Livia blinked at him. "Cause of the kiss?"

"Yes...and other things."

Livia closed her eyes. "I was photographed with him when we walked into the parade together."

"That's not really what kicked things off—" Justin drawled. "It was how he greeted you before the match."

"Before the match?" Livia asked, confused. "What'd he do?"

"He didn't greet you formally—" Justin said.

"Oh. Oh, you mean the chin thing?" Livia asked. "Isn't that an insult or—"

Justin laughed. "No, Livia. It means you're dating. Are you? Are you dating him?"

258

"No. But he's used to not greeting me like that because of school and work before that."

"Okay, that's what he said but he knows better. He knows people would assume you were dating. So I wondered if…perhaps he had tried to reveal it when you didn't want him to?"

"No, we're not dating," Livia insisted.

"Okay, I believe you, Livia," Justin said easily. "But…is there anything you want to tell me? I confess to being really curious."

"About what?" Livia asked.

"If there's anything between you and Corvin? He's out in the waiting room—" Justin gestured.

"That's just the type of person he is—"

"No," Justin shook his head. "He's the type of person who'd want to avoid people spreading rumors. Typically, he'd keep his distance in case he accidentally conveyed an interest in you. He's careful about that sort of thing. So careful that he wouldn't be sitting in a public waiting room to hear that you'd recovered unless he was in a committed relationship with you."

Livia shook her head, confused. "No."

"Then I suspect he likes you," Justin said, simply.

Livia thought deeply about that. "I wonder if it's that thing I said to him—"

"What did you say to him?"

Livia cleared her throat. "I told him I wouldn't be his friend unless he agreed to be my friend everywhere and in front of everybody. That I wouldn't tolerate him acting like a different person at school and in Caesarea."

Justin's mouth slowly turned up in a pleased grin. "Really?"

Livia explained, "So, he's just being a good friend."

"Clearly," Justin half laughed. Livia got the feeling that he didn't believe her even though he said he did.

"Is there a point to this conversation?" Livia snapped.

Justin sighed and stood up. "I'll let Corvin and your brothers know you're alright. You know you can contact me if you need anything?"

"Yes," Livia said.

He nodded to her. "You fought well today. I'm proud of you, Livia."

"Thank you."

Then Justin walked out of the hospital room.

Livia had hoped that Corvin would come in with her brothers but he didn't. Hyrum and Lucas fussed over her. She asked if Corvin was with them. Hyrum reported that he left as soon as Dr. Tullius came out and told them she'd be fine.

A nurse came in and gave them Dr. Tullius discharge orders—lots of water and sleep—and then checked them out of the clinic.

"You won an award," Lucas told her on the way home.

"Did you?" she asked.

"Yeah, but yours is better." He laughed.

"What is it?"

"Usually, it's called primus bellator. Since you're a girl it will be prima bellatrix. It goes to the warrior who gets the most 'kill' hits in the game."

Livia laughed. Lucas and Hyrum fed Livia and sent her straight to bed when they got home. She took a quick shower and slipped into her bed. She didn't wake until late morning the next day. She took a hot bath and got dressed. When she came into the kitchen in search of food she almost felt like her normal self again.

Lucas was sitting at the bar and looking at his phone. When Livia pulled out a frying pan, he abandoned his phone and confronted her.

"What are you doing?" he asked.

"I want an omelet," Livia said.

"Well, go sit down. I'll make it for you," he said.

Livia glared at him. "I'm fine, Lucas."

Lucas glared right back. "How about we err on the side of caution when it comes to your health, Liv?"

Livia huffed. "I can cook an omelet."

"So can I," he argued.

So, Lucas made Livia an omelet even though she bickered with him the entire time he did it. Then he set the plate of hot food in front of her with a fork. She took a bite and her eyes teared up.

"Does it really taste that bad?" Lucas sighed, defeated.

Livia shook her head. "It's good."

"What's wrong then?" he asked.

Livia sniffed. "It's nice to have someone do something for me."

Lucas rolled his eyes. "Liv, you're impossible."

"Thanks," she choked.

He came around the counter and ruffled her hair. "Thanks for fighting with me yesterday. I'm sorry you got hurt."

"I'm fine."

"It's okay not to be fine, Liv," Lucas said.

"But I am. I'm fine," she insisted.

"I'll be back to check on you in an hour," he pulled a cup from the cupboard and filled it with water. Then set it down next to her plate. "Don't forget to drink some water."

Livia muttered at him resentfully and he laughed as he walked into the next room.

Livia decided to take a chance on checking Tabula. She figured if Justin was warning her she might need to know what was going on. She pulled up her account. A distorted pinging sounded as the program tried to notify her of over 300 notifications all at once.

Instantly overwhelmed, Livia almost shut down the window and walked away. Livia browsed before she read deeply and found that professional photos of the reenactment were posted. There were a lot of Livia as she'd fought the longest and they were all embarrassing. She had dirt on her face, sweat pouring off her temples, her hair was askew, and the worst? She looked like she was wearing a potato sack. She tied up the stupid stola and made herself look ridiculous.

Livia pressed her palms to her burning cheeks to cool them down. When the strategy didn't work, Livia downed the water Lucas set down in front of her instead. Having partially restored her composure, she continued browsing. She ran into the photos of her with Corvin.

There was photographic evidence of her wrapped up in his crimson cloak, his lips pressed to hers. Livia couldn't stop staring at the image. His red cloak swept to her ankles so she didn't look like she was in a potato sack anymore. Her crazy hair was tamed under Corvin's long fingers, as he cradled her face between his palms. There was something so tender in Corvin's entire countenance and so eager in hers. If she'd seen that photo of someone else and they tried to explain they weren't dating, Livia wouldn't believe them.

Livia swallowed at the anxiety that tightened her throat. She'd revealed her secret to everyone. She liked Corvin. Livia went to Corvin's page to see a bunch of their SARP associates and his family leaving thrilled comments that they were dating. Corvin had gone through and responded to each one clarifying that they weren't dating. Livia realized many of the comments on her page were the same, congratulations. They'd been sitting there days and she hadn't responded. It struck her in a moment how awful that looked. Corvin refuting they were dating right and left on his page and Livia remaining silent. Panicked, she went through each comment and did the same thing Corvin did. It took her over an hour and by the time she was done she had sweaty palms and a racing heart.

She was still recovering when her phone rang. She answered without looking at the screen. "Hello?"

"Livia," Corvin's warm-toned voice traveled through the phone. "I need to see you. Are you up for that?"

Livia thought she'd have a heart attack. She clutched the fabric of her shirt in her fist. Why was he calling? Was he mad? Should she agree to see him?

"T-tonight?" she stuttered.

"If you're feeling alright? I understand if you're not up to it."

Frantic thoughts pinged through Livia's brain. Sometimes you had to confront people's anger. Right now, Hyrum and Lucas were here. If Corvin wanted to have it out, she preferred to do it when her brothers were around to back her up. Maybe insisting on her own terms would be enough to discourage him from coming in the first place.

"I'm only up for it if you come to me. I'm not up for going out," she said.

"So, if I bring over ice cream?" he said this with a casual tone.

Livia hesitated. She hadn't intimidated him. Was she ready to do this?

"Liv, you there?" Corvin asked.

She rushed to fill her silence. "That'd be fine."

"I'll see you at 7:00," he said.

Before Livia could figure out a way to change plans, he ended the call. That evening, Livia had dinner with the family. Afterward, she kept looking at the clock and then finding something to clean.

"Stop that," Hyrum snapped at her. "You're supposed to rest."

Livia glared at him. Staying busy was the way she dealt with her anxiety and she was super anxious about Corvin coming over.

"What's going on with you?" he asked.

"I have someone coming over at 7."

"Who?" Hyrum asked.

"Corvin."

Caecilia's gaze immediately focused on Livia. "Is there something wrong?"

"No...just eating ice cream," Livia said.

Caecilia's eyes narrowed, suspicious. "Whatever you say, Liv."

Livia sighed. She didn't blame Caecilia. She didn't believe herself. Livia didn't know what to do. There was dust on the black splash. Livia found a rag and went to rinse it under the water.

"Go rest," Hyrum barked.

Livia gave him a pleading look. He only glared and she had to abandon the rag in the sink. It was 20 mins of eternity until the doorbell rang. Livia rose to answer the door but Hyrum beat her to it.

"Corvin." Hyrum greeted him with a handshake. "Nice to see you."

Corvin grinned. "We seem to keep missing each other, right?"

"Life has been crazy." Then Hyrum added wryly, "But you don't seem to have the same trouble with Livia."

"I've heard Caecilia has been better?" Corvin said, side-stepping that conversation.

Livia's face flamed with embarrassment. How could Hyrum say something like that?

"Yes." Hyrum nodded. "Cil!"

Caecilia stepped out of Hyrum's study and greeted Corvin with a hug. "Hey, Corvin."

"You look wonderful," Corvin told her.

Caecilia snorted. "Pregnant, you mean."

Corvin's face lit with playfulness. "Wonderful, I mean."

Caecilia playfully smacked his arm. "It's good to see you."

"I'm happy you are doing better. Mom was worried about you," Corvin said.

"She called me," Caecilia said. "Always so encouraging and kind."

"You let us know if you need anything," Corvin said. "We'd be happy to help."

Caecilia looked down. "Oh, that is so kind."

"I mean it," Corvin said.

Caecilia shook her head. "You're all so busy—"

"But not too busy to help you through this pregnancy," Corvin said. "I'll be gone soon but I am sure the girls would run to help. The little ones are older now. Verity is in kindergarten. Mom would appreciate the companionship."

Caecilia drew her chin back. "Is she lonely?"

"Few people understand the pressures of being materfamilias but you'd come fairly close," Corvin said.

Caecilia nodded. "I'll call her?"

"Please, do. She needs friends," he said.

"Hyrum and I will be in the study here," Caecilia said. "Feel free to interrupt if you and Liv need anything."

"Thank you," Corvin said. Then he looked at Livia.

Caecilia pulled Hyrum into the study with her and closed the door, not entirely. It hung slightly ajar. Livia met Corvin's gaze across the entranceway. A spark lit in his eyes when he saw her. Livia tried to interpret what that meant. Then he stepped toward her and scattered all her thoughts completely.

There was something about the way his body moved in a pair of jeans that sent butterflies dancing inside her. Goosebumps raised on her forearms in anticipation of his touch. Livia honestly didn't know if she was excited or

264

scared and that made her flinch back when he lifted his arms for a hug.

Corvin froze. His face adopted his blank mask. "Still sore, Liv?"

"I-I'm not sure," she said honestly, looking down.

His expression didn't change and he lifted the grocery bag he brought with him. "Want some ice cream?"

Livia looked at it. "What type is it?"

It was Corvin's turn to be flustered. "I didn't know what flavor you liked," he said, pulling it open so she could look inside. "So, I got those single-serve ones in a bunch of different flavors."

Livia smiled. "Clever."

"Glad you think so," he said. "Wasn't sure how you'd interpret it..."

Did Livia see a flash of insecurity on his face? She must have imagined it. "Let me get some spoons."

"How was your day?" Corvin asked as they took their first bites. Livia had selected chocolate. Corvin had selected salted caramel.

Livia wasn't certain how to react to how normal and friendly Corvin was acting. She'd expected him to be simmering with anger and frustration. Instead, he was calm and relaxed. "It was boring. Lucas and Hyrum won't let me do anything."

"You'll be back to normal soon enough," Corvin said. "Why not take advantage of the time to rest?"

Livia shrugged. "Gotta keep up my reputation and all—"

Corvin laughed. "I think you've thoroughly established your reputation."

"And yet," Livia muttered. "You're still here to yell at me."

Corvin did a double-take. "Yell at you?"

"Of course, you're angry."

Corvin looked confused and Livia tried to figure out if it was an act or not. "Why would I be angry?"

"I distracted attention from your father's speech."

Corvin waved a hand to dismiss that. "We went over that mess with Gaius. I think the consequences were severe enough to change the way he acts from now on."

"And Bella?" Livia challenged.

265

Corvin looked displeased. "What about her?"

"She's—I'm her friend?" Livia said.

"Are you?" Corvin asked, an eyebrow raised.

Livia sighed. "She is mad at me."

Cause she's jealous of our relationship," Corvin agreed. "But that's her problem, not ours."

Livia sighed. "How do I fix it?"

"You can't. She's blaming you for something you can't fix," Corvin said. "Even if you decided to never speak to me again I still wouldn't get back together with Bella."

"So…"

"She's going to have to get over it," Corvin said, shrugging. "You might have to wait for her to be ready to be friends again."

"But you're not angry with me over it?"

Corvin sighed. "Livia, I don't have any reason to be angry over it. If anything, it's you who should be angry with me. Are you?"

Livia's feelings swirled inside her and a thread of anger was there. "You waited in the hospital to see if I was alright but you didn't come to see me? If you weren't angry why did you do that?"

Corvin took a couple of deep breaths. That vulnerable look flashed across his features again. "I'm sorry. I didn't know you wanted me. I had to leave, though."

"To where?" Livia demanded.

"Cassia's parents hold a memorial every year on the anniversary. I went."

Livia's chin drew back in surprise. "You were at the graveyard?" she asked.

Corvin nodded. "Yes."

Livia tried to figure out if she was uncomfortable with this. It hurt to be passed over for a dead woman. Yet, it wasn't fair to prevent him from participating in a personal tradition that brought him comfort.

"It upsets you," Corvin said.

Livia nodded. "A little but I understand and it's okay."

"Are you sure it's okay?" Corvin pressed.

"It's not something you need my permission for Corvin," Livia said.

He tilted his head to the side and looked at her. "But you wanted me there at the hospital?"

"Yeah, I'm—" Livia gulped. "Sorry about the kiss, Corvin."

His expression softened. "I wish it had gone better for you. I'm supposed to be the one apologizing."

Livia shook her head. "No, it's my fault—"

Corvin shook his head. "I shouldn't have overestimated your endurance. It was a miscalculation on my part. I am sorry."

"And, now we have those rumors to deal with," Livia muttered.

"That's why I'm here," Corvin said, and a sense of purpose erased his vulnerability. "To discuss the rumors."

Dread filled Livia. "What rumors?"

"You are well acquainted with the rumors," Corvin said. "Since you told everyone on Tabula we weren't dating...yet."

"Yet?" Livia asked, confused. Then she pulled her phone into her hand and scrambled to sign in. She put her hand over her mouth as she realized what she'd done. Over and over she'd told people she and Corvin weren't dating...yet.

"Oh no!" she cried. "Corvin—I-I was trying to fix it and I made it worse!"

She put her phone face down on the counter and covered her face with her hands, mortified.

Corvin laughed. "So, Livia, let's talk about this yet."

"Oh, please don't tease me!" Livia cried. "I'm so sorry!"

"I'm not teasing right now. I'm making honest inquiries. Was it a mistake or did you mean something by it?"

"Oh my goodness. I'd never do that," Livia said. "I am so sorry!"

Corvin's expression flashed with hurt. Then Livia realized he took it to mean she'd never date him, which isn't what she meant to say.

"No, wait," she put down her spoon and pushed her ice cream away. "That didn't come out right—I mean..."

Corvin's face was a mask. "What did you mean, Liv?"

"I mean to say that I..." Livia hesitated. Her mind was racing so fast words wouldn't come to her. "I'm trying to say that..."

Corvin let the silence stretch out a long time.

Livia bit her knuckle. "Okay, I can do this...I don't want to be the girl who says things online that...makes you feel like—" Livia tried to explain a different way. "My mom she manipulated my father and I don't...I wouldn't play games that make you feel stuck...with me. So, I'm saying it was a mistake. It wasn't intentional to trick you or part of a twisted strategy—I'm so sorry," Livia said.

Corvin tilted his head to the side. "So, you're very bothered by the idea that I'd interpret it as a deliberate ploy to get my affection."

"Yes, that's not the type of person I want to be." Livia gestured with her hands to emphasize her point.

"So, you're not saying that you'd never date me," Corvin said.

"I was not trying to say that," Livia confirmed.

Corvin pushed his ice cream aside and leaned onto the countertop with his forearms. "So, you might date me?"

Livia's heart thudded in her chest so hard she was certain it was visible to Corvin. "I-" she whispered. "T-that's complicated..."

"In what way?" he asked.

Livia decided to deflect the conversation a bit. "Corvin, you can't convince me you want to date me."

"I do want to date you," he said, firmly. "I feel like you understand me significantly better than a lot of people in Caesarea."

"You think I understand you?" Livia asked. "I find you pretty confusing, actually."

Corvin grinned. "I'm willing to answer questions."

He paused here as if she'd start an interrogation immediately.

Livia couldn't pluck a single question from her frantically spinning thoughts. "Can this be a long-term offer?"

"For as long as you wish," Corvin said. He studied her before speaking again, as if calculating how frank to be with her. "Livia, I'm tired of hiding my feelings for you. I think about you frequently when we aren't together and I would love to spend more time with you. Obviously, my powers of observation are fallible and so you may correct me, but I think that you like me too. Am I wrong about that?"

Livia cleared her throat. "My feelings are…I'm not sure I trust them."

Corvin looked confused. "What do you mean?"

Livia laughed. "I mean, I've had them a long time and—"

That made Corvin smile but he didn't interrupt her. Instead, he gave her the space to gather her thoughts again. Livia wished he wouldn't because she could hardly think. Her heart raced and the thoughts in her head were blurry and hard to pin down.

When Livia didn't immediately continue Corvin asked, "How long, Liv?"

Livia met his eyes and realized this was the moment of truth. It was time to tell him. "Since we met. I mean…not…not the first *instant* we met. Not like that—"

"That wasn't a moment for romance," Corvin confirmed.

"But somewhere in between then and when you left ten days later," Livia gulped.

"So, when you reference these feelings," Corvin encouraged. "You mean what?"

"I'm not sure," Livia whispered. "I spend a lot of time trying not to feel them."

Corvin laughed. "Why, Liv?"

"Well, at first, I was too young for you," she said.

Corvin nodded. "Granted. But you're not too young now. I'm a little older but not that much older. It's less than ten years."

Livia closed her eyes. "Then I was embarrassed because…what a cliche, right? Girl falls in love with the officer who saves her. I thought it was some psychological weakness—"

Corvin considered that. "I understand what you're saying. But it's been two years, Liv. Your immediate physical safety is about as secure as the average person now. You don't need to be in a relationship with me to meet your basic needs. So, I don't think you need to be concerned that being with me is automatically unethical."

Livia opened her eyes. "That's true, isn't it? I couldn't get over that. That the way my attraction started…I needed you to protect me."

Corvin nodded. "Do you feel like that still?"

Livia sighed. "Not the same way. It is different. It's something that sounds…nice, convenient. But I don't feel terrified to be without you the way I did at first."

Corvin's brow furrowed. "You felt that way, Liv?"

Livia nodded. "So, it scares me a little to be put in that position again."

"I had no idea," Corvin said.

"I wanted to beg you to stay the day you flew out," Livia said.

Corvin sighed. "I hated leaving. The squad was broken up about it for weeks afterward. We didn't want to make it harder for you to get along with your mother when you were still a minor, though. She'd asked us not to contact you."

Livia nodded. "I know."

"I wish you'd said something," Corvin whispered. "I could have written letters. Maybe that would have been enough to ease your fears…"

Livia shook her head. "That might have been worse."

Corvin looked into her eyes. "We can sit around all day and intellectualize all the circumstances but it won't change the fact that emotionally I abandoned you."

Livia looked at her hands and didn't say anything.

Corvin said, "I can understand if a romantic relationship is too hard an ask after all that. But at the same time…will you give me a chance to be there for you now? To regain your trust, Liv?"

Livia inhaled. "But I'm not even done with my list yet."

"What list?" he asked.

"The 'why we can never be together list'."

Corvin smiled a bit. "What else is there, Liv? I mean, what you just told me is already a lot."

"I worry we grew up too different," Livia said.

"We did," he nodded. "But everyone does, Liv."

"No, Corvin," Livia said. "Not as dramatically different as we did."

He leaned forward to rest on his forearms. "Liv, sometimes that can be a good thing for a relationship instead of a bad thing—"

270

"How?" she demanded.

Corvin hesitated before he answered her question. Then he spoke with a frankness that surprised her. "I'm always afraid that I'll marry a girl who won't ever question me. That she'll go along with everything I want and I don't want that, Livia. That sounds so boring to me. I crave an intellectual challenge…that's the best way I can describe it. I've tried to make things work with traditional Caesarean women and…eventually I feel trapped… intellectually, I mean."

Livia's narrowed her eyes. "So, you think fighting with me is some intellectual game—"

"No," Corvin shook his head. "No, Liv, I am saying collaborating with you will be a worthy intellectual challenge."

"Only people from TARP would say something like that," Livia muttered.

"Sounds like you're already familiar with my conflict resolution strategies. I say that puts us ahead of the game, Liv."

Livia took a deep breath. She thought Corvin was being too optimistic, but she didn't know anyone else that would be as prepared as Corvin to face the challenges she worried about. Hyrum did say that sometimes you have to take a risk on people.

Livia said, "In theory, let's say I agree to this—"

Corvin grinned. "Continue."

Livia narrowed her eyes. "Are we going to match?"

Corvin groaned. "Liv, that takes so long. Let's just date."

"I don't want to," she said.

Corvin looked alarmed. "To date? Or you don't want it to be informal?"

"I don't want to be informal," Livia clarified.

Corvin sighed. "Look, you were the one complaining about lawyers and inequality before. Being informal is the most equal way to do this. We're dating right now, not getting married. Let's keep the complications out of it."

"So, you're not serious about dating me," Livia challenged.

"That's not true. Look, Liv, there's a lot of pressure and serious discussions involved in signing a match contract. I don't see the point of putting you through that when it's not necessary. So unless you can explain what benefit you'll get out of the situation I won't do it. It's not fair to you."

"First," Livia said, putting up a finger. "I'm already an outsider in Caesarea. If I'm going to be part of this community I need to follow the traditions and rules of the community."

Corvin sighed. "Using my words against me now, are you?"

Livia smiled. "Second, we both know there are people in Caesarea that aren't going to be happy that I'm dating you."

"Forget them," Corvin slapped his palm against the counter.

"I want to show them that I'm not going to mess around with you. That I'm serious about respecting you and your family. That I'm not irresponsible like my mother."

Corvin quipped, "Liv, you're the complete opposite of irresponsible."

Livia ignored his teasing. "Third, if we're going to do this I want to have the serious discussions. I'm not going to be played, Corvin. You're not going to wish-wash your way into this relationship because you're lonely and then leave me high and dry. You're going to prove to me that I'm worth your time and effort," Livia insisted.

Corvin stiffened. His eyes widened and his lips parted to say something but nothing came out. Livia was sure she'd offended him.

"Are you still in?" she asked.

He laughed. "I said I wanted this, didn't I? Someone who'd stand up to me? Way to not disappoint, Livia."

She grinned but there was little mirth or flirt in it. "Well?"

Corvin leaned in his close, his hazel eyes intent on hers. "Liv, I'll agree if—" Corvin paused for emphasis— "you talk to Gaius about it before we leave for Cornelia tomorrow."

Livia frowned. "Why?"

"So we have an idea straight off how he will work with you. If you have a bad experience bringing it up with him we'll reevaluate, deal?"

Livia figured that was fair. "Deal."

Corvin inhaled, and his eyes roved her face. "Let me know how your discussion with him goes."

Livia nodded. "I will."

Corvin said, "You don't have much time to talk to him. We leave for Cornelia tomorrow at 2:00."

"I'll figure it out," Livia said.

Corvin nodded. He reached out to touch her.

Livia flinched away.

Corvin froze and pulled his hand back. "Too soon?"

Livia swallowed a knot of emotion. "Yeah, I'm sorry—"

"No, that's okay. You deserve time to recover. I'll see you tomorrow. You keep taking care of yourself, okay?"

Livia nodded. "Thanks, Corvin."

* * *

Livia texted Gaius almost immediately after Corvin left. *Remember when you asked if I had anyone I was interested in matching with?*

Gaius responded instantly. *Yes.*

Livia: I want to talk.

Gaius: Right now is the only time I can talk

Livia: I am at Hyrum's

Gaius: I'll be there in 10 min.

Hyrum got to the door before Livia did. "Gaius? I didn't know you were coming over. Is everything alright?"

"Livia and I have a matter to discuss."

Hyrum gave Livia a concerned looked.

"It's okay Hyrum. I asked him to come over," Livia said. "If we need you we'll call you in—"

Hyrum's eyes narrowed at being dismissed this way, but he didn't object.

Gaius removed his jacket and took a seat in the front room. Livia sat down across from him, feeling nervous.

"Livia," Gaius said. "How are you?"

"I'm doing fine."

He raised a single eyebrow. "Are you? Really?"

"I have a question—" she hedged.

"I have one too," he quipped, grinning.

"What's the procedure to start a match?" Livia asked.

Gaius folded his hands together. "You tell me who you have an interest in and I make the appropriate inquiries and then it goes from there."

"Goes from there? How?" Livia asked.

"If the response to our inquiry is positive, the woman submits her request first and the man responds," Gaius said. "So you'd submit a letter stating interest. The man would respond with a letter of reciprocal interest. Then invite you to submit a match contract proposal and they'd accept it, reject it, or ask us to negotiate."

Livia inhaled a deep breath. "Okay."

"Are you going to tell me his name?" Gaius asked.

"I like Corvin Tullius."

Gaius grinned, pleased. "I like Corvin too."

"You do?" Livia asked.

He nodded. "Tell me about him. Do you talk often?"

And soon an hour had passed and Gaius had dragged out the entire story.

"I'd like to speak with Lars if you'll permit me," Gaius said. "It sounds like Corvin knows the letter of interest is coming so there's no point in delaying."

"Okay," Livia said. "Should I arrange to be with you while you talk?"

Gaius shook his head. "No."

"Fine," Livia agreed. "Let me know what they say?"

"Of course." Gaius stood. "I'll be in touch."

* * *

Livia was in the thick of studying for finals three days later when Gaius forwarded an email from Lars.

Livia,

Gaius Pius the Paterfamilias of Taurus house has communicated your interest to pursue a match with Corvin Tullius. This serves as notice that Corvin holds a reciprocal interest in pursuing a match. We look forward to receiving your match proposal. We request to receive your offer by January 31st. If circumstances prevent submission by that date, please notify us in writing and a new date will be negotiated.

Highest regards,

Lars and Aurelia Tullius

Livia hit reply to let Gaius know she received the news. Then she sat back and let the happiness wash over her. Corvin had been serious about dating her. He'd called her last night to chat. When he only asked her questions about her plans and how her studying for finals was going she doubted he would follow through. He did though and Livia got ready for her day in a distracted haze. She grabbed her purse and bag and set out for lunch. She crossed campus. She came to the staircase in front of the student center. She looked up and froze. Corvin stood at the top of the stairs as if he was waiting for her.

Livia climbed the stairs eagerly. She stepped in front of him.

"I thought you were holing up in the library to write a paper today," she said.

"I thought I'd take my lunch break with the strongest woman on campus," he teased.

Livia rolled her eyes but she laughed.

"As long as that's alright with her?" Corvin asked.

"I'd like that," Livia agreed.

"You'll have to tell me what's good to eat," he said.

Livia took a deep breath. "I got an interesting email today."

Corvin's expression didn't reveal anything. He asked with an emotionless expression. "Was it good news?"

Livia laughed at him. "Corvin, stop doing that!"

He didn't break. "Doing what?"

"Pretending like you don't know what I'm talking about!"

A slow smile spread over his face. "You heard from mom and dad?"

Livia couldn't help smiling back. "Yes."

"So, it went okay?" Corvin asked. "Mom and Dad said Gaius was pleasant to work with, surprisingly."

"He was really supportive of the whole thing," Livia said. "So, now what do we do while we wait? What are we between now and then?"

"Whatever we want to be," Corvin said. "Of course, I think we should be a couple to make the most of it. If you feel different I'd like to accept the challenge to become better friends."

"I'd like both," Livia said.

Corvin jerked his chin toward the door. "Let's start with lunch then."

"Wait." Livia stepped closer to him. "There's one more thing I want."

"What's that?" Corvin asked.

Livia lifted her hands to his cheeks and went up on her tiptoes. "A do-over?"

Corvin's hands rested lightly on her waist. "Granted."

Corvin lowered his lips to hers. Livia braced herself for another lightning strike but she experienced only softness. Livia pulled away a moment to breathe, to put down her defenses. She leaned up to press her lips to Corvin's again and met once again with his tender mildness.

Livia tangled her hands into his curly hair and lingered over the kiss as long as she dared in public. When she pulled back she couldn't suppress the smile that turned her lips as she stared into Corvin's golden-flecked hazel eyes. Her heart thudded with a dozen emotions. Happiness and excitement sent chills down her back but there was a deeper sense of rightness taking root in her. She was willing to take risks to be with this man. Even if it meant rooting out and facing all the demons from her past.

"Much better," she murmured.

"You're still conscious," Corvin teased. "My appeal must be wearing off."

Livia stepped away and flicked his bicep. "Not funny."

He was laughing though. "For the record, I liked the second time better."

Livia took his hand and tugged him toward the cafeteria. "Come on before I turn into a hungry Taurus."

About the Author

Emily Debenham lives in Pennsylvania where she is continually amazed at how easily things grow here after growing up in the western US. She has a double major in Latin and History teaching.

You can connect with me on:

- http://emilydebenham.com
- https://www.instagram.com/gamila.walrus
- https://www.patreon.com/emilydebenham

Made in the USA
Monee, IL
26 April 2023

32424612R00166